S0-GQE-616

THE
TRAITOR

THE
TRAITOR

Joe B. Johnson

JBJ TRUE PRESS
Chicago

The Traitor. Copyright by Joe B. Johnson. All rights reserved. Printed in the United States of America. No part of this book may be used or reproduced in any manner whatsoever except in brief quotations without written permission from the publisher. Address all such requests to: JBJ True Press, 25 West 103rd Place, Chicago, Il. 60628.

ISBN: 0-9622969-0-2

First edition

Blacks who breach the secret covenant among blacks that "Blacks don't air their dirty laundry in public," usually are punished.

To those blacks who have the courage to defy such defeatist demands in the interest of improving the lot of blacks, this book is dedicated.

Chapter 1

When late set clerk Jimmie Jones stepped off the elevator on to the fourth floor at the Metro City Main Post Office (MMPO) building at 10:12 PM for work, mailhandler Bessie Black screamed: "There he is! the traitor." Then she slapped him across the face and slammed him hard against the corridor wall. "He's the smart ass nigger who say in his suggestion, what he call the Blockbuster, that he want to save the taxpayers some money. But what do he really want to do, ladies?" she yelled in a cheerleader style to the three women clerks accompanying her.

And they dutifully yelled back in words she surely wanted to hear: "By taking jobs away from blacks, that's what he wants to do."

These were the Hatchet Ladies: Blanche Mims, Mamie Smith, Dolly Jean and Bessie Black. Blanche Mims was The Beautiful One; she had the title of the Late Set Sweetheart. Mamie Smith was the Unlearned One; she had little education. Dolly Jean was the Confused One; devastated from her divorce, she became a Bible toting Christian zealot. And Bessie Black was the Take Charge One; with less education than even Mamie Smith, she was the fiery leader of the Hatchet Ladies.

They were a group of MMPO black women workers banded together to fight for the rights of MMPO women workers, especially MMPO black women workers who composed ninety eight percent of the total workforce of 20,000. The total city wide postal workforce was 35,000.

Jimmie, the author of a ninety eight page suggestion, headed quickly down the corridor, south, toward the men's locker room. The four Hatchet Ladies followed after him and took turns at giving him

2

good swift pushes. It was like a cancerous disease, he thought, a massive dark cloud blinding them of the realities of life. Most black people, it seemed to Jimmie, cared nothing at all about efficiency and productivity. Totally consuming them, were thoughts only of jobs.

"Yeah," sweetheart Blanche Mims interjected, giving Jimmie a good swift push, "he wants the letter sorting machines (LSM's) to work more. But with letters coming through the mails in all shapes and sizes, he says the machines can never work to full capacity. So he suggested in his Blockbuster, what he calls Standardization."

"What do he mean by that?" unlearned Mamie Smith asked. Then, instead of a good push, she hit him hard in the jaw with her fist.

"He wants Congress to pass a law that all letter mail be the same size," Blanche Mims responded, giving an answer that was almost right.

"That's crazy!" Mamie Smith yelled, and gave Jimmie a sharp, vicious kick in the groin. "They can't make people do that. People use whatever size they wants to. We ain't in slavery no more..."

"What he really said was that there should be a minimum and a maximum size-standard," confused divorcee Dolly Jean cut in, correcting Blanche Mims, and pushing Jimmie, too, but only lightly. "He did not say that all letter mail should be the same size."

"Why are you defending this traitor," Blanche Mims yelled, pushing Jimmie again. "Are you sleeping with him or something?"

"I'm not defending him," Dolly Jean shot back. "I was just telling you what the suggestion actually said."

More women workers began to gather around and follow Jimmie. They were taking turns pushing him, too. Working on a job where women out numbered men ninety eight to two, he was severely out gunned.

But, anyway, as he staggered from the effects of the swift pushes the women were giving him, and the hard licks and kicks Mamie Smith was giving him, he looked back over his shoulder and said to Blanche Mims: "She's telling you like it is. That's what I really said."

"Ain't nobody talking to you," Mamie Smith growled and hit him with both fists fast in the ribs. Then she asked Blanche Mims, "Do you know what else he said in his blockbuster suggestion? He said that couldn't none of us blacks working here get a job working nowhere else."

Dolly Jean was about to inadvertently risk the embarrassment of

being chided again for correcting one of her colleagues in Jimmie's
defense. He broke in and spared her the pain.

"What I said," Jimmie explained, "and it was stated in the introduction of the suggestion and not in the body of it, is that Metro
blacks should be proud that the post office exists because many of
them working here could not qualify for jobs in the private sector
paying salaries as high as those that they are receiving here. And I
don't hesitate to regretfully put myself in that category. With my
few skills, I am painfully aware that I'd have a hard time finding a
job out there paying the kind of money I'm making here." He turned
and curtly asked: "How about you, Mamie Smith? What could you
do out there to demand the kind of money you are making here?"

"There's lots of things I could do out there," the Unlearned One
said, pushing him only, this time, but hard. "And make more money,
too, than this little old piece of change I'm making down here."

Dolly Jean eyed Mamie Smith with accusing suspicion. So did
Bessie Black and Blanche Mims.

Jimmie, as everyone else did at the MMPO, knew of Mamie
Smith's limited education. It had been rumored that MMPO supervisory jobs were for sale. Obviously, clerk jobs were for sale too, he
figured. No way could Mamie Smith have legally passed the test,
not the one he took, anyway. Normally, he did not practice the art
of embarrassing people. But, unlike that of the others, her attack on
him had been more brutal. She deserved it, he thought. "Name me
something you could do out there that would bring you this kind of
return," he challenged her. "One thing. Anything."

"Ain't none of your business what I could do out there," she
feebly retorted. "Cause you's a dummy, don't think everybody else
is, too. I can do lots of things," she informed him, then took a stiff
verbal jab at Jimmie. "But taking jobs away from black folks ain't one
of 'em. Talking 'bout them old LSM machines ought to run more.
They run too much now, working the mail that we suppose to be
working. If they gonna work all the mail coming in here, then what
we gonna do? You and that old Bill Brown, our jive ass Postmaster,
is jes alike, want them old noisy machines going all night, deefening
everybody. We don't need them machines no how. We can handle
this mail. And you talking 'bout making everybody use envelopes
the same size so we can run 'em more. I don't know how much more
we can run 'em. They run all night now, as it is."

Dolly Jean's new found religious teachings about such things as honesty brutally crashed through her apparent thin crust of hatchet lady loyalty. "No they don't, Mamie," she inadvertently disagreed. "On our shift, those machines run only about 2 or three hours a night." Then she squeezed her little black Bible tightly under her arm and quickly clamped her hands over her mouth trying futilely to hold back the escaping words. It was as if she was standing squarely in the center of a Sunday morning pew at her saintly family church where she had accidentally made some profane and ungodly statement.

Bessie Black, leader of the Hatchet Ladies, was a mailhandler and worked in a different section from the clerks. "Shut up, Dolly Jean," she stormed at her. "Mamie is right. They do run them machines too much. I see yall manual clerks sett'n over there, most every night, with nothing to do, 'cause them damn machines done worked up all the mail. And if this black traitor ass nigger here, Jimmie Jones, gets his way, they ain't gonna need yall 'round here at all for nothing no more," she said and gave Jimmie a good swift push.

Bessie Black was exaggerating the possibilities of LSM machine operators replacing manual operators, but only by modest degrees. The initial standard for manual distribution clerks had been 3 trays of mail per clerk per hour. It was now reduced to 2 trays an hour, but the department, even on good days, was lucky if it got one and a half trays an hour. Conversely, LSM operators, working with letters that were machine ready were capable of sorting some five trays of mail an hour.

They finally reached the guardpost at the end of the corridor. A conglomerate of hands gave Jimmie one last rushing push. And grasping for a moment of deliverance, Jimmie flashed his badge for the two guards there to see, peeled smartly off and quickly dashed into the men's locker room. Ah, relief, he comforted himself. But there, too, he'd meet another waiting, welcoming party, the two principals of whom were his lockerroom buddies, Ronnie and Oscar. And the first to see him entering was Oscar. "There he is," Oscar quickly announced.

Jimmie remembered that "there he is" were the same three un-courtly words that finger pointing Bessie Black had yelled out at him back at the bank of elevators. She had wanted everyone to know that this was Jimmie Jones, the guy who wanted the machines going full blast all night, as she put it, to "take jobs away from blacks." To let him know what she thought of his idea, and of him generally, following those three uncourtly words, she branded him with the two condemning words: "The traitor."

Will Oscar do the same? he wondered. Does he think I'm a traitor? What about Ronnie? How does he feel about it? Does he think I'm a traitor, too?

"Mr. Medicine Man," Oscar said completing his salutatory remark, "come on in here."

"Yeah, let's talk about it, Mr. Medicine Man," Ronnie added, backing Oscar up.

Bessie Black and her Hatchet Ladies, in the second phrase of their salutatory remark, had branded him a traitor. Ronnie and Oscar were now giving him the title, Medicine Man. It doesn't seem as condemning as the traitor, he reasoned, but what does Medicine Man mean? What are my buddies trying to tell me?

Jimmie remembered that his wife Mary Belle constantly asked him: ("Why don't you jes go on down there and work lak everybody else? Why you got to try to run everything everywhere you go?")

Are they saying, too, that I am a smart aleck, a know it all? No, Jimmie disagreed. In this great big city, only my loving wife Mary Belle thinks I'm a dummy. No one else. Those guys don't think so, either. But what do they really mean by the distinction, Medicine Man? I don't quite get it, he said.

He did have an idea, though. Yet, he questioned them anyway. "Medicine Man?" he asked, "what do you fellows mean by that?"

"Well, medicine is what people takes when they's sick and wants to get well," Oscar explained. "And uh, the guy who gives 'em the right kind uh medicine they needs to get rid of the flu or the bad cold, or whatever they's got, well, he's the Medicine Man..."

"And that's you," Ronnie cut in, "Jimmie Jones. You told black Postmaster Bill Brown and his black staff just what's wrong with this place..."

Jimmie was pleased to know that his buddies did not feel the same way Bessie Black and her Hatchet Ladies did about his Blockbuster. However, he cut Ronnie off: "I was sure that you guys, like everybody else around here, had branded me a traitor, too. That you think I came up with my suggestion simply in order to make black Postmaster Bill Brown and his black management team look bad.

Look fellows," Jimmie emphasized, "The Blockbuster is 98 pages long. It took me months to gather that amount of information and then get it into some kind of order. Blacks took over in May of this year. I started work on my Blockbuster back in the summer of 1966, more than a year ago."

"We know all about that, Jimmie," Ronnie agreed. "We know when you started working on your Blockbuster. You even discussed one of your suggestions with me, Consolidation, remember? You told me how wasteful you thought it was that the primary and secondary Out Going Letter Sections (OLS), (which process out of town first class letters,) were split up, OLS primary up on the ninth floor, and OLS secondary on the 8th floor. I agreed with you. Don't you remember? And you took a wild guess that the Postal Service could save about a million dollars a year by consolidating them, by moving OLS secondary up on the ninth floor with OLS primary.

"You also talked about the consolidation of junk mail operations. You said that these operations needed consolidating even worse than OLS first class operations. You told me that junk mail was being worked on almost every floor. And I had no reason not to believe you. And that was long before anyone around here had any notions whatever of a black administration coming in here," Ronnie agreed. "But it wouldn't make any difference anyway..."

"Naw, hell naw," Oscar cut in. "Black or white, if the place is fucked up, it's fucked up. And you told 'em it was, too. 'Course they knowed it was. It's been that way all the time, ever since I been here. So, if the black dudes don't want to be criticized for the way things is, then they ought to change 'em. Lak you told 'em 'bout rewrap. You said the answer was simple. And it is. All they gotta do is tell the people how they ought to wrap they packages, and if they don't wrap 'em that way, don't take 'em, that's all.

"That't the way them private parcel dudes out there operate. If you take a package to them that ain't right, they tells you quick. 'We don't take 'em lak that.' That's why when they brings a package to your house, it's all together, man. Ain't nothing missing. That's why they's taking so such business away from Uncle Sam..."

Jimmie cut in. "You're right. People can trust them to deliver their packages safely," he said.

"You ought to go up there, sometime, up on the six floor and see all the mess spilling out over everything up there," Oscar continued.

Jimmie smiled in amusement. "I've been up there, "he told Oscar. "That's why I made the suggestion. Ronnie's been up there, too."

"Show yall have. Show yall have," Oscar apologized. "I don't know what I was saying. But uh, yall knows what I mean." And he continued, still, as if talking to someone who had not been "up there." "Most uh the time you wonder how the people got the packages to the post office in the first place, 'cause you look, and you look, and can't find no wrapper nowhere, jes a lot uh jumbled up mess floating 'round all over everything. And they got all them people up there with wrapping paper and glue and tying machines and stuff trying to get that crap back together some kind uh way.

"And lak you said in your rewrap suggestion, some uh them people go and sue the post office for losing that mess they was lucky enough to get in here in the first place, 'fore it busted up and spilled all out in the street. And lak you say, too. The PO gotta pay 'em 'cause they can't find the shit to get it all back together and put it back in the container it ain't never had. Boy, if the general public knowed what was going on down here, the way these people fuck up their money, they'd want to come down here and start kicking some asses. And I wouldn't blame 'em, neither. So, I'm with you all the way on that rewrap deal, Jimmie," Oscar told him.

"Lak you say, it ain't no big problem. It's simple. All they gotta do is tell them dummies on them windows down there in that lobby, who been taking in all that shit that scatters all over the damn place, is to take it if it's wrapped up good. And don't take it if it ain't wrapped up good. And lak you say, the PO will save a whole lot of big bucks if they do."

"Well, fellows," Jimmie said in appreciation, "it's nice to know that I didn't shoot a complete blank, that out of 20,000 people working down here, at least two agree that some of my ideas are worthy of consideration."

"We aren't the only ones, Jimmie," Ronnie corrected him. "There are lots of others..."

"Yeah," Oscar interrupted, "everybody working down here know this place is all fucked up. They was scared to say something when whitey was running it. And now, with blacks in the driver's seat, you better not say nothing. 'Cause it ain't gonna be jes the 20,000 black folks working down here breathing down your neck, it's gonna be every black dude living in Metro City with his foot up in your ass.

8

So don't be making no waves"

"Thanks a lot, friend," Jimmie said, forcing out a smile. "Just what I need."

"Oh, I'm sorry, Jimmie. I wasn't thinking. I was uh..."

"Look at that time, man," Ronnie cut in, eyeing the big round white and black clock hanging on the west wall. "Getting close."

"Yeah, we better start making it on down to the time card racks," Oscar agreed.

As usual, Ronnie and Oscar went on a few minutes ahead. Jimmie would wait until the gathering workers retrieve their time cards from the racks and move away, then he'd go and get his time card.

Finally, he closed and fastened the door of his locker. But before starting for the exit, he stopped and jotted down some notes in his little black book, a kind of diary he maintained. Notably, he entered the early, general reaction to his Blockbuster, including the lone, surprisingly favorable reaction by Ronnie and Oscar.

Finally, he made his exit out through the south passageway of the men's locker room and headed for the time card rack. By now, only about a minute and a half to hit time, his card would probably be the only one left in the rack. He'd not have to waste time and effort looking through all fifty or so others to find his time card which was almost never in its proper slot. The timekeeper, usually in a big hurry, just didn't play the game that way.

He was thinking now about Bessie Black and the Hatchet Ladies being angry about him submitting a suggestion such as his Block-buster. Their basic complaint was that it would cause some blacks to lose their jobs, and that it would be embarrassing to black management in that it was highly critical of them.

But Ronnie and Oscar knew. So did his wife Mary Belle. Jimmie had begun working on the suggestion long before black management took over the Metro City Post Office. As he took his time card from the time card rack and headed toward his work section, he recalled that cold winter night in 1966 when it was first rumored that Metro City was probably going to get its first black Postmaster.

He picked up the phone to talk to his wife, who said, "Hello, you black sonofabitch, finally decided to come to the goddam phone, huh?"

"I'm sorry Mary Belle," he said. "I got here as soon as I could."

"Your post office whore didn't want you to leave her, huh?" she shot back.

He ignored her cynicism and said calmly: "There's big news down here tonight. It's being rumored that we're going to get a black Postmaster, and the workers are using the phones here to call outside to tell their friends and everybody about it."

"Who is he, you?" she asked, giggling.

Again he disregarded her cynicism. "His name is Bill Brown," he answered.

"Not Jimmie Jones?" she sneered. "Well I'll be damned. How they miss you, somebody who know all about the post office and every damn thing else, too?" She paused for a moment, then added, "Oh yeah, speaking about knowing it all, I read some of that shit you got wrote down in this folder."

"What folder?"

"This here folder you got in the bottom dresser drawer. What you calls Blockbuster, or something lak that. And I played them tapes, too, you got in there."

"I've asked you quite often not to tamper with things like that of mine."

"Ah hell, I'm your wife aint I? I'm suppose to look at your stuff if I wants to."

"Yes, but, Mary Belle, you are too careless with such things. I don't even have to come home to know that the manuscript is scattered all over the drawer, all mixed up, page 10 following page 3, page 15 following page five. And no doubt the tapes are twisted and creased and hanging all out the drawer. How about it? Right?

"I don't know, maybe it is. I didn't have time to be messing 'round with that crap all day. 'spent too much time as it was reading and listening to that shit. Got it back in the drawer the best way I could," she said, breaking out in hysterical laughter and adding: "Boy, you really got your nerve."

"And what is that suppose to mean?" Jimmie asked curiously.

"I was just remembering some of that shit you got wrote down telling the Postmaster what he ought to do," she said, but warned: "'course you gonna have a different Postmaster by the time you gets all that crap together. So you gonna have to erase that white man's name off and put that spock's name on there. You sure it ain't gonna be you, huh?" she sneered again.

"Is it really necessary for me to tell you no again?" Jimmie asked angrily.

In a sneaky, grinning voice of mockery, she asked: "Anyhow, why don't you jes go on down there and work lak everybody else? Why you got to go and try to run everything everywhere you go? You got more sense than all the people in Metro City and Washington D.C., too."

Metro City was divided into 55 postal zones. Galova township was located in zone 48. Mail headed for Galova township, as was mail for all other postal zones, was given two sortings at the main Post Office, a primary sorting and a secondary sorting.

The primary sorting for Galova township was done in Galova Section-48P (GS-48P). The secondary sorting was done in Galova Section-48S (GS-48S).

GS-48S was Jimmie's work section. Normally, its workload did not begin to build up until around midnight when GS-48P completed the primary sorting of Galova mail.

When Jimmie reported at 10:12 each night for work, usually there was little or no mail for sorting in GS-48S. But there was set up work, such as supplying the section with hand trucks, tying machines, mail sacks etc. for dispatching the mail. Jimmie and 7:12 clerk Slick despicably referred to such duties as Man's Work. With banter, they frequently played a little game of mockery about it.

"There is no mail in here," Jimmie said to Slick who was there patiently waiting for him to come in and pose that very question. "Why are you here? And why do they want me in here?

"Is you uh man, or is you a woman?" Slick asked Jimmie.

"What's that got to do with me comimg in here early, when there's no mail?"

"It's got everything to do with you coming in here early, mail or no mail," Slick shot back, feigning irritation. "Now, tell me, is you uh man, or is you a woman?"

Jimmie uprighted his shoulders, wrinkled his lips and rammed out his chest. "I'm a man," he barked out in a voice deliberately huskier than his own. Then he pointed to the false muscles he simultaneously made in his outstretched arms. "Can't you see, brother? I'm a man. Dammit. I'm a man."

"Okay! Okay! Be cool," Slick mockingly calmed him down, while trying desperately to hold back his own snickering laughter. "Then, that answers your question. You's in here early 'cause you's a man. 'Cause you and me's got work to do. Man's Work."

"Man's Work?" Jimmie mockingly asked as he, too, tried unsuccessfully to hold back his squeezing out laughter.

"Yeah, Man's Work. And don't come telling me we's all making the same pay and they ain't no such thing as Man's Work. 'Cause that ain't the way it is down here. On pay day? Yeah. When it comes to getting that check. Everybody's equal. But on any and all other days, including pay day, when it comes to doing the work, you is either uh man or uh woman. If it's heavy and dirty work, it's Man's Work. Down here, that's the way it is, brother. Believe me, that's the way it is."

"Do I hear somebody from the 7:12 set complaining about MMPO working conditions?" Jimmie asked, continuing with their mockery of what he considered management foibles.

"Now there you go," Slick charged, "jealousy will get you nowhere. Anyway why don't you go on and say what you mean? The O.T. (over-time) set. I can't help it if they's got a lot of money that they wants to give away. So, I ain't complaining, not really. But if it looks lak I am," he stipulated with a big smile on his face, "I'm complaining for yall 10:12s. And for all them other sets that don't get no O.T. 'til Christmas time. It hurts me to be making all this good money when yall ain't and cain't." He broke out into loud laughter and added, "It ain't fair. It jes ain't fair."

"But on some of those overtime nights, when you sit for long periods doing nothing because there isn't a letter nowhere in sight, don't you feel just a little bit guilty?" Jimmie lectured Slick. "I think I would. And you should, too. For example, during vacation time, especially July and August when most everybody in Metro City is away and writing no letters, calling overtime, in my opinion, is much like a midnight mugging. The Metro post office draws a gun on the taxpayer, pulls him up into a dark alley, takes his wallet and, then, just for the hell of it takes the butt of its gun and clubs the taxpayer over the head several times. Yeah, Slick, if I were on 7:12, I'm not saying I wouldn't take the money, but I'd sure feel guilty as hell. And I can't bring myself to believe that you really don't, too."

The overtime scenario was a part of their little game of mockery, too, yet, each time they pulled it off, Slick showed genuine signs of emotional discomfort. He squirmed on his seat and stammered in his speech. "You right, Jimmie. Uh. You right. I do. I mean, I do feel kinda guilty, sometimes," he said, shaking off his nervousness. "But then I start thinking 'bout my expenses: my house note, my car note, my wife's car note, my son's car note, my daughter's car note, their college tuition, my golfing losses, and uh," he started stammering again, "and, well, with all them pretty little girls out there, a man's gotta have some fun sometimes, too. So, when I think about all them bills and things and stuff I gotta pay and do, well, the guilt sorta jes goes on away."

Jimmie was pleased to have the little game of mockery to play with Slick. It took his mind off the Blockbuster and the negative reaction shown to it, especially by the Hatchet Ladies and the sympathizers who joined with them to follow him to his locker room. But now the little mockery game had ended. He would have to face some kind of Blockbuster reaction from Slick. What will he have to say about it? Jimmie wondered. Will he be negative, too, like the Hatchet Ladies and their friends? Or will he be understanding like Ronnie and Oscar?

"Hey, this suggestion you made?" Slick called out to Jimmie, "what everybody's calling the Blockbuster, what made you do that, man?"

Oh oh, here it comes, Jimmie told himself. I don't like Slick's tone. I wasn't sure, but I thought he'd understand. Most of the things I included in the suggestion, at one time or another, I have discussed with him. And I thought that he agreed with me that something should be done about them. "What made me do it?" he responded, repeating Slick's words.

"Yeah, man, what made you do it?"

"What do you mean, what made me do it?"

"Just what I said, what made you do it?"

"I did it because it needed doing, because I guess I didn't think anyone else around here was ever going to do it. You don't approve of it, huh?"

"I ain't said that."

"No, not in words. But I'm sensing from your general reaction, that you don't. You disappoint me, Slick," Jimmie scolded him. "As much as you and I talked about adverse conditions around here, I thought you were genuinely interested in seeing some kind of change. I guess I was wrong. But tell me, what don't you agree in particular with?"

"The whole idea," Slick responded, surprising Jimmie, "that's what, the whole idea."

"Come on, Slick, you got to be kidding. You mean I didn't say, at least, one thing you agree with? In 98 pages, not one thing?"

"Naw, I ain't saying that. You said lots of things I agrees with."

"But you just said you disagreed with the whole idea. How can you disagree with the whole idea and, at the same time, agree with some of the items contained in it?"

Slick got cute, Jimmie thought, as he went on to explain precisely what he meant. "The idea, man," Slick said. "The whole idea," he repeated, placing great emphasis on the word idea. "All that time and money you wasted writing up that shit."

"What do you mean?"

"I mean they ain't gonna do nothing 'bout it. That's what I mean. They ain't gonna do nothing to change nothing 'round here. Never. And you can believe that. That's what I'm talking 'bout."

"Well, I'm glad we cleared that up," Jimmie said, in a tone expressing much relief. "For a minute there, you had me worried."

"Ah you knowed what I was talking 'bout. You jes wanted me to spell it out."

"You said you agreed with lots of the ideas in the Blockbuster. Which particular one do you think came across real well, better than any of the others?

"Well, lak I say, they was all good. You know how I feels 'bout all that shit. I think they ought to change everything you said they ought to change."

"But I mean," Jimmie insisted, "if you had to reach into the bag and pull out only one, one that holds great interest for you, which one would it be?"

"Well, lak I say," Slick repeated, "they's all good. But you know what my main peeve is: no parking facilities. You and me, we talked 'bout that a lot. And you told 'em good, too, 'bout that. 'Course a couple of things you said in the Blockbuster 'bout parking me and you never talked 'bout before."

"Oh yeah, what's that?"

"Well, I knowed 'bout, uh. Well, me and you, we talked 'bout how some Metro City private businesses who don't have no more'n 25 employes have a lot for 'em to park they cars in. And what a shame it is that down here at the PO where 20,000 people work, the government ain't got nowhere for us to park. And me and you, we talked something awful 'bout these old greedy parking lot owners 'round here, how they's robbing postal workers blind. We said that we pay more to park in they little old dirty, greasy lots over here on these crummy back streets than people pay to park in them nice clean lots downtown..."

"And you and I discussed how these enterprising lot owners enter into collusion with the city, too," Jimmie interrupted. "They demolish deteriorating, unprofitable buildings and construct parking lots on the land. Then they use their clout at City Hall to get no-parking signs installed on all neighboring streets, forcing Metro Main Post Office workers who don't want to walk long distances no option but, for a fee, to park in their lots..."

"Yeah, and we talked about how them robbers would starve to death, too," Slick cut in, "if it wasn't for us post office folks. 'Cause lak you say, most of them cars you see in them lots all day is post office folks cars."

"Also, you and I discussed how from five o'clock in the afternoon until 8 o'clock the next morning, all the cars in those lots are postal worker cars," Jimmie added. "Because during that time, except for us, this part of the city is a ghost town."

"And we wasn't lying, neither," Slick agreed. "And yeah, me and you, we talked about all uh that before. But something else you wrote about in the Blockbuster we never talked about was: you said that there is 30 parking lots 'round here. Man, I knowed it was a lot of 'em, but I ain't had no idea it was that many."

"You said there were a couple of things I included in the Blockbuster that you and I had not discussed," Jimmie reminded Slick. "What is the other one?"

"Well, you said some of them parking lots is on government land, didn't you?"

"What I said in the Blockbuster was, I had been informed that indeed many of those lots are constructed on land leased from the government. I have no absolute proof of this, but the information came to me from a reliable source. I have no reason to disbelieve it. I tried to get a clarification from the Postmaster's office. Needless to say, they flatly refused to give it to me."

"Well I didn't know that," Slick said in bewilderment. "You never said nothing to me 'bout that before. Many times we talked 'bout parking, too, and you ain't never mentioned that."

"I didn't know before," Jimmie apologized. "I found out about it only during the time I was putting the Blockbuster together. I must admit, though, I wasn't a bit surprised. I had assumed as much."

At midnight, GS-48P had finished the primary sorting of the first batch of city first class letter mail. Segments had begun arriving in GS-48S to receive its secondary and final sorting before being sent out to carrier station 48. Jimmie and Slick had trucked it in and women clerks were being called in to help sort it.

As the women filed in to take their seats, Slick sounded a warning.: "Hey, Jimmie?"

Yeah?"

"Don't look now," he cautioned, saying, "Up front."

But Jimmie did look now. And what he saw up front, surrounded by her myrmidon Hatchet Ladies, was the prancing, bellicose Bessie Black. And on her cheerleading direction, like a professional singing group from a glittering Las Vegas stage, they all pointed and started chanting in an ordered rhythmic pattern: "There he is, the traitor. There he is." Over and over they chanted. Passing workers, chanting, too, stopped and gathered around them. Shortly, the front part of section-48S became a wall of people. Among them, about one hundred, there was one man. He stood well to the rear of the crowd. But like all the rest, he, too, pointed and yelled out loudly: "There he is, the traitor. There he is."

Willie Moses, GS-48S supervisor, did not make a verbal show of his disapproval of Jimmie's Blockbuster, but he loudly acquiesced his support for the opposition. Picking up a handful of papers from his lecturn, he briskly headed toward the office to attend a staff meeting that had not been called.

At the direction of cheerleader Bessie Black, the chanting suddenly came to a halt. "Lak I tells yall all the time, black men ain't no good," she told the crowd. "You know what he said in his bullshit Blockbuster? Huh? Do you?" she urgently tried to rev up the crowd.

"He wants standardization in letter mailings in order to maximize machine usage," someone in the crowd said in a cajoling manner, but no one laughed.

"Yeah, he wants to take jobs away from blacks by running the machines 24 hours a day," someone else added. "That's what he wants."

"Yeah, that he do," Bessie Black agreed. "But that ain't what I'm talking 'bout, now. I'm talking 'bout what else he said. If you don't know, well, then I'll tell you . . ."

"Yeah, tell 'em, Bessie," unlearned Mamie Smith interrupted. "Yeah, go on tell 'em."

"It's about us black ladies," Bessie Black began, "how he ain't got no respect for us . . ."

"You got that right, Bessie. He show ain't," Mamie Smith said, cutting in again. "He lak all the rest of 'em," she agreed. "And what you alway say about 'em ain't no lie, neither. Black bastards. They jes ain't no good. That's all. Jes ain't no good."

Mamie Smith borrows a line from What Jimmie tagged Bessie's Black Gender Credo, which she repeated almost daily: ("The black bastards jes ain't no good. They ain't got no education. Cain't take care of their family. They's mean and hateful. Always beating on yuh. They ups and leaves you with a house full uh kids 'cause they can't make ends meet. And most uh the time, they acts lak a child. Black bastards. They jes ain't no good. That's all. Jes ain't no good.")

"He say us black ladies," Bessie continued, "ought to be made to lift these old heavy dispatch bags up on them trucks and push them old, big heavy trucks on over to the freight elevators, and do everything else the men do 'cause we make the same money."

"Show did," Mamie Smith said. "It's a shame, I tell you, it's a shame."

Dolly Jean nervously squirmed about the floor, pushed her Bible further up under her arm and squeezed it tightly, a posture she occasionally assumed as a matter of conscience. It was quite obvious that she had a great desire to directly refute the argument Bessie Black and Mamie Smith were putting forth. And rightfully so. Jimmie did note in his suggestion that some black male MMPO workers did indeed complain about having to do all the heavy and dirty dispatch work while black female MMPO workers receiving comparable pay did none. But the plan he presented as an instrument to solve the problem was not that black female MMPO workers be forced to do the heavy and dirty dispatch work.

His argument was that to classify all male secondary clerks dispatcher and require them to perform all dispatch duties and not do the same by female secondary clerks was discriminatory. He labeled the practice a form of force by pointing to what he termed the Comparable Paradox.

"On the fifth floor, only one floor above city letter section, is the Equal Employment Opportunity (EEO) office," Jimmie stated in the Blockbuster. "The EEO says that 'any postal employee... who believes he is being discriminated against because of race, color, religion, sex or national origin may file a complaint,'" Jimmie quoted, then stipulated that the EEO, headed by a woman, received a volume of complaints everyday from women charging the Postal Service with discrimination because they claim it awards most supervisory and management jobs to men. These are the same women who refuse to perform dispatch-work for which they are being paid.

Jimmie noted in the Blockbuster that male clerks were beginning to complain about the dispatch-work dilemma. It was a thankless job, some of them charged. The women did not appreciate the fact that the men were doing their part of the dispatch-work as well as their own. But what really galled some of the men clerks more than anything else, perhaps, was that, when it came to doing dispatch-work, which the guys jokingly preferred to call Man's Work, some of the women clerks would start ordering them around.

So to solve this problem and simultaneously ease the growing tension between the sexes, because of the responsibilities attached to it, Jimmie suggested the dispatch job be given rank, upgraded in pay and assigned to one particular qualifying individual, male or female. To justify his suggestion that the dispatcher job be given rank and upgraded in pay, he outlined the responsisilities of the job exclusive of the so-called Man's Work part of it. If a dispatch is late leaving the main installation; if it is late arriving at its destination; if any part of it is late arriving at its destination; or if it is mislabeled and is mis-sent to the wrong destination, the dispatcher is held responsible, Jimmie noted.

Dollie Jean, apparently, had no more love for Jimmie than Bessie Black, but the fairness-side of her personality seemed to have revealed her utter discomfort in hearing someone deliberately lie about someone else's actions, even about Jimmie's actions.

Obviously, this was why she nervously squirmed about the floor and tightly squeezed the Bible that was neatly perched under her arm. She wanted to explain exactly what Jimmie had said in his

Blockbuster about dispatch work. But with Bessie Black, the Hatchet Ladies and the crowd of one hundred women supporters who were all fired up and seemingly ready to handle anything that might happen to displease them, Dolly Jean thought it better to keep her fairness-side muffled and out of sight.

"What yall think about that, huh?" Bessie Black screamed into the crowd. "Can you believe it? Jimmie Jones wants us ladies to load them ole heavy sacks of mail up on them dispatch trucks. Then, with them old rusty wheels binding on 'em 'cause they ain't been greased in ten years, he wants us women to push them trucks over these old bumpy pot-hole floors all the way over on the other side of the building to them freight elevators."

Once again , Dolly Jean went into her squirmimg Bible squeezing act. Bessie Black was lying again about what Jimmie said in his Blockbuster, she surely must have been thinking.

"What yall think, ladies?" Bessie Black screamed out again. "Lak I tells yall all the time. The black bastards jes ain't no good." Then cheerleader Bessie Black yelled at the crowd: "What did I say?"

And they yelled back: "The black bastards just ain't no good."

"And Jimmie Jones, the traitor, What about him?" Bessie Black interjected, "he ain't no good neither. What did I say?"

"Jimmie Jones, the traitor," they responded. "He ain't no good neither."

The little question and answer game, played by Bessie Black, her Hatchet Ladies and the one hundred black women gathered around her continued non stop. The lone man had disappeared. In the fashion of a song writer improvising on the spot, and tacking on fragments from her black gender credo, Bessie Black hooked up all the elements of their harangue into a song and played it back nursery rhyme style. Pointing their fingers at Jimmie and chanting in low tones on a single note over and over, they droned out the words: "There he is, the traitor. There he is, Jimmie Jones. He ain't no good neither. The black bastards jes ain't no good. Jes ain't no good."

In the thick floating heat of the droning mass of voices, one member of the revelers, a tiny shadow of a woman, broke out through the crowd, rushed into GS-48S and started banging Jimmie over the head with her small strapless purse. "You traitor," she yelled at him. "You dirty, stinking traitor. Turning against your own people. You ought to be shot," she screamed. Then, as fast as she had run into the section, she dashed right back out.

Slick was sitting on the sorting case right next to Jimmie. He hopped up from his seat, caught Jimmie by the arm and said: "Come on, man, let me get you out of here. You lucky it was one of them little ones. If it had been one of them big mammas coming in here on you, you would have been in big trouble. 'Cause They totes rocks and and guns and things 'round in they purses. If one uh them konks you on the head, we gonna have to take you out of here on a stretcher."

Jimmie and Slick went out through the back of the section and took a break. So did the noisy crowd move away from the front of GS-48S, including Bessie Black and her Hatchet Ladies. But they did not stay away. Official break-time at the MMPO was fifteen minutes. When Jimmie and Slick returned to GS-48S, Bessie Black and her Hatchet Ladies returned also, followed immediately by the noisy crowd.

"Look, man, here they come back again," Slick alerted Jimmie.

Walking back to his case, but falling slightly behind Slick, Jimmie fearfully viewed the crowd reassembling at the front of the section.

Bessie Black saw Jimmie coming back into the section, but she asked anyway: "Where is that damn traitor, Jimmie Jones?"

"Here he comes now," Johnnie Mae answered in a scraggly, masculine voice. She was a GS-48S female clerk with man like features who had come into the station at midnight with the other GS-48S female clerks. As usual, she was sorting mail at the fifth case.

In order to get back to the third case where he had been sorting mail, Jimmie was obliged to pass right by Johnnie Mae's case.

"There he is!" Hatchet Lady Blanche Mims yelled. "The traitor, there he is."

This time, instead of framing the raucous stance of a high school cheerleader, Bessie Black took on the classic-raised-arm posture of a symphony conductor: "What did Blanche say?" she conjured the noisy crowd. "Huh? What did she say?"

And in contradiction to the quiet tone of Bessie Black's patrician posture, the noisy crowd loudly bellowed back: "There he is, the traitor! There he is!"

The intense warlike cries coming from the one hundred angry black women, encouraged by Bessie Black and her dedicated Hatchet Ladies, had begun to unsettle Jimmie a bit. In approaching his case to resume his mail distributing duties, he decided to visually observe the unruly crowd. He would try to judge the extent of their anger in order to determine if they really were becoming as violent as they sounded. At the moment, he was thinking and noticing nothing else.

Johnnie Mae's premeditated actions were quick, sure and painful. She wheeled on her swiveling stool, slammed her big flat foot between Jimmie's legs, and tripped him fast to the floor. Pondering the possibility of some one coming in again from the angry crowd outside, instead of this surprisingly bizarre in-station occurrence, Jimmie was unprepared to break the fall. Like a one piece store case manikin, refusing to bend, he fell flat on his face. His body went numb, the low hanging flourescent ceiling lights, seemingly, flicked on and off. He felt warm sticky blood spouting from his nose. He sensed someone tugging about his shoulders. And, from what seemed a long distance away, he faintly heard a voice asking if he was okay.

It was the scraggly bass voice of Johnnie Mae, the tinge of mischief now displaced by shrouded mockery. As quickly as she had tripped him to the floor, she now left her stool in maudlin pretense to attend to him. She carefully lifted up his head several times, but, with force, she deliberately let it fall back to the floor. She rammed him violently in his sides with alternating knees and, in that scraggly bass voice, she asked him again if he was okay.

Jimmie felt Johnnie Mae running both of her fleshy hands underneath his body and begin raising him up from the floor. She was a big, strong woman.

Suddenly, he sensed that his body was fast falling again. Also, it felt weighted down. And, with more force than he had ever known, his body banged back down to the hard parquet floor. For a few minutes he thought he would die. Johnnie Mae had not only let Jimmie fall back to the floor. She had let herself fall to the floor, too, squarely on top of him. Still lying there with 210 pounds of solid flesh squashing Jimmie beneath her, in that scraggly voice, she mockingly asked: "Is you okay?" Later, it seemed forever to Jimmie, Johnnie Mae rolled over off of him and got to her feet. She bent back down, slid her ebony banana-fingers under his belt, lifted him up from the floor and stood him up against her sorting case.

She was sorry about the whole thing, she said. She had first tripped Jimmie to the floor because in swiveling her stool about she did not see him coming. She dropped him back to the floor because she lost her grip. And she fell on top of him because her feet slipped on "all this ole loose twine and paper and crap all over the floor."

Brushing dirt and lint from his clothes and emotionally licking his wounds, Jimmie headed back out to the men's room to wash his face and clear his head. And without any verbal screaming and frantic hand waving direction from Bessie Black, the one hundred angry women sniggled in perfect unison.

When the battered Jimmie returned, Bessie Black, her Hatchet Ladies and the one hundred unsympathetic noisy women were still there waiting. They weren't through with him yet. Not by a long shot. Johnnie Mae's little comedy skit had momentarily brought jocular sniggles to their snarled up faces. But those jocular sniggles had now faded. They were dead serious again.

"Hey, Mr Traitor," Bessie Black yelled at Jimmie, "You in big trouble. I guess you know that by now. You done went and said a lot uh thing in your Blockbuster, as you calls it, that a lot of us black folks don't lak. Right ladies?" she called out to her colleagues.

And they agreeably answered: "Right, Bessie. Right."

"They ain't gonna take it sett'n down," Bessie Black continued. "And you can believe that. They ain't gonna let you get away with the shit you done gone and put down in your Blockbuster. And me and my close lady friends is gonna be right there with 'em," she said, pointing to the Hatchet Ladies, one after the other: Blanche Mims, the sweetheart of the Late Set; Mamie Smith, the Unlearned One; and Dolly Jean, the confused Bible toting divorcee.

"But you can do something about it," she assured Jimmie. "You hear me, nigger!" she shouted at him.

Jimmie did not respond. He sat down to his case and started throwing mail.

"Here's what you can do, Mr. Traitor. You can go down there to the Suggestion Committee and tell 'em that you want your Blockbuster back, that you didn't mean all them things you said about black folks. That will get you off the hook with us. How 'bout it? Gonna do it? Huh?"

Jimmie still did not respond to Bessie Black. But, in a soft tone, he did ask Slick: "What does she mean about all those things I said about black folks?"

"The word is out that you think black folks can't run nothing,"

Slick told Jimmie. "That's what she's talking 'bout. The workers say your suggestion makes the black administration look bad."

"I'm giving you a chance to get these people off your back, nigger!" Bessie Black strongly urged Jimmie. "You better come on in out of the rain while you can. Take my word for it. If you don't. Things ain't gonna get no better for you. So, if I was you, I'd come on in now, 'fore they really do get bad."

Jimmie hadn't responded to Bessie Black because he wasn't sure of just what he should say, or how he should say it. He had had two very negative experiences already tonight, the tiny shadow of a woman clubbed him over the head with her purse. Queen bee Johnnie Mae, as Slick chose to refer to her, tripped him to the floor. And, with her 210 pounds of solid weight, she sprawled flat on top of him. There were 100 angry black women out there gazing predaciously down the GS-48S aisle at him, ready and waiting for the slightest provocation to pounce on him. If he unfortunately chosed the wrong words, it could set them off. Wild and unruly, like a ochlocratic mob seizing one whom they consider a satanic ruler, these 100 ill advised, treacherous black women, outnumbering him and his buddy Slick 100 to two, could storm into GS-48S and maul him to death, and Slick, too, if he tried to help, before any one else could get there to rescue them. So, not knowing just what to say or just how to say it, Jimmie thought it better to say nothing at all.

"How 'bout it, Mr. Traitor?" Bessie Black prodded him. "Is you gonna do it? Is you gonna go down there and get your Blockbuster back? That thing can cause a lot of black folks to lose they jobs. And you know it," she accused him. "Is you gonna go and get it back? Huh?"

Jimmie still did not respond. This time he didn't even ponder the question whether he should or not. He just didn't.

"Okay, Mr. Traitor, with your smart ass. You asked for it. And you gonna get it," Bessie Black threatened him. "Come on over here, Blanche," she ordered, and Blanche Mims obeyed. "Did you do what I told you to do?" she asked.

"Yeah, I've got it right here," Blanche replied.

Bessie Black had ordered Blanche Mims to: "draw up one of them what cha call it things 'cause I don't know how to do it, and you do."

Blanche Mims started reading from a sheet of paper she held in her hand. It was an ultimatum. It did not demand that Jimmie withdraw the entire suggestion. But it did demand that he retract several entries which they thought would surely cause a loss of jobs to blacks. Also, and this was at the top of the list, they demanded he retract the statement that the low educational level of the average black Metro City postal worker would prevent him or her from finding a job in the private sector paying a comparable salary.

"This is what you gotta do," Bessie Black shouted out to Jimmie. "And not tomorrow. Today. If you don't. Well. Me and my close lady friends is gonna want to know why. And the way we gonna ask you why, you ain't gonna lak. So, black bastard, you better get on your bicycle right now and be on your way."

Chapter 2

A call over the loudspeaker ordered Jimmie to report to the detail desk.

There were 55 primary sections and 55 secondary sections on the floor, including Galova Section-48S (GS-48S), Jimmie's section. The detail desk was situated squarely in the center of the floor, primary sections to the north, secondary sections to the south. If Jimmie walked down the main aisle to the detail desk, he knew workers in each of the other 54 secondary sections would yell traitor at him as he'd pass. So he sneaked down the back aisle.

When he arrived there, the clerk gave him a small slip of yellow paper and said: "You are to call this number immediately. The person whose name is on the slip said that it was an emergency."

It happened every Tuesday night. So Jimmie didn't rush. In route to make his call, he took the back aisle behind the 55 primary sections. He would avoid traitor-calls from workers there, too.

But the telephones were located in the north end of the building by the candy counter. From the guardpost to the phones there was no back aisle. Most employes were in their sections working. But he did meet some coming down the corridor and they gave him the traitor-call.

When he got there, he found all six telephones busy. He was not necessarily displeased. A few minutes wait would not remove the problem, but it would push it back into time giving him a few more minutes of freedom from tension and aggravation. A short distance away from the candy counter, he leaned against the corridor wall to relax, and to try to hide from more traitor-call hecklers.

The candy counter was 30 feet long and ten feet deep. With a single opening only on the corridor side, and sunken into the wall, it depended on the cafeteria situated behind it for its very topography. Physically, the candy counter was so much a part of the cafeteria that when it was closed, a stranger would not know it was there.

The device that camouflaged the counter when it was closed was a huge three foot thick overhead swinging door. Painted the same color as the corridor wall, unless separating seams were examined closely, the pulled down candy counter door created the illusion of a solid wall. Jimmie saw the monstrous, rolled-up overhead door perched high against the ceiling. And he shuddered at the thought that if by some strange twitch of fate it should come crashing down, how flatly it would splatter the bodies of the two lines of people standing beneath it.

Suddenly, his mind started playing awful tricks on him. He saw the figure of someone he knew very well step into one of the two lines of people. It was Mary Belle, his wife. Along with those people waiting in line she, too, stood directly beneath the huge, overhead door. Jimmie saw the safety catch on the door give way. He saw the big door start sliding for the crash. He heard people screaming. And he saw them scurrying, trying to get out of harm's way. But his ominous mind saw the specter of Mary Belle just standing there, unable to move. He closed his eyes tightly and mumbled inaudibly as if asking someone to forgive him. Wishing harm to come to others was something Jimmie hardly ever did, not even to Mary Belle. He felt guilty and ashame.

As he stood there waiting, he continued watching the two lines of people as they filed in to buy candy, cigarettes and gum. He was sorry about the errant, wishful thought of the big, heavy overhead door crashing down on Mary Belle. But he was not so abased that he was urging any of the six phone users to hurry and finish so he could talk to her. In fact, he was still dealing with the crashing door mirage as the impulsive thought seemingly tried to wedge its way back into his mind.

Suddenly, from one of the two waiting lines came an amusing distraction. A short, bald man, buying a package of cigarettes from the blind, candy counter clerk, said, "Sorry, sir but twenty is the smallest I got."

The blind clerk took the money and replied: "That's okay, Bill, we can change ten dollars."

The short, bald man shot back, "You can change what? And what did you call me?"

The blind clerk rubbed his hand through his thin graying hair several times, smiled at his black, female clerk companion and told her to: "Tell him what I said, Bernice."

The black female clerk tapped her ebony forehead lightly with her long, slender forefinger and said, "Tell him with the money, honey."

The blind clerk counted out $9.60 to the short bald man: a five dollar bill, four singles, two quarters and one dime. And he said, "Cigarettes, forty cents."

"Give me the rest of my change!" the short, bald man demanded, ripping open the cigarette pack. "I want ten dollars more!" he yelled.

The blind clerk yelled back at him. "That's all you get here, Bill! Good night, Bill!"

"I want my ten dollars," the man said again "And quit calling me Bill '

"Don't you ever give up, Bill?" the blind clerk pleaded. "After ten years, it gets a little tiresome." Then he stipulated: "And out of all the fake voices you've tried over those ten years, this one beats all. My two year old, if I had one, wouldn't have any trouble knowing who you are, Bill."

The blind clerk, his black, female companion clerk and the two long lines of waiting customers all broke out in hardy laughter. The short, bald man, sneaking out through the crowd, tried desparately to cover his mouth. He was laughing, too.

The blind man yelled after him. "Hey, Bill! Better luck next time."

Finally, one of the phone users finished her conversation, hung up the receiver and walked away. Jimmie reluctantly strolled over to take her place. He had thrown the small wadded yellow piece of paper into the garbage. He knew his own telephone number. So he positioned himself and started dialing. He heard the click of the receiver being picked up on the other end.

"Hello, you black sonofabitch," the harsh salutation roughed through the line at Jimmie. And with it came the belching effects of odious sour mash. Mary Belle loved her beer. "Finally decided to come to the goddam phone, huh?"

Mary Belle was not really a bad girl. Deep beneath the bluster and profanity, she was gentle and warm. On some very rare and unguarded occasions, she surprisingly revealed it. But, like so many Metro City 31 year old black women, a goodly number of whom worked right there at the MMPO, Mary Belle had been lied to, disappointed, beaten and estranged. Her first husband left her with three children. Her second husband left her with two more.

Jimmie got the idea that perhaps Mary Belle's brash treatment of him was meant in some way to make him pay for the sins perpetrated against her by her two previous husbands. Her cold, coarse indifferent attitude would create distance between them, he presumed she thought. It would give her a certain amount of independence. If Jimmie should likewise happen to estrange her, because she was detached, she would suffer little pain. On each occasion of her attacks on him, Jimmie would resign himself to an area of hurtful understanding.

"I'm sorry Mary Belle," he said calmly. "I got here as soon as I could."

"Your post office whore didn't want you to leave her, huh?" she shot back.

He disregarded her cynical remark and said calmly: "I didn't come to the phone to listen to a lot of profanity, especially from someone who claims to be a lady. And I don't plan to listen to anymore. If you have some particular reason for having called me, I will discuss that with you. If not, I will hang up."

"Now, you look here, motherfucker, goddamit. You don't go getting so highfalutin with me, talking all that proper shit, sounding like a fucking sissy. You my husband. I can call you anytime I gets ready."

"I just told you about that profanity. You know I don't like it. I don't like it at home, in public places or on the telephone, either. And if you don't stop it and tell me why you called, I'm going to hang up."

"Don't get mad, now. You know what I called you for. Now don't you, baby?" she said in a low voice.

"No, I don't know why you called," he said, but he did. And he tried to straighten out his face, as he lied, as if she could see him through the telephone line.

"Ah, Jimmie, don't be like that, baby," she drooled. "You do know. Now don't you?"

"I know nothing of the kind," he answered sharply.

"Tomorrow," she said. "Just you and me, baby. All alone in the house, all the kids away."

Her five kids were by previous marriages. "All the kids away? Where?" he questioned her.

Jimmie could hear Mary Belle breathing hard. He could hear her muted voice hissing through her tightly closed lips. He could sense the consternation building up in her.

And in one big puff of anger, she screamed back through the line at him. "Tomorrow is Wednesday, goddamit! You black sonofabitch, you know what day it is. The kids will be in school, as they is everyday, and I'm off."

Jimmie thought that he could not agree with Mary Belle more. She really was off.

"Jimmie, please," she whispered . "I'm sorry I said that, baby. I really am. You knows I am. Don't hang up. I'm just so worked up, thinking about tomorrow. I go the whole week thinking about nothing but Wednesday, my day off. My day at home alone with you."

Occasionally, Mary Belle was successful in catching Jimmie of guard. For a moment her purring words held him captive. Spoken by anyone else, such words fluffing against his longing ears, would have sunken deep into his waiting groins. Titilating it to its very tip, they would have made firm his rock-throbbing phallus. But coming from Mary Belle, those warm mating words were without substance, empty. And they left him cold.

Yes, he knew why Mary Belle had called. He knew exactly what she wanted. And the thought of it, the whole repulsive idea of his being at home in bed with her all day, nauseated him.

"And what do you do every Tuesday night when I calls you?" Mary Belle complained. "You makes a fool out of me, pretending you don't know what day tomorrow is. Why do you do that to me, Jimmie?"

"Mary Belle," Jimmie said to her, then thought to himself: God only knows why her mother named her Mary Belle. There is nothing merry about her. And her raspy voice certainly doesn't sound like a bell, not one in tune, anyway. "I've got to get back to my work section," he said, giving her his intended final notice.

"Not yet, baby," she pleaded. "let's talk some more about tomorrow."

"What is there to talk about?"

"Don't be so mean. Don't you have no feelings?"

Jimmie had feelings all right. Feelings of nausea and disgust. Like all Tuesdays when she called him, those feelings would linger throughout the night. And, on his arrival home the next morning, they would be amplified by her who would torment him for the rest of the day. "Mary Belle, I've got to go now," he said calmly.

"Okay, Jimmie, I'll let you go, " she said "But I'll be waiting. I won't sleep a wink all night, not 'til you gets here."

Jimmie hung up the receiver and walked away from the phone. "Okay, Mary Belle,"he said. "You liar. You bare faced liar."

Jimmie returned to GS-48S. Realizing that he had been gone for a considerable time, he went directly to his seat and began distributing mail into his sorting case at an unusual rate of speed.

Slick was anxiously awaiting his return. "Hey, man," he said. "You know the nice broad I was telling you about? The sharp new chick that's so stacked up? Well, she come in while you was gone."

Rapidly thumping mail into his case, and not really listening to what Slick was saying nor remembering anything he had told him about the "nice broad," Jimmie said, "Oh yeah? She did, huh?"

Slick motioned his head backward and said in a quiet voice, "Yeah, there she is, right behind us, over there, sett'n up on the front case. Didn't you see 'er when you come back in?"

Jimmie didn't answer. Letters bouncing off the metal backdrop of his sorting case, emulated the sounds of rapid fire coming from an army rifle range. He was busy trying to bring his work output up to the level of his station mates who had been there working all along. But more importantly, the idea of being home all day Wednesday with Mary Belle was the thing really bothering him.

"Hey, Jimmie," Slick persisted. "Man, I don't know what's got you so shook up, but whatever it is, what I'm trying to show you will take your mind off it right quick"

"Yeah? It will, huh?"

To get Jimmie's attention, Slick reached over and grasped him by his right hand, abruptly stopping him from sorting the mail. "Hey, man? Over there. On the front case. The fine new chick I was telling you about. Goldie."

"Goldie!" Jimmie shot back, the name coming from his anxious lips even faster than the letters zipping from his rapid mail throwing hand. It was as if the name Goldie held for him some kind of warm, memorable significance.

Slick quickly released his arm, backed off slightly and viewed him strangely. "Yeah!" he replied. "Goldie! That's her name." He turned and faced the row of cases behind them. "Say, Goldie?" he called to her. "This here is Jimmie, the dude I told you about, the one who passed the supervisor's exam." Turning back and facing Jimmie, he said, "She agreed with me. She say you ought to go on and take it 'cause she think you would make a good supervisor, too."

Jimmie was flattered by the confidence his two station mates had in him. But how did they know whether or not he'd make a good supervisor, especially Goldie, the new girl? She had just met him. She didn't even know whether he was a good clerk or not. In reality, she knew nothing at all about him, not even what kind of person he was. Momentarily, he lowered his head in fleeting dejection. Again he wondered if Mary Belle was the only person in Metro City who thought him a dummy.

"Hey, man?" Slick asked. "Ain't you gonna thank the pretty lady who don't know nothing 'bout you for feeling the same way I do 'bout you making a good supervisor?"

Jimmie turned and faced Goldie at the very moment she turned and faced him. His eyes loomed large, his hands became sweaty and his heart pounded uncontrollably. It was Goldie all right. His Goldie. The only woman he had ever loved, and probably ever would. Finally, with a shaking voice, he managed to say, "Thank you. Thank you very much."

"You are more than welcome," she said, and added, "I do believe you'd make a good supervisor. You know that, don't you?"

"See? I told you," Slick said. "And she means it, too. She ain't gonna lie." He paused in admiration, and stipulated, "She's nice."

Jimmie was proud and still excited, but talked in a more controlled tone, now. "Yeah, I know," he said. "I agree with you. Goldie is nice. In fact, she's one of the nicest persons I've ever known."

Slick looked at Jimmie in astonishment. Then, he picked up a letter from his ledge and just stared at it for a moment before throwing it into the case. This definitely is not their first meeting, his facial expression seemed to say. "When I introduced you, I thought you was jes meeting her," he questioned Jimmie, then he probed them both: "How long yall knowed each other?"

"A long time," Goldie said, with a seeming catch in her throat.

For a moment she said nothing more. She just stared over at Jimmie. And he just stared back at her.

Their eyes locked in tight, especially Jimmie's eyes. And he thought that in seven years she had not changed one iota: the golden complexion glowing from her warm face; the dark brown hair streaming down her back; the yellowish brown eyes twinkling at him, especially now locked in; the thin, sensuous lips calling out to him; and that warm smile that smiles even when she doesn's smile, they were all there.

"A very long time," Goldie stipulated. "1945 to be exact. Jimmie had been discharged from the service only a short time. We met and fell in love." She paused for a moment, then continued. "And he's the only man I've ever loved." But, then, she quickly threw her hand over her mouth as if trying to keep the words from coming out. She was a married woman. And now, so was Jimmie a married man.

Jimmie wanted to change the subject. "No, Slick," he reverted to the previous discussion. "I don't want to be a supervisor..."

"Yeah, man," Slick cut him off and awkwardly tapped two letters together. He looked at Goldie and Back at Jimmie as if trying to figure out some kind of puzzle. Then he leaned over to Jimmie and said in a low tone, "That's what I want to tell you, man. You on the list. You play your cards right and you got it made. No problem. You on the list!" he repeated with great emphasis.

"But I didn't make a big score," Jimmie replied. "I don't even remember what it was, about 70, I think."

"But, man, with your years of service, that would push you up to about 87 or something like that." With a look of disgust on his face, Slick took his thumb and pointed over his left shoulder at Willie Moses, GS-48S supervisor. He was standing at the front of the unit at his small desk, which was really a podium. For it had no seat. "See that dummy up there fumbling with them papers, trying to look busy and intelligent? They say he didn't even make 70," Slick charged.

"But you have to make 70 in order to qualify," Jimmie disagreed.

Slick leaned over a bit closer to him. "That's the shit they tells you, man. But all you have to do is have some bread and know the right people."

"I've heard that," Jimmie agreed. "But I've never met anyone who knows who takes the money. Neither have I met a supervisor who will admit that he paid out money to get his job."

"All you got to do is act like you wants it," Slick insisted, "and that you don't mind paying for it. That's all. And you won't have to worry about looking for them. 'cause they'll come looking for you..."

Johnnie Mae, whom Slick referred to as the Stud Bee, in a masculine scraggly voice, yelled at him from the fifth stool where she sat plucking hairs from her top lip with a shiny pair of metal tweezers. "Hey, motherfucker, what the hell you whispering 'bout over there?" She rocked her 210 pound frame backward on her stool and peeked around the clerk sitting on the fourth stool next to her and on around Jimmie so as to see Slick who was sitting on the second stool.

As usual, such language coming from the mouths of women, embarrassed Jimmie. He took a quick look over Johnnie Mae's way, then turned back.

Johnnie Mae's shoulders were massive, as if padded. But her apparent solid torso, with a breast that had no visible signs of mammaries, tapered quickly to meet narrow hips then ballooned so that her expansive behind completely hid the top of the rest bar she sat on. Her gums, peeping from behind thick lips, purpled at the edges. Her big fat black face glowed of excessive oil. And her bloodshot eyes, like school yard marbles, danced about in their sockets.

Johnnie Mae yanked another hair from her top lip and yelled at Slick again. "Hey, motherfucker! talk out loud, Dammit. So everybody can hear what you saying."

Jimmie had switched over to clerk and come to work at the Main Post Office back in 1961. Prior to that he was a postman out at the MidSouth carrier station. As he had done for six years, he tried hard once more to sink himself down into the foam rubber padding of his restbar. It was a part of his up-bringing. He simply was not accumtomed to hearing such language coming from the mouth of a woman, especially in so public a place.

"Big lard ass woman lover," Slick growled, but not loud enough for Johnnie Mae to hear him. "Always thinking somebody's talking 'bout her. She's thinking that 'cause she's always talking 'bout somebody."

As he had done on each such occasion over the six years he had been there, Jimmie spoke in a quiet tone. "Little vulgar, huh?"

And Slick answered him as he had done on each such occasion over those six years. "Ah, man, that bitch say the first thing come into her mind. And it don't make no difference who she talking to, neither. It could be the Postmaster hisself. It wouldn't make her no difference. That's why I told Supervisor Moses to seat 'um the way they's sett'n. See? I got Goldie and Julie Mae sett'n up on the front 'cause they's nice. And down on the other end, I got Mrs Reames, 'cause she's a church going lady. Got this bitch in the middle, away from them good and decent people.'Course, you know she's gonna start walking in a minute. And it ain't gonna make no difference then."

Jimmie looked over at Goldie. Their eyes met again. She dropped the letter she was about to throw into the case, and slid down from her restbar to pick it up. There were other letters on the floor. She picked them up, too.

"Goldie, you start picking up letters off the floor 'round here, and that's all you'll be doing all night," Slick told her. "I used to pick 'em up. No more, baby. These people 'round here throw mail all over the floor, kick it 'round and walk on it and everything else. Supervisor Moses say something to 'em about it, they cusses him out. And he don't say nothing else to 'em, just runs on back up there to the front. That's why they need some good supervisors down here like you would make," he said to Jimmie watching supervisor Moses from the sides of his eyes. "Look at that dummy," he sniggled. "Up there fumbling with them papers like he's some big executive. And ain't gonna make no move to do nothing about the mail or nothing else unless somebody tells him to.

The detail clerk, over the loudspeaker, interrupted. "All stations in secondary, pick up your mail in primary," she said. "Replace bascarts."

The first pick up at midnight of mail from GS-48P for GS-48S usually was a large one. Jimmie and Slick normally used several hand trucks of a 40 tray capacity to bring it all in. Later pickups were smaller, requiring only bascarts, mobile containers similar to super mart carts, with a capacity of about ten trays of mail.

"Okay, Slick, there you go," Johnnie Mae yelled out.

And Slick snapped back, "I hear 'er. Think I'm deef?"

"Well, all right, then. Let' go. Get that mail in here so we can work it"

"Ah shut up, woman."

Jimmie looked toward the podium to get Supervisor Moses's reaction to Slick and Johnnie Mae's discussion. Moses just stood there gazing toward the back of the unit. At what, Jimmie could not tell.

In the meantime, Slick started looking back and forth at Jimmie and Goldie Again. Finally, he leaned over to Jimmie and asked, "Hey, man," and smiled to soften the blow, "what do a fine babe like Goldie want with a dude like you? I mean, don't get me wrong, now. You's a all right guy. I mean. You wear sharp clothes and you got some smarts about you, and you stand up to whitey but..." He looked at Jimmie's receding forehead, his protruding chin, his rolled back lips. Then, at Jimmie's total visage. Slick's brow furrowed and quickly smooth out again. Jimmie's inky face reflected the dancing light that came from the high hanging flourescent lamps like Mississippi black top beaming back at an August noon day sun.

"I mean, man, ah, well, what I mean is, a pretty yellow gal like Goldie. With that personality she got. I mean, man, that babe can have anybody she wants to."

It ripped through Jimmie once more. To him, one of the most horrifying things about being black was not that black was black, but that black was ugly. He swiveled about on his restbar as if to check the face of every individual person within eye shot, those on his side of the section's aisle, those on the other side of the aisle, and those rushing to and fro on the floor's main center aisle.

When he'd undoubtedly find one, he would say to Slick: I know what you mean. It's because I'm very black. But you make it sound like I'm an oddity, a strange phenomenon. Then he would point to a face and say to Slick, Look at that chick over there, she's as black as I am. And look at that dude walking down the center aisle with that red shirt on. He's even blacker than I am.

But, although he'd checked around, as he had done hundreds of times before, Jimmie knew that he would not find anyone blacker than he, neither would he find anyone nearly as black as he. Not even Johnnie Mae nor Bessie Black, with their separate deep soot pitched complexions, was as black as Jimmie. Of the total 20,000 employes working in the Metro City Main Post Office building, he'd not find one. He knew that before he swiveled the first time, but he swiveled anyway. One time-, two-, three Then he severely reproached himself.

That's how it always was. Even when he'd go looking down on 57th and Peach Street, 65th and Burly Grove, he'd find no one as black as he. Even if he went over on the westside where blacks were arriving fresh out of the blistering sun of the southland, it was the same. He'd still find no one as black as he. Jimmie thought that, except for him, the admixture of his race had been total. He was the only true black man around, the only blue blood in the entire hemisphere. Indeed, he was a Puritan.

He pushed out his chest, erected his shoulders high, turned back to face Slick squarely and said in a clear, unwavering voice, "Now what were you saying?"

"I thought I told you to go and get that mail," Johnnie Mae yelled again at Slick. This time she was standing right behind him.

With his face all wrinkled, Slick turned, looked up at Johnnie Mae and said, "If you in such a big hurry for that mail, why don't you go on out there and get it yourself?"

"I ain't suppose to go and get it," she said, plucking another hair from her top lip. Then she worked hard at trying to be dainty. "I'm a lady," she said. "That's your job."

"If it's my job, then, you let me handle it. Okay?'

"But we need mail in here."

Slick leaned over and looked at the case where Johnnie Mae had been working. The ledge was three quarters full. "What's that down there on your case?" Slick asked, then pointed to four bascarts that stood in the middle of the aisle loaded with mail. "And that?" he shouted.

"Yeah, but the night is..." Johnnie Mae started saying to Slick, but turned and walked across the aisle to Goldie instead. "Naw, naw, baby, not in there. "She reached over Goldie's shoulder and fished a letter out of her case. "Don't throw them specials in," she ordered her. "Air mail neither. They ain't worked with the regular mail. They gets special treatment. Hold 'em out and take 'em up front. You'll see two boxes up there, one for specials and one for air mail. Put 'em in there A man'll be around later to pick 'em up," she informed Goldie.

Goldie slid down off her restbar and reached for the letter.

Johnnie Mae's six foot, 210 pound frame towered high over her who was only about 5 foot two.

Viewing this scene, Jimmie could plainly see why Slick had referred to Johnnie Mae as the section stud bee. Her shiny black hair was cut short, shorter than Slick's. And it was comb-fried down to her square head like a solid piece of very thin fabric. Not one strand stood out free of the others. And down below the wide shoulders were a bare flat chest, a tapered torso, narrow hips, well separated thighs that were too slinder, and an over size pelvis that bulged against her flush fitting skirt like a stimulated jock trying to break out of there.

"You don't have to walk up there for one letter," she said, taking the letter from Goldie's hand and tossing it into the right corner of the ledge of her sorting case. "Leave it there until you gets a lot of 'em. Then take 'em up there."

Slick glanced over at the letter and snarled, "That ain't no special no more. I tells yall that all the time. It's coming back."

"I don't care. You still hold it out," Johnnie Mae fumed at him.

"What cha gonna hold out a special for that's coming back?"

"'Cause the order said so. It said don't work Specials and Airmail letters with the regular mail. Hold 'em out, 'cause they gotta go separate. Don't you remember nothing, dummy?"

"Yeah, I remember the order," Slick berated her. "But they thought you knowed better than to hold out them that was coming back." He turned and pointed to Jimmie. "This man's been at both ends of the line. He carried mail for eight years, and he been down here clerking for six years. Tell 'er that ain't no special no more, Jimmie..."

Johnnie Mae cut in. "I don't care nothing 'bout him being no carrier," she snorted. "What they do out to the stations and what we do down here is two different things. And 'bout him being down here six years, that means he been doing it wrong for six years."

Slick gave emphasis to his reply by bobbing his head up and down. "A coming back special is a coming back special. And it don't make no difference if it's down here or out there. It ain't no good no more. It..."

Johnnie Mae cut in again, this time to give Slick a lesson in correct postal terminology. "Return special," she said. "Return. "Not coming back."

But Slick ignored her intended correction. "See, man," he said to

Jimmie. "That's why we get so many complaints in this station. They won't listen to nobody. I tell 'em all the time. But they jes won't listen. They even hold out coming back certified and air mail letters, too."

"Return, dummy. Return," Johnnie Mae corrected Slick again.

And Slick came up just short of making an embarrassing mistake. "Okay, boss ma, ah, lady."

"The order she's talking about," Goldie asked Slick, "where is it, now?"

"It was through here a couple of weeks ago," Slick responded. "When they gets complaints they types 'em up and brings 'em down here. They gives 'em to the clerk on the first case. She reads 'em and passes 'em on to the next clerk. And if they don't wait, the last clerk gives 'em to the supervisor, and he takes 'em back up to the office."

"Suppose you didn't remember what the order said, and you wanted to refer to it?" Goldie asked.

"It don't come back, baby," Slick warned. "It don't come back. You jes have to try to remember what it say..."

Turning back around, Johnnie Mae interrupted. "And if you got any smarts about you, you can remember it, too..."

Slick did not respond to Johnnie Mae's accusing remarks. "And you got to read it fast," he said. "'Cause most of the time the general foreman or the detail clerk brings 'em down here. And they dance around up there holler'n 'It ain't no newspaper article, read it and pass it on down.'"

"Yeah, that's 'cause you sets there holding it and reading it over and over..." Johnnie said as Slick cut in.

"Ah, naw I don't. I try to see what the damn thing is saying. But I don't read it no over and over."

"Ah yeah you do. And you still don't know what it say."

Goldie asked, directing her question to Slick: "What if you are not in the section when the notice is circulated?"

Slick pushed out open palms, and cocked his head to one side. "If nobody don't tell you, you don't know."

Johnnie Mae slapped Slick lightly several times on the back of the head and, with her thumb, pointed over her shoulder toward the northend setups. "The mail," she said. "When you gonna go get the damn mail?"

Slick had this nickname partly because of his thick, coal black, slicked down hair, and partly because he was considered an all around cool cat. He was over six feet tall, with a long oval face and a long narrow nose. His chin was square, his eyes dark brown, and his skin complexion was light brown. His coal black hair was slicked down tight to his oval shaped head. And he wore a matching mustache, not slicked down tight to his full blown lips, but standing aloft thick and coal black. His nails were long, clean and neatly polished. The skin of his hands looked baby-soft, and so did the skin of his face.

Slick knocked Johnnie Mae's hand away. She giggled. "Don't do that, woman, goddamit," he shouted at her. "I done told you 'bout that." Johnnie had not mussed up Slick's slicked down, coal black hair, but he carefully ran his hands over it several times anyway.

"You think you so great," Johnnie Mae told him. "You waits 'til everybody else comes back from the setups, then you goes strutting up there, so everybody can see you with your long skinny ass. Mr. Moses!" she yelled to the supervisor. "They got mail for us out there in primary. Make Slick go get it."

"Slick's real name was Henry Reed. Supervisor Moses walked half way down the aisle and said, "Mr. Reed, will you please go and get the mail?"

The job description for clerk at Metro City Post Office stated clearly that: "All clerks are required to load and push hand trucks short distances, and must be able to lift waist high objects weighing up to 80 pounds."

But if a man clerk disobeyed a supervisor's order to perform dirty and heavy jobs for the women, he could get fired. Obviously, this was going through Slick's mind when he gave Johnnie Mae a vicious look, and pointed an upright thumb at her and snapped in a very low voice, "up you, bitch!"

Nevertheless, he didn't hop down off his stool and go running scared to get the mail. He sat sulking for a few minutes. Then, as if the incident hadn't happened, he slid down from his restbar and, as Johnnie Mae had outlined, made his announcement: "Well, I guess everybody has jes about thinned out up there now. 'Go out here and get this mail." He pulled a pair of heavy leather gloves from his hip pocket. They were lined with a pair of brown jersey gloves to keep his long, neatly polished nails from getting broken off, and to keep his baby soft hands from getting scuffed up. He fingered them on and headed for the setups.

"And make it quick," Johnnie Mae heckled him.

"Want me to go with you, Slick?" Jimmie asked.

"Naw, I'll get it by myself. You stay here and watch Johnnie Mae. Don't let her be messing with Goldie telling her to hold out them coming back specials. They ain't no good no more, they's suppose to go right in with the regular mail."

"Don't listen to 'em, Goldie," Johnnie Mae said. "He don't know what he talking 'bout."

"Ah go on back to your case, woman. Leave Goldie alone," Slick growled. "Goldie know what she doing. I done broke her in."

"You broke her in?" Johnnie Mae asked, looking up at the ceiling. "God help her." Then, she asked Slick. "What did you tell her?"

"I told her everything I know about the operation of this section."

"And that ain't too much," Johnnie Mae said. "What about the Galova Bank, and the Bank of Galova? You tell her they ain't the same?"

"Yeah."

"Did you tell her that some of the bank of Galova mail goes direct to the main office and the rest go to two different departments?"

"Woman, go on back to your case and set down," Slick snapped. "If you ain't gonna throw no mail, get out of the way and quit bothering the other people so they can throw some."

Slick nudged Jimmie, winked his eye and pointed to Goldie. "Be cool, brother," he said, and left.

Johnnie Mae reluctantly went back to her seat.

Jimmie and Goldie continued to throw mail, but mostly they just sat on their separate stools and stared out the corners of their eyes at each other. Finally, Jimmie asked, "How long have you been working down here?"

"About 3 months."

"What made you decide to start working?"

"Oh, lots of things."

"Well, I must say, for a person who has never worked before, you seem to be adjusting quite well."

Goldie patted the fabric covered foam rubber padding of the restbar next to her. The occupant was out on a break. "Sit over here until she gets back."

As usual, Jimmie's moves around Goldie were very careful. When he was seeing her, she was a married woman. They had plenty of sex together and she loved it, but she was not permissive. For that reason, he respected her and never wanted to do anything that would seem to make her look or feel cheap.

"You are not still afraid of me, are you?" she asked.

"Afraid of you?"

"Uh huh."

"What is that suppose to mean?"

"You wouldn't be able to figure it out in a million years, would you? I've always heard that action speaks louder than words," she challenged. "So, obviously, you are still afraid of me."

Jimmie looked down at himself in surprise. He didn't realize that he had not moved over to the vacant seat beside her. He slid quickly down from his stool, rushed over and hopped up onto the vacant one beside her.

Goldie's golden face lit up with approval. "So, I am wrong," she proclaimed jokingly. "You are not afraid of me. But it took some time for you to make up your mind."

"I was thinking about the clerk on this case," Jimmie explained. "I wouldn't want to make a misthrow on her case and then see the case checkers come around and find it and penalize her for it."

"Jimmie, the considerate one. Always looking out for the other person."

"Well, now. Look who's talking. Of all people. Have you got a lot of nerve?"

She tried to stare him into looking her way, but now he would not. "Yes, I remember," she agreed. "You don't have to remind me. 'Goldie, the altruistic one.' That's what you used to call me." She paused for a moment, then said, "But from what I hear, though, you don't have to worry about making a misthrow in anybody's sorting case."

"How so?"

"Obviously, you know this scheme inside out. This is an 8 week scheme. They tell me you threw it in only one week."

"Not quite," he corrected her. "Nine days to be exact."

"Well, give or take a day or two," she quipped. Then, after a moment of silence, her face took on a somber look. And she spoke in a hurt tone: "How is she, Jimmie?"

"How is who?" he hedged.

Goldie's face flushed slightly. "Don't do that to me, Jimmie," she pleaded. "You know who I mean. Your wife. How is she? Is she nice?"

Jimmie lied. "Oh yeah, she's nice."

"Are you happy?"

Goldie's questioning was causing Jimmie some discomfort. He squirmed on his seat and lied again. "Yeah, I'm happy."

Goldie went on, really giving him the third degree. She tried again to stare his eyes around to meet hers. But no luck. "Do you love her?"

This question, even more than any of the others, irritated Jimmie. He vigorously squirmed on his seat. His eyebrows dropped. And he snapped. "Sure I love her. I married her, didn't I?"

Goldie squeezed her lips tightly together. Her face looked bloated. There was no doubt that her mouth wanted to fly wide open in an immense smile of happiness. Jimmie's sharp, snappy response had given the real answer she wanted to hear. She continued trying to stare him into looking at her. Finally, she succeeded.

He turned, faced Goldie and looked deep into her eyes. "I'm sorry," he said. "I didn't mean to snap at you like that" He blinked his eyes rapidly, turned away and cleared his throat. "I am happy, though," he tried to convince her. "I really am."

Goldie's yellowish brown eyes opened wide. "You never could lie," she said with great confidence.

Jimmie turned and faced Goldie again. For a brief, helpless moment, without saying a word, he gazed deeply and lustfully into her eyes.

Goldie's sensuous lips quivered as if in great need. Her somber look became warm and inviting. And her voice scaled to a whisper. "I love you," she said.

Jimmie quickly changed the subject. "How is Paul," he asked.

Goldie sank deep into her seat. The warm inviting look on her face became somber again. And her whispering voice shot up to a level of Sad protest. "Same as always." she said.

"I speak of that dude as if I know him well," Jimmie said with no real regret. "And I've never even met him."

Goldie disagreed. "Yes you have. You met him."

"When?"

"The night I had Alice to bring you over to the house to the party."

"Oh, yeah, I remember," Jimmie acknowledged. "Sure did." Then changed to: "Now, that's who I really should be asking about. Alice. How is my buddy? Does she still envy you for having a business, three six flat buildings, a nice home and two big cars?" he asked, then hurriedly added: "And a husband and an outside man?"

Goldie scolded him. "Alice is a nice person, Jimmie. She didn't really envy me."

"Yeah, I know. I didn't mean it in that sense. I was only kidding."

"But if she did envy me, then," Goldie explained, "she can't envy me now. For those other things you mentioned, maybe yes. But for having another man, no. I haven't had a man, not really, since you got..." She paused and frowned as if she thought the word she was about to say was going to bring a bad taste to her mouth. But then, she said it anyway. "Married. Not for seven years."

"What about Paul?"

"I still say I haven't had a man since you walked out on me.'

Jimmie didn't tell Goldie that he had gotten tired of the fact that he could see her only when it was convenient for her. True, she had suggested numberless times that she leave Paul and come to him, and that each time he had rejected the idea. He discouraged her only because he knew that leaving a business, three six flat buildings, a nice home and two big cars to come and live with him in a one room apartment would eventually bring her only regret. He didn't tell her that, either.

"I remember that night," he said, "the night of the party. Paul thought Alice was my girlfriend. We came in arm in arm, smiling at each other We really made it look good. I even kissed Alice on the cheek a couple of times."

"He knew "

"He did?"

"Uh huh."

"What did he say?"

"Nothing. But he knew, especially after I danced with you, and you pushed me away because you said I was getting too close for comfort."

"He said something about that?"

"No. But Paul is not only an older man, he is an inadequate man. Inadequate men watch and see everything. Paul pretends he doesn't, but I know he does. It was different when we first married, though.

Like his cleaning business, his three six flat buildings, his nice home and two big cars, I was only another possession for people to come over and gawk at. He constantly invited friends, and just customers too, to come over to the house for drinks, mostly men. 'I just wanted them to see my pretty wife,' he'd say.

"Not being able to fill the shoes of a full time sexual mate did not really bother him. But, then, you came into my life. I don't think I changed, at least not that much. When I was seeing you, I respected him and our home. And I still do. I prepared his meals on time, with a great variety of foods, as I had always done, which he enjoyed, as he had always done." She paused, seeming to express gratitude, then added. "He says I'm the best cook in Metro City..."

"I agree with him on that score," Jimmie interrupted.

"But, then, he began to change. I could see the hurt," she continued "Although he never mentioned it, I could tell that he knew another man was in my life. He just didn't know who it was until that night."

Chapter 3

It was two A.M., lunch time for the late set. Now Jimmie would get a cross section opinion about his Blockbuster by listening to comments of employes from other work areas. He was sure he'd get more criticisms and objections. He was also hopeful that he would get an approval here and there.

He had written an introduction and summary of the 98 page Blockbuster in which he discussed in detail the shortage and disrepair of tools and implements, and of worker attitude and management foibles.

He leaned heavily on worker apathy, spelling out in detail how it adversely affected efficiency and productivity at the Metro City Main Post Office. Because of the general MMPO worker low educational qualifications, compared to those in the private sector earning equivalent salary, Jimmie thought that instead of exhibiting a high degree of apathy that MMPO workers should show signs of appreciation. So far, only his locker room buddies, Ronnie and Oscar, had whole hardily approved of the Blockbuster. Even Slick, his section mate, expressed reservations. He thought the idea itself was a mistake. "They ain't gonna do nothing 'bout it," he had told Jimmie. Now, to Jimmie's surprise, Slick came up with another reservation.

All the GS-48S clerks, except Jimmie and Slick, had gone to wash up for lunch. With just two of them there, obviously, Slick reasoned that one more small reservation, especially a personal one, would not further jeopardize Jimmie's already precarious standing with workers at the MMPO.

Jimmie noted in the Blockbuster introduction that: "It was but a few short years ago that fathers and mothers of many present day postal employes were bootblacks, carwashers and house maids. With large families to support, and existing on a mere pittance, they lived in the squalor of a single room. Regarding school, their children were early dropouts.

"Today things are different," he said "Metro City postal employes live in comfortable homes, they fly private airplanes, they split Lake Michigan's surf with high powered boats and they operate big businesses. Custodians and charwomen are no longer fixed in their substratum positions. And their sons and daughters are graduating from Yale, Harvard and the University of Chicago.

"I don't have no high powered boat to split Lake Michigan's surf with," Slick objected.

"Then you have no complaint," Jimmie silenced him. "I was referring only to those who do," he added and pointed to the men's nearby washroom. "You go ahead. I'll be along in a minute."

Slick left, and Jimmie took his little black book (a kind of diary) out of his pocket and was about to jot something down in it when he was interrupted.

Supervisor Moses was one of only two blacks living out in Dunes township, an upper class suburban area. Each night he parked his big gold limousine 10 blocks away from the post office, then boarded a bus the rest of the way to work. With all GS-48S clerks, now gone, except Jimmie, he had sneaked down the aisle to Jimmie's case.

"Mr. Jones? Just a minute please," he said in a whispering tone. "you'll have everybody out there in Metro City thinking we postal workers are rich, that we all drive luxury limousines and live in $100,000 homes."

"I'm sorry if I gave you that impression," Jimmie told him, then left the section and headed out for lunch.

On arrival at the privately operated cafeteria, Jimmie found conditions to be the same as always: due to the large number of people working at the Metro Main Post Office, due to bad planning and due to the short paid, slow, uncaring help, lines at lunch time were usually long and restless.

Jimmie stepped into one of the lines behind clerk Minnie Lee who, with costume diamonds sparkling from her ears and fingers, was dressed as if she was going to a party. It was a mistake. About Jimmie's comment in the Blockbuster that some large and now affluent black postal families had once lived in the squalor of a single room. She wanted to know: "Why did you have to bring that up?"

Molly Curtis, whose expression on the job forever suggested she felt guilty about something, stepped into the line behind Jimmie. She tapped him gently on the shoulder and spoke softly to him. "Everybody does it, why shouldn't I?" she asked, then hastened to add: "But I'm not as bad as some. I do stay on a break longer than 15 minutes sometimes. I don't always work as hard as I should, and I don't pick up mail other people drop on the floor, either. But I pick up what I drop. And I certainly would pick up a burning letter, whether it got caught from my cigarette or not. And I'd put it out, too."

Jimmie finally got his lunch, paid the cashier, went directly to one of the 50-foot-long dining room tables and began eating. Again, the cafeteria food successfully defended its title. And the knowledge that Mrs. Georgia Rogers, with her tray of lunch, was headed to his table, added to its unsavory flavor. Bessie Black's Hatchet Ladies and their 100 crowding allies had lambasted Jimmie with their objections to the Blockbuster and had given him an ultimatum. Molly Curtis, Minnie Lee, Supervisor Moses and even Slick had made their confessions. Now Georgia Rogers, a fanatic weekend Christian was coming to drench him in her fire and brimstone. He braced himself.

"Mr. Jones, may I sit with you?" she asked. "I want to talk to you."

"Be my guest," Jimmie reluctantly accommodated her.

Georgia Rogers was a plain woman who wore no makeup because of religious reasons. And like most MMPO people, her demeanor for six days was sort of plain and common, too. She sat down and doodled considerably with her napkin and silverware before saying anything else. Finally, she forked up too much food and crammed it into her mouth as if to get the strength and courage from it to say what was on her mind. "It's about your suggestion," she said, swallowing her food quickly.

Oh, oh, here it comes, Jimmie told himself. And he really didn't want to hear it. Like Bessie Black, with her Hatchet Ladies, Georgia Rogers also had a following on the job: a group of saved black women. If they, too, objected to the contents of his Blockbuster, there'd be only a few left who didn't. As Slick had said, it seemed that it had all been for naught.

"I know all about your suggestion, probably more than most of the workers," Georgia told Jimmie. "A friend of mine works down in the Awards Committee Office. She described it to me in great detail, especially the introduction and summary." She took another bite of food, this one a bit smaller, and chewed it several times. Her large brown eyes searched Jimmie's face, as he anxiously awaited her assessment. "You painted a clear picture of the conditions down here," she said. "And you didn't pull any punches. But I want to ask you one question."

This was it for sure, Jimmie thought. He waited for her line of objection. But, then, he had a feeling that this God fearing woman who surely believed in fair play, a day's work for a day's pay and all those good and honorable things, just might be on his side.

Bessie Black and her Hatchet Ladies filed past with their trays of food and took seats at the 50-foot-long dining room table directly opposite Jimmie and Georgia. Separated, estranged and divorced from their discrete husbands, their faces were grim as if they were reliving some of their past, unpleasant, marital experiences. Except Dolly Jean. She sat there, read her bible, twitched, squirmed and giggled freely at nothing that was apparently funny.

"Twenty four hours," Bessie Black said to Jimmie, referring to the time she had given him to call back the part of his suggestion in which he had noted that black MMPO workers, with their low educational level, could not find work in the private sector making comparable pay. "Mr. Traitor? You got twenty four hours," she stipulated.

"Where did you get the courage to do such a thing?" Georgia Rogers asked Jimmie.

"Oh, I, uh..."

"Don't misunderstand me," she interrupted. "I think it was a splendid idea. And so true. Especially what you said about unskilled blacks not being able to find jobs in private industry making this kind of money. I know I couldn't," she said looking up at the ceiling. "And God knows I'm thankful."

It was the next morning. Jimmie was on his way to Pete's parking lot to get his car and head for home. He had not shown any signs to Bessie Black and her Hatchet Ladies that he intended to suggest to the Awards Committee to strike any segments from his Blockbuster. He had begun to think that they were simply bluffing anyway, just trying to throw a scare into him with the hope that he would fearfully react favorably to their wishes. The idea sounded logical to Jimmie, but not convincing. And rightfully so. When he reached Pete's parking lot, he was greeted by four tires on his car that were very very flat.

It was a devastating discovery. One flat he could handle. He could jack the car up, take the spare out of the trunk, throw it on and, in minutes, be on his way home. With two, or even three flats, there was a slim possibility he could handle that situation, too. Maybe he could find Ronnie and Oscar and borrow their spares. Including his, he'd have the necessary three. But he needed four. And the only other person he knew from whom he thought he could possibly borrow a spare tire was his section mate, Slick. But Slick was home in bed, fast asleep. He was a 7:12 clerk, and had left for home 3 hours before.

So, with four flat tires, there was nothing he could do but get a service station guy over there with an automatic pump to inflate them for him. Yes, that's what he'd eventually have to do. But now, he couldn't even do that, not at that hour. It was 6:42 in the morning. The nearest service station was more than a mile away and it was closed, would not reopen until 9 A.M. He decided to just go on to the nearby Dover Avenue subway station and catch a train home. He'd get a couple of hours sleep. Then he would come back and pick up the car.

But, before leaving the parking lot, Jimmie found that his devastating discovery of four flat tires was far worse than he had first imagined. On second inspection, he made another devastating discovery. The four flat tires were not only flat, they were ripped to shreds. Now, going home and coming back later was the only logical thing for him to do. No way did he have enough money with him to pay for road service, four new tires, and their installation.

So, heading for the subway station, Jimmie started recapping the onerous events of the night: first, Bessie Black, her Hatchet Ladies and 100 thirsty black female colleagues crowded at the front of GS-48S to hurl insulting remarks at him. Second, a sprig of a woman violently clubbed him over the head with her small purse. Third, stud bee Johnnie Mae tripped him up, bounced his limp body about the floor and slammed her 210 pound frame on top of him. Now, this morning, four flat tires. Nothing else bad could possibly happen to him before he got home, so he thought. But he was wrong.

Down on the platform waiting for the southbound seven AM B

train, along with scores of other home bound Metro City postal workers, were Bessie Black and the Hatchet Ladies. They huddled at the foot of the escalators as if waiting for him to arrive. Why are they here waiting for a train, he wondered. They each have a car. He had thought that the four flat tires were indeed of their making. Now he was sure.

"There he is, the traitor," Bessie Black yelled out. "See 'em? Right there, coming down them escalators, with his little ole briefcase under his arm, looking lak he think he somebody, and ain't nothing but a jive ass clerk lak the rest of us? (but she was only a mailhandler.) Hey, Mr. Traitor?" she called out to him, "what cha doing down here riding the train with us? What's wrong with your au-to-mo-beel?" she stretched out the word.

Jimmie plowed through the crowd to the outer section of the subway boarding platform in order to be one of the first to get on the train and get a seat. Otherwise he'd probably have to stand most of the way home, almost an hour. Bessie Black and the Hatchet Ladies followed Jimmie and stood directly behind him.

"One little push and the third rail could solve our problem," Bessie Black said. "It would get rid of the traitor bastard for good who hates his own people. Somebody who wants to see 'em out of work, on relief, out in the street and nowhere to stay."

Jimmie wasn't standing dangerously near the platform's extreme outer edge. But if Bessie Black or any one of the Hatchet Ladies should give him a good running push, indeed, he could land out there on the highly electrically charged third rail. He felt a cold kind of pain rush through his entire body.

For a second, like very thin strips of bacon sizzling in a big black early morning skillet, he saw himself out there on that third rail smoking and frying. It was an unsettling thought. The wisest and safest thing for him to do was to just move away. But that kind of response would express fearful concern. He was all man, not a squeamish person or some very small child. Anyway, should he attempt to move away, the Hatchet Ladies would surely try to block him.

Such a turn of events would make matters even worse. He would not move away. He'd stay put, right there. He slid his right foot quickly, but cautiously along the concrete boarding platform out in front of his left foot to brace against a possible push from behind.

And he prayed earnestly for the train to hurry and pull in. But then he quickly stopped his praying, not because he really didn't want the train to come. He had to get home. It was because the regular tracks on which the train would arrive were much closer than the third rail. A slight shove from the hands of a ten year old boy could do the job. Suddenly, he saw himself being crushed to bits beneath the mammoth wheels of the speeding train.

"Black traitor bastard, I ought to," Bessie Black mumbled.

As unlearned Mamie Smith cut in with: "Go on, Bessie. Do it. Go on."

"Yes, Bessie, go on, do it," Sweetheart Blanche Mims urged her. "It would be no more than what he deserves, and no less than what black people should get."

Reading her Bible, chewing gum and giggling, Confused Dolly Jean said: "What traitors sow, so shall they reap. So let the good times roll."

"Go on, Bessie," Mamie Smith pleaded again. "Go on, do it."

A roaring fast clucking sound came rushing through the dimly lit subway tube. It was the 7 AM B train. Running late, it was coming in at full speed. Pushing firmly against his extended right foot, Jimmie frantically tried to brace himself. Could he ward off a good fast running push? He thought so. Even as strong as mailhandler Bessie Black was, he still thought he could do it. But what if one of the Hatchet Ladies should help Bessie Black? he asked himself. Or worse, suppose the four of them tried it together? He didn't think they would dare take that chance, though. One could very likely go over the side with him. Well, he had to do what he had to do, he concluded. But did he?

All he really had to do was to walk away from his position in front of the Hatchet Ladies. And if they tried to block his move, all he had to do, then, was to keep persistently walking on his way. No, he would not do it, he firmly decided. Even in the gravest of adversity, which this certainly was, he still could not do it. What would it say so loud and clear about manhood?

It didn't matter anyway, now, as to what Jimmie thought about moving away to one side, and about manhood at all. The onerous redhot third rail was patiently waiting to fry him to a crisp. Bessie Black and the Hatchet Ladies were ready to unhinge his firmly planted feet. And the wheels of the late running 7 AM B train were rapidly coming to smash his body to bits. And seconds later, like a school boy's lofty kite soaring in a Chicago March wind, Jimmie's body went flying swiftly through the air. But Bessie Black didn't like what she saw. She stamped her feet and popped her fingers as if she had just thrown snake eyes in an ally crap game. "Well I'll be damned!" she blurted out, "Can you believe that?"

"It's incredible!" Blanche Mims said. "How could it have happened? I see it with my own eyes, but I still don't believe it."

Dolly Jean squeezed her Bible tighter against her body and exclaimed, "It's a miracle, that's what it is, a miracle."

Disbelieving that he was still alive, Jimmie was sprawled on the concrete platform busily examining his body. Not only was he still alive, but his body was not burnt from landing on the third rail. And there were no missing limbs from having fallen beneath the wheels of the fast moving train. He remembered flying through the air, though, and slamming up against a broadside of some kind and bouncing back away from it. What really did happened, he wondered.

Had Bessie Black and the Hatchet Ladies joined forces and pushed him so energetically that he sailed clear across the two nearby rails and on past the third rail? Had he slammed up against the wall on the other side of the tracks and fallen back onto the narrow concrete apron below? No. Impossible, he disputed. That wall must be 30 feet away. No way they could shove him that far. But he hit a broadside of some kind, he remembered.

Maybe I'm still on the boarding platform, he thought. The train was late. It was coming in much faster than it would have under normal conditions. When they pushed me, the front of the train had passed by and I slammed up against one of the following coaches, he figured. Yeah, lucky me, he said in thanksgiving, and warmly patted with his hands the hard, concrete surface beneath him. I landed up against the train and fell back off onto the boarding platform. That's what happened.

And this is the way Jimmie thought it really did happen. But he was wrong. And when he looked up and saw Tiny Stark standing in front of him, he realized that he probably was wrong.

Tiny Stark was a 10:12 security guard at the MMPO. As with Jimmie and hundreds of other 10:12 MMPO workers, his tour of duty ended at 6:42 AM as well. Like hundreds of other late setters, he rode the subway home, too, the 7 AM B train. And like Jimmie and many more, he usually worked his way to the outer section of the subway boarding platform in order to be one of the first to get on the train to get a seat. Tiny Stark, especially Tiny Stark, did not want to stand not one minute, to say nothing of the full hour it sometimes took for him to get home.

As a security guard minding his post, Tiny Stark stood on his feet most of the night. At the end of 8 hours, he was very tired. The pleasure of sitting, whether for a full hour on the soft foam rubber padded seats of the 7 AM B train, or for just a few minutes on the hard unpadded wooden benches of the men's locker room, he welcomed it. It wasn't the standing so much in itself that tired Stark out. He was a big man. The nick name Tiny, given to him by his colleagues, was a misnomer. Standing at the far end of the pole, he was the direct opposite of tiny. He weighed over three hundred pounds.

Tiny Stark was that "huge broadside of some kind" that Jimmie remembered having slammed up against and bounced back away from. Ramming his way through the crowd at the last minute before the train's arrival, as he usually did in order to get a seat, Tiny Stark reached the outer area of the subway platform and stepped squarely in front of Jimmie at the very instant Bessie Black and her Hatchet Ladies gave him the big push.

Happy to be all in one piece, Jimmie went home and slept part of the day, came back and got his car, went back home and back to work that night.

He had worked two nights now since submitting his Blockbuster to the Awards Committee. It was the next morning after the second night, and he was on his way to the parking lot. The first night had been a night of mishaps for him. The second night was no different. The 100 angry black women did not crowd at the front of GS-48S and remain there for a long period. They came and stayed only a short time. Then, Bessie Black and her Hatchet Ladies went out on a recruiting spree. For the full 8 hours, workers in groups from all 12 floors, as sightseers do at a big city zoo, filed by GS-48S and gawked in and chanted: "There he is, the traitor. There he is."

Somehow, though, Jimmie had made it through the 8 hours of this second night. It wasn't easy. But, at least, unlike the first night no one inside the building bodily attacked him. And that was good.

Now if only his four tires were not flat again this morning, things would not be too bad at all. There would be no subway incident, because he would not have to go down there. He didn't worry about finding four flat tires, though. He didn't think the perpetrators would resort to the same tactics two nights in a row. Bessie Black and her Hatchet Ladies surely were through for this second night, he reconciled himself. They were off somewhere planning their strategy for the third night. On his way home, he'd try to figure out what it could possibly be.

As he left the building for the parking lot, Georgia Rogers, a member of the saved black women's group who was happy with her post office job, called out for him to wait. If only there were more Metro postal workers like her, he wished to himself, he'd not be taking the tremendous amount of abuse that was being dealt out to him. But abuse or no abuse, he wasn't going to change his position. Not one iota of the Blockbuster would he retract. The Hatchet Ladies could come up with whatever they chose.

"My car is parked in the north end of the lot right beside yours," Georgia Rogers imformed Jimmie. "So we might as well walk along together." Then, without any direct reference to the material cited in the Blockbuster, she broached a conversation regarding the negative attitude of Metro City black postal workers.

"It's a shame," she started out. "We blacks fight hard for a better life. Yet when we get it, we don't know how to deal with it. The Metro City Post Office hires more blacks than all the private institutions of this city put together. And we have an intelligent, educated black Postmaster. But we don't half come to work. And we don't work for him after we get here. If they brought a white Postmaster back in here, we'd take to the streets in protest.

Jimmie agreed with Georgia Rogers in her opinion about the thankless attitude of the general MMPO black workforce. But, because she was a black woman, he did not mention to her one segment of the workforce which he thought was the most thankless of all, black women.

He thought that, instead of being abusive and domineering of MMPO black men, that MMPO black women should be thankful that the MMPO black men perform their part of the heavy and dirty work. He believed that big, strong 210 pound man-like women such as Johnnie Mae, who was able to pick him up off the floor with one hand, should especially be thankful.

He smiled and noted to himself that it was a strange situation. He, Slick, Ronnie Oscar and all the MMPO black men had had a chance on many occasions to ligitimately complain to management about this problem. But they didn't.

Management, only several weeks before, had made a reproduction of the clerk job description and circulated it throughout the building. Well, not really circulated it, but a copy of it was placed on every supervisor's desk in plain view for all workers to see. Heavily underlined in those copies were the words: "All clerks must be able to lift waist high objects weighing up to 80 pounds."

"Wow! that really must be a good story," Georgia said, as they entered the parking lot gate and headed north.

"Huh?" Jimmie responded.

"Standing by your car, reading a book, isn't that your wife?" Georgia Rogers asked.

Jimmie looked. It was Dolly Jean, leaning against the front fender of his car reading her Bible and bobbing her head up and down while listening to music that must have been playing only in her mind, he thought.

Dolly Jean, though a pretty girl, neatly trim and who normally dressed in vogue, was not the brightest of Metro postal workers. They all knew that. But, at 6:42 in the morning with everybody else trying to get out of the parking lot for home, why was she just casually standing there reading her Bible? he wondered. And of all the cars in the lot, leaning on his?

Georgia Rogers grasped his arm and held it tightly as if in great fear.

Jimmie had never liked the idea of carrying a gun. Although he would not admit it even to himself, he was an emotional person. Therefore, he was afraid that if he was carrying a gun and some innocent soul should unexpectedly burst out of the shadows on him some dark night, he might accidentally shoot him. But he was carrying a gun that morning and he was going to use it, if need be.

Suddenly, someone ducked out from behind Jimmie's car. It was Bessie Black, leader of the Hatchet Ladies, with the other hatchet ladies following close behind her. They all had long switch blade knives which they hurriedly popped open.

Dolly Jean opened her switch blade and joined them. Forming a sweeping curved line, they walked toward Jimmie and Georgia in a swaggering stride. The dancing glare from the long shiny blades of the switch knives played devilish tricks with the dim turned down lights of the early morning parking lot. And it created for Jimmie and Georgia, a scary scene.

"Okay, Mr. Jimmie Jones," Bessie Black scoffed. "Me and my close lady friends here told you to call back that part of your Blockbuster where you say MMPO black workers is too dumb to find work out there in private industry paying the same money lak we making here. And we told you, too, that if you didn't we was gonna ask you again in a way you wasn't gonna lak. 'Member that?" she added, briskly waving her switch blade through the air at Jimmie, confirming to him that he was right in speculating that she and her Hatchet Ladies were the culprits who ripped up his tires.

"You didn't do it," she hammered at him. "Plus you and that jive ass Postmaster Bill Brown had to go and plan on spreading that lie all over town. We knows 'bout that, too. So now, Mr. Traitor man, we's gonna spread your black ass all over this here parking lot, piece by piece. How you lak them there apples, huh?"

Bill Brown, who had diligently worked his way up through the ranks all the way from mailhandler to Postmaster, had sought Jimmie's permission to reproduce the introduction and summary of his Blockbuster, which dealt primarily with worker apathy. He wanted to post a copy on each bulletin board of every postal facility throughout the city.

"I like what you said," he had confided in him. "And although we could pass the word on as you suggested we do, I think every Metro City postal employe should have a chance to read it for him or herself just as you said it, not a paraphrase. Maybe it will open up their eyes as to just how lucky they are."

Bessie Black and her Hatchet Ladies continued their slow, sure footed pace toward Jimmie and Georgia, adroitly bending the two ends of their line to eventually encircle them.

"Come on and take your medicine, Jimmie baby," Unlearned Mamie Smith said. "Be a good boy. Don't fight it. And there ain't no use hanging on to that old sanctified and holy broad, neither. 'Cause she can't help you none. And they ain't no use looking 'round for nobody else. 'Cause they ain't nobody else 'round here who gives a damn 'bout what happens to your black ass. So, come on, let's get the show on the road."

Jimmie had his hand in his pocket, palming his gun. He knocked the safety off and shook himself free of Georgia.

"That's right," Bessie Black approved. "We don't want her, just you, baby. So, come on."

Mamie Smith was the first to slash at Jimmie. He faded to the left side. She missed. "What cha running for," she gabbed at him. "Might as well get it now, as later. 'Cause you is gonna get it. Ain't nowhere you can go to hide. Not now, baby." She pointed to the two circling ends of their line. "We got cha covered. You jes making it hard for yourself by dragging it out like this. Come on, baby and let's get it over with now. It'll be easier that way."

The four Hatchet Ladies were standing between Jimmie and his car. In the process of forming a circle in which to enclose him, they had now reached a posture that represented the letter U: confused Dolly Jean on his left side; Unlearned Mamie Smith on his right side; Leader Bessie Black on his right front; and Late Set Sweetheart Blanche Mims on his left front.

"Come on, Jimmie baby, let's get the show on the road," Mamie Smith urged again. "Jes you and me. Let's start it off, huh?"

Jimmie coiled his fingers closed-tight for a more secure grip on his gun, but did not yet extract it from his pocket. "My advice to you," he said very quietly, but with much resolve, "all four of you, is that you close your knives, find your cars, get in them and go home. Because that's what I'm going to do. So, please step away, to one side," he demanded, motioning with his left hand.

"You ain't done what we told you to do," Bessie Black snapped. "So now, you gonna pay."

"No, I didn't do it," Jimmie shot back. "And I don't intend doing it. If I had lied about what I said, I probably would consider retracting it. But I didn't lie. I told it like it is. Many MMPO workers, most of them in fact, could not find a job out there in the private sector making half of what they make here. Let me tell you something of significance, if I may. I was down to the Postmaster's office yesterday..."

"Yeah, we knows you was down there," Bessie Black cut in, reminding him. "I just told you that. You and him with his jive ass down there plott'n to tell everybody in town how dumb we is. White folks in this town think that already anyhow. And you and Bill Brown's gonna tell 'em that they's right, putting that shit on bulletin boards all over town. It's a damn shame. Talking 'bout we ought to be happy we getting this little ole hand out they's giving us for coming down here doing this ole tiresome work every night."

When Postmaster Bill Brown took office, he presented a three point program, things he said he wanted to accomplish. At the top of the list was: to reduce the use of sick leave. Of the 20,000 employes working at the main installation, 2,000 were absent from work each day, he said.

"The bulletin board thing is not what I'm talking about," Jimmie told Bessie Black, cutting her off. I'm talking about the Letter For Leave Program."

"What about it?" Bessie Black asked sharply.

"You are aware of the program, aren't you?"

"Yeah, shit, I know 'bout it. Everybody know 'bout it. So what?"

"Well, the way the program works is that those persons guilty of using excessive amounts of sick leave, or those suspected of using sick leave for unauthorized purposes, are requested to write a letter expressing in detail specifically why they thought the sick leave was necessary."

"Yeah, yeah, we told you we knows all 'bout that Letter For Leave shit," Bessie Black ripped back at Jimmie. "If you stalling for time, Mr. Traitor, it ain't gonna do you no good. Your black ass belongs to us. You had your chance and wouldn't take it. Now it's too late.

"I'm not stalling for time. What I'm trying to do, if you and your friends will only listen, is to reveal to you the evidence to support my claim..."

"Support what claim?"

"The claim that many blacks working here could not get a job in the private sector making the kind of money they are making here..."

"You jes a damn lie," Unlearned Mamie Smith interjected. "you can't prove nothing. You black bastard, you jes won't learn, will you? That's why your black ass is in a sling now, why we's gonna slice you up in little biddy pieces and scatter 'em all over this lot. 'Cause jes lak white folks do, you thinks all black folks is stupid, too. And jes lak them, you's always trying to prove it. We jes as smart as they is!" she screamed out hysterically.

"Shut up for a minute and listen to what I have to say!" Jimmie scolded her.

"You don't tell me to shut up!" Mamie Smith exploded back at Jimmie. "Goddammit, don't nobody tells me to shut up, 'specially you. You damn traitor. Anyway, I'm tired of listening to your shit. Your time is up, baby," she warned. "Right now. Come on, ladies, let's get his ass," she ordered, and slashed at Jimmie again. He faded to his left side again. She missed again.

But nervous and fidgety Dolly Jean, surprised and excited by Mamie Smith's effusive order, did not. Awkwardly rushing in from his left side, Bible in one hand, switch knife dangling in the other, she caught him on his left forearm, spouting blood, but pricked him only superficially.

Jimmie looked down to quickly assess the damage. And when he did, Mamie Smith on his right side, for the first time, moved into a close striking position.

She raised her switch knife high into the air above her head and yelled: "Now we got 'em! Come on, ladies! let's finish his black ass!"

Nervous, fidgety Dolly Jean, on the left, this time, raised her blood dripping switch knife above her head, too. And she moved closer in.

Late Set Sweetheart Blanche Mims moved closer in, too. She held her switch knife even higher and yelled even louder than Mamie Smith had done: "Jimmie Jones!" she exploded out. "Your time has come! Let him have it, ladies!"

Two nights before, in front of GS-48S, on the rallying orders of Bessie Black, the choral singing Hatchet Ladies chanted in unison their monotonous little "traitor" song. This morning, in the dimly lit parking lot, on the excited orders of Sweetheart Blanche Mims, the switchblade wielding Hatchet Ladies, hummed in unison a morbid song of death.

Lucky for Jimmie the Hatchet Lady U had not yet become a circle. With Mamie Smith on the right side of him, Dolly Jean on the left side, Bessie Black on the right front and Blanche Mims on the left front, the southend of the U was open, and no one was standing behind him. Not even Georgia Rogers. Frozen in fear of what she was sure was going to happen, she stood far in the background and well to one side.

The switch knives of Sweetheart Blanche Mims, Unlearned Mamie Smith and Confused Dolly Jean started falling fast throught the air in Jimmie's direction. Jimmie saw them coming and moved swiftly backward out through the open south end of the Hatchet Lady U just in time to elude their butchering, blood-letting fall.

Twice now, Bessie Black's command of the Hatchet Ladies had been wrested from her. First, it was Mamie Smith odering the Hatchet Ladies to strike out at Jimmie after he had told her to shut up and listen. Then, in support of Mamie Smith, exploding out to Jimmie that his time had come, it was Blanche Mims.

That was probably why Jimmie got nicked on the arm by Dolly Jean. He was caught off guard. He had expected the order of charge to come form Bessie Black. Instead, it came from Mamie Smith. In fact, even before Dolly Jean nicked him, Mamie Smith, on her own, had made a solo charge at him but missed. He considered himself pretty lucky. But now, he would not have to worry about any further preemption. Bessie Black was about to reclaim her position as the sole, fiery leader of the Hatchet Lady Gang

"Okay, ladies," she chimed in with great authority, "Goddammit! who's running this show 'round here? Everybody? Or jes me?"

"Just you, Bessie," Dolly Jean said in a quick, withdrawn voice. Mamie Smith and Blanche Mims agreed, but not so readily, nor so tractably.

"I don't want nothing else to happen 'round here unless I say it happen," Bessie Black demanded. "Understand me?"

They all said yes again. And again, Dolly Jean more willingly.

"It ain't gonna make no difference to this here traitor," Bessie Black admitted. "But I jes wants to hear what else he got to say 'bout this here Letter For Leave Program. Go on, man, say what you was 'bout to say, but don't take too long. It's gett'n late. We gotta go home. You gotta go home, too, ain't cha?"

"Yeah, he's going home alright," Mamie Smith joked, pointing the glittering blade of her switch knife to the sky. "Up yonder to his maker, that's where he's going. "

"Now, it ain't the traitor, it's me, I'm telling you to shut up," Bessie Black said to Mamie Smith, violently shaking her switch knife at her "And I mean it. Jes shut up your mouth 'til I tells you to say or do something.

"Don't let the ladies shake you up," she comforted Jimmie in low gutteral tones, and laughing. "We ain't gonna kill you yet. That is, not this morning. We's jes gonna rip you up a little bit. 'Cause we wants you to know that we mean business 'bout you calling back what you said 'bout us black folks being too dumb to get a job anywhere else but at the Post Office. But if you don't call it back after our little meeting this morning," she warned him, "I can't tell you nothing 'bout what might happen to you the next time around. So now, go on and say what you was gonna say. And make it quick."

Jimmie thought for a minute of what Bessie Black had just said about their not wanting to kill him this morning but that they only wanted to rip him up a little bit. Did she expect him to believe that? he wondered. If not to kill him is her plan, she should pass the word on to the other Hatchet Ladies. The way they were raising their switch knives up to the sky and brashly thrusting them down, not to kill, apparently, was the farthest thing from their minds, he thought. And as for her, only the morning before, joining with them, she had tried to push him in the path of a moving subway train. Only the broad 300 pound body of Tiny Stark stood between him and his bone crushing death.

Explaining how the Letter For Leave worked, he finally said: "Postmaster Bill Brown wants to know just who the people are that habitually abuse their sick leave privileges. Also, He wants to know what their attitude about the job is, what their situation at home is, and just something about themselves in general..."

"That ain't none uh his damn business," Bessie Black interrupted. "He ain't got no right asking people questions lak that."

"You're right," Jimmie said, agreeing with her. "He shouldn't ask such questions, especially without the permission of the employe. And he didn't..."

"But you jes said he did," Bessie Black cut in.

"No I didn't."

"You jes a bare faced lie," Mamie Smith said.

"Shut up, Mamie, goddammit!" fiery leader Bessie Black shouted at her. "I ain't gonna tell you no more."

"What I said was," Jimmie explained, "is that these are some of the things he wanted to know, but I did not say he specifically asked employes about them. Except in a few very rare cases, workers who have used more sick leave than they have earned, and still use more, are required to write a letter explaining why they think the sick leave taken was necessary. They are instructed to include in the letter the nature of the illness, the method of treatment used to relieve it, their current physical state, etc.

"Postmaster Bill Brown admitted that the Letter For Leave Program contains a clandestine element," Jimmie revealed. "He hoped that from reading such letters, other significant information about the employe could be learned. And right he was", Jimmie regretfully admitted. "The Postmaster read through several of the letters, ran off copies and gave them to me. One continuous thread that closely knits each and everyone of the letters to all the others was the low educational level of the black sick leave abusers. This leads one to wonder about the educational levels of those black employes who are not sick leave abusers. It also asks the question: how did these people ever qualify on the entrance exam. For example, this letter here," he said pulling a photo copy out of his pocket. "It was written by someone whose name I will not reveal. And it tells the story far better than I can. Just listen to this," He invited Bessie Black and her Hatchet Ladies as, under the dim parking lot lights, he slowly started reading it.

" 'I had a bad cole and I was coffin something awful. I should uh went to the doctor, but I didn't. I took some casta oil and stayed in bed 'til I got rid of it.' The letter goes on," Jimmie said, looking over at Mamie Smith who showed nervous signs that she was quite familiar with every word that appeared in the letter. "But I have more than a enough in that short space to prove my point. So far, the writer of that letter has made six errors. She mispelled the words: cold, coughing, terrible, and castor oil. And instead of saying she should have went to the doctor, she ought to have said, I should have gone to the doctor.

"Now you can see why I can't retract that statement," Jimmie said, "because I didn't lie. What I said was the truth." He took more photo copies from his pocket. "And these letters prove it," he added, fanning them about.

"Truth and proving it ain't got nothing to do with it," Bessie Black said. "You say black folks is ignorant. I don't lak that. And my close lady friends here don't lak it neither. And you is gonna take it back, nigger!" she said, inflecting her voice and shaking her switch knife at him. "And Goddammit, I mean that."

"But you don't understand," Jimmie pleaded. "That's just the point, knowing the truth of the matter. Education, efficiency and productivity go hand in hand. But education must come first. So, especially in the technological age we live in, if black people are to become more efficient and productive, we must, accordingly, raise our educational level."

"Ah, shit," Bessie Black objected. "Don't nobody need no college education to do what we do down here every night. Anybody with any common sense can do it. And that goes for all the jobs down here: mailhandler, clerk, supervisor, and that damn jive ass Postmaster job, too. They's all the same. Ain't no difference."

What Bessie Black said, overall, was dead wrong, Although Jimmie had to admit that somewhere inside of it, there was definitely a sparkling element of truth. At the Metro City post office, there was little or no creativity, and virtually no curiosity about certain built in inadequacies. Although some standard orders and regulations devised in Washington might have been appropriate for use in some small town post offices, they added greatly to the already high level of inefficiency and low productivity in most big city post offices. However, officials at Metro City Post Office did not question such misguided wisdom.

But the larger question here involved the pernicious black man's malady which Jimmie referred to as the Infinite Peer Syndrome, where black shoe shine boys and car washers considered themselves the equals to black lawyers and doctors. Here, mailhandler Bessie Black had made no distinction between the requirements needed to do her job and those needed to do Postmaster Bill Brown's job. In fact, she flatly stated that there was no difference.

This concept of a one and only educational, economic and social level for all blacks, among all blacks, by all blacks was one of the main factors that retarded the general growth of black people, Jimmie thought. That's why he stood firm in his conviction. "What I said in the introduction and the summnary of the Blockbuster was the truth," Jimmie said and bristled. "I know it's the truth. You know it's the truth. I stand by it. And I will not retract it, for you, nor for anyone else. Education, efficiency and productivity. That's the key. That's our one potential salvation.

"Ah shit, man, we don't want to hear that crap," unlearned Mamie Smith told Jimmie. "To hell with education, efficiency and productivity, and all that bull-shit. What black folks needs is jobs..."

"No more talk," Bessie Black cut in. "Mr. Traitor? One more time. Is you gonna call back what you said 'bout all black folks working here being ignorant?"

"I did not use the term ignorant, neither did I say all blacks," Jimmie corrected her. "But what I did say was the truth. And I just told you. I stand by it. And I will not retract it."

"Okay, ladies, he's all yours," Bessie Black ordered. "Get his black ass. And get it good."

And on her order, Unlearned Mamie Smith was the first to slash at Jimmie. All total, though, this was really her third time. The first time she had slashed at Jimmie, he moved to his left and she missed. The second time, he moved to his left again, and Mamie Smith missed again. But Confused Bible toting Dolly Jean, positioned on his left side, did not. She inflicted a flesh wound on his left forearm. This third time, coming up, Jimmie remembered that, indeed, Dolly Jean was on his left side, and even closer than before. But the Hatchet-Lady-U had not yet closed to form a circle. The south end was still open. Jimmie treaded backward very quickly.

"Come back here, you black sonofabitch," Mamie Smith yelled out and hurriedly followed after Jimmie, slashing wildly with her switch knife, up and down and from side to side.

Jimmie started backing away, faster and faster, but not quite fast enough. One of Mamie Smith's wild down slashes ripped through the sleeve of his coat and on through his shirt, landing high on his right arm, up near the shoulder. He felt the sharp shooting pain and saw the fast spouting blood.

Mamie Smith took on a beastly posture. Her forehead wrinkled with deep furrows, her eyes grew large and glassy, and she snorted loudly through flaring nostrils. "You got your nerve, you black bastard. Who in hell do you think you is, reading my letters?" she snapped at him, slashing up and down and from side to side with her shiny blood dripping switch knife. "You ain't gonna read no more of my letters. Goddammit, you ain't gonna read no more." She slashed at Jimmie again. This time, she missed.

But Jimmie didn't miss. He realized that no matter what Bessie Black had said about just ripping him up a little bit, this Mamie Smith character was a killer. And he wasn't taking any more chances with her. As she raised her gleaming switch knife high above her head and pointed it directly at his neck and started down with it, he pulled his small pearl handled gun out of his pocket and fired one shot, hitting her directly in the heart

But Mamie Smith, swinging her switch blade wildly from side to side and baring her teeth like a mad dog, kept coming.

Jimmie backed away and waited, thinking that from the direct hit in the heart, she would soon go down. But she didn't. She kept coming. He coiled his finger tightly around the trigger of his gun preparing to shoot her a second time. Unlearned Mamie Smith was even tougher than she sounded, he thought.

"You black sonofabitch you ain't gonna read no more of my letters!" she shouted again. "You hear me? 'Cause I'm ripping your black ass to pieces." She started hopping up and down, stamping her feet and snorting and grinning. Suddenly, she sprang forth. Her entire body left the ground and she sailed through the air in the direction of Jimmie. Though a courageous act, it failed. He stepped to one side and, like a slab of cold beaf, she fell flat on her face.

Blanche Mims was the next Hatchet Lady to slash at Jimmie. He fired and blasted her squarely in her heart, too. And like Mamie Smith had done, she tried to stay on her feet long enough to get to Jimmie. She didn't make it. One step forward and she helplessly colapsed.

Jimmie thought he could feel the parking lot pavement slightly cave in under her weight.

Georgia Rogers screamed: "Mr. Jones! my God! what are you doing?"

Dolly Jean was the next Hatchet Lady to step forward and slash at Jimmie.

Georgia Rogers obviously knew now that Jimmie wasn't going to quit firing as long as they were coming at him. She yelled for Dolly Jean to run, to go back, or to at least, stop. But Dolly Jean was giggling, twitching and bobbing her head up and down to the rhythm of music only she was hearing. With her Bible in her left hand and her glowing switch knife in her right, she showed no signs of having heard Georgia. She kept right on coming.

Georgia Rogers rushed up to Jimmie and grabbed his firing hand. "Don't shoot!" she screamed. "Don't shoot! Dolly Jean is in some kind of daze. She doesn't know what she's doing."

Dolly Jean kept coming. And the long blade of her switch-knife, kept glowing. Jimmie backed away, dragging Georgia with him.

"Go away Dolly Jean! Go away!" Georgia screamed. But Dolly Jean would not go away. So Jimmie shook himself free of Georgia and dropped her to the parking lot pavement right along with the other two of her blood thirsty friends.

There was only one Hatchet Lady left, the brash, fiery leader Bessie Black. "You just saw what happened to your 'close lady friends,' as you refer to them," Jimmie said to her. "So if you don't want the same thing to happen to you, you'd better do what I'm about to do, get in your car and go home." Looking, cautiously, back over his shoulder at Bessie Black, Jimmie headed for his car.

She started walking away, too. But, after taking only a few short steps, she quickly turned and started for Jimmie.

"No! Bessie, no!" Georgia Rogers screamed and jumped in front of Jimmie, as he wheeled around and raised his gun to shoot. "Go back! Go back!"

Obviously, Bessie Black had noted that Jimmie aims for the heart. She ran to where her colleagues lay, doved to the ground, yanked Dolly Jean's Bible, which she had death-clutched, from under her arm and quickly placed it over her heart. Using her switch blade holding-hand, she adroitly sprang back to her feet.

Jimmie pushed Georgia Rogers to one side and hurriedly got off a shot that hit Bessie Black in her abdomen.

The impact of the bullet, momentarily, halted her pace. She cringed and grasped her abdomen with her Bible holding hand, carelessly presenting a situation that Jimmie expertly took advantage of.

He aimed and got off a good clean shot that traveled swiftly and directly to her heart.

Bessie Black staggered over a short distance but did not go down.

Killer Mamie Smith was a tough cookie, Jimmie thought, but Bessie Black was incredible. Her chest must be made of steel, he said.

"Mr, Jones!" Georgia Rogers yelled. "My God, man. Don't you have any mercy at all?"

Bessie Black's eyes got glassy and began to close. She blinked them open again. Her body looked weak and began to sag. She straightened it back up. Apparently, she knew that Jimmie's six shooter had only one bullet left in it. She must have counted them. ("One for Mamie Smith, one for Blanche Mims, one for Dolly Jean and two for me. Five from six leaves one.")

She slammed the Bible up over her heart again and plodded on toward Jimmie. Seemingly on her mind was: If I can hold on and absorb another hit in the abdomen before I go down, I'll get to him and take his black ass down with me.

"No! no!" Georgia Rogers screamed again. "Go back, Bessie, go back." Bessie refused to go back. Georgia ran over and caught her by the arm, accidentally knocking the Bible out of her hand. It fell to the ground.

"Look what the hell you done gone and did," Bessie Black feebly mumbled out. "You stupid ass." She pushed Georgia away. Apparently, she intended to try and quickly pick the Bible up before Jimmie could get off another shot.

But before she could even start into the crouch, Jimmie banged his last bullet dead center of her heart. And that second shot in the heart did the trick. Bessie Black, finally joined her three colleagues sprawled on the parking lot's early morning pavement.

The four women Jimmie had gunned down in Pete's parking lot were not his friends. They were not innocent souls that had bursted "out of the shadows some night" accidentally exciting him into shooting them. They were women with criminal intentions and surely had earned some form of severe punishment. But Jimmie had not killed them.

He turned to see what Georgia Rogers was doing, or to see if she was still there. She stared at the four fallen women, then at Jimmie. Her face was filled with the mixture of pity, terror and hate. Jimmie smiled at her. And like gun slingers of the old west did after finishing off their would be ambushers, he blew the imaginary haze from his smoking gun and gently patted its cooling barrel.

To Jimmie, Georgia Rogers's stare at him was as violent as the gleam from the hatchet ladies switch knives had been. "Mr. Jones! How could you?" she shouted.

Jimmie walked over to where she stood. "This is not a real gun," he explained to her. "That is, I was not shooting real bullets. These women are only stunned," he added, taking her by the arm. "So, let's you and I get going for home before they start coming out of it."

Chapter 4

Metro City's first black Postmaster Bill Brown had been on the job for more than a year now. Yet, Metro City black postal workers, and Metro City black residents, too, were still asking the question: "Why, after 200 years of white domination in the Metro City PO, was this job given to a black man?"

MMPO clerk Mike Davis was the first to speculate. He was expounding to a group of workers on break in the men's locker room. Among them were Jimmie, Ronnie, one of his locker room buddies, Slick, his section mate and about 40 other workers. Oscar, another one of Jimmie's locker room buddies, was expected but had not arrived.

"Bill Brown was appointed to be a front man only," Mike Davis said. "As long as he's Postmaster, and as long as he's black, he'll never have any say. Behind the scenes, whites will make all the decisions," he charged. "And that's all he's been doing since he's been down here, carrying out the white man's orders."

"What white man's orders?" one of the men asked.

"You know what white man's orders," Mike retorted. "The Boss, Ed Riley himself, that's who. You know nothing ever happens in this town unless he lets it happen. That's why they call it the Consesus City," he stipulated, "because it's a town of only one mind, Ed Riley's mind."

Ed Riley was the colorful Mayor of Metro City. Depicted by the Media as the last of the big city bosses, and backed up by the most powerful political machine in the nation, Ed Riley loved Metro City as if it were a living blood relative.

In 1967, the civil rights movement was a potent force in America.

With its sit-ins, demonstrations, marches and boycotts disturbing the normal flow of human activity, in the home, school, worksite, and the market place, it had affected the lives of every man, woman and child. Compared to many other cities, though, Metro City had been a relatively quiet metropolis. Maybe there was some truth in Mike's suspicion that Ed Riley might have had something to do with Bill Brown's appointment.

Of all the business establishments and institutions in Metro City, the Post Office hired the highest number of blacks. About 98% of its 35,000 employes were black. Among the 20,000 main installation workers, there was much unrest. As noted by the Star, Metro City's leading newspaper: "The Metro City Post Office is plagued by overstaffing, absenteeism, a dozen unhappy postal unions, and a totally disgruntled workforce. Also," the Star added, "numerous complaints have been filed about the very few blacks in authority, and the alleged sexual harassment of black women workers by white male supervisors."

Riley was an astute politician and was no doubt aware that the sligthest incident of racial strife starting at the Post Office could spill into the streets and clog up the machinery of his Consensus City.

Mike Davis thought that black man Bill Brown was given the Postmastership in order to keep the peace. "The Metro City PO is supposed to be a federal institution," he said, " but it's located here in Metro City. That makes it Ed Riley's PO. So, he got on the phone to Washington one day and, as if he was talking to one of his stooges down there at City Hall, he told the President of the United States to send him a black Postmaster.

"And we got a black Postmaster. Not because Riley wanted us to have one. And not because he loves us. But because he didn't want a bunch of niggers running loose like wild animals tearing up his town. So you can believe it," Mike Davis added confidently. "Bill Brown is a front man. He's in there just to keep blacks quiet. And he ain't gonna be able to make no decisions before first getting the okay from boss man Ed Riley."

Clerk Mitchell Wade agreed with Mike Davis that Bill Brown was probably appointed Postmaster to play the role of a front man and didn't have any real authority, but he didn't buy Mike's theory that he was made a front man simply to keep the peace among the races. "Naw, it's more than that," Mitchell Wade said. "It's a conspiracy, that's what it is. I can understand what you're saying, though, Mike. All these people bunched up here together, with most nights not enough mail to keep us busy, it does get a little tense in here sometimes. People get touchy. They mouth off at each other. Sometimes there is a little skirmish here and there. And those few white supervisors that are left after the turnover, are tough. Frequently some black women complain that they are abusive. They do piss you off sometimes".

"Quite frequently, conversations between white supervisors and black women workers do get pretty heated," Ronnie agreed.

"Yeah," Slick joined in, "'specially when they comes back off one uh them thirty five minute breaks. Take Johnnie Mae back there in my section. Now she know she's only suppose to stay on a break 15 minutes. But, man, that broad'll go and stay thirty five minutes and come back and swear she's been gone only thirteen." He looked over at his section mate Jimmie for confirmation, then went on. "'course our supervisor Mr. Moses is black. He lets her get away with it..."

"Yeah, I know," Ronnie said, cutting back in. "That happens all over the place, black women workers taking advantage of black men supervisors. That's why they hate those white supervisors. They won't let them get away with it. In my section they play a little game on our black supervisor. If he questions one about staying too long on a break, first, she'll give him the line about: 'I'm not a man. Certain times of the month, it takes a lady a little longer in the washroom.' If that doesn't work she'll start talking loudly as if he's attacking her. And all the women in the section, 25 or thirty, crowd around asking, 'what's he doing to you?.'

"My supervisor is a big man. He stands over six feet. With this lone woman standing before him looking totally helpless and all the other women in the section crowded around staring him down as a big bullie, now he's embarrassed. So he tucks his tail and says, "Okay, all right. You go on back there now and throw some mail for me."

"That's really something, man. I know what you mean," one of the men said. "It happens in my section, too. But let's get back to this front man thing," he urged Mitchell. "You say its a conspiracy huh? what do you mean by that?"

Mitchell Wade was the kind of blue eyed mulatto that could pass for white anytime he chose. But that was outside. Inside, he was blacker than Jimmie Jones himself. He hated his caucasian complexion so much so that he wore his long coal black hair streaming down his back to hide his almost lily white neck. And he maintained a heavy beard that seemed to cover all of his face except his eyes. It was a kind of mask that Mitchell wore ("He wears all that long, black, thick ass hair all over his face to make him look more lak a nigger," Slick had said.). Constantly on the stump fighting for the black cause, he was considered a fanatic by many MMPO workers. Their claim was that he thought every move the white man made was designed to conspire against blacks.

"Well how about it, Mitchell?" Ronnie asked with a kind of smirk on his face. "What's the conspiracy this time?"

"Yeah, come on, Mitchell, tell us," several of the men asked together, giggling.

"Go ahead," Mitchell said. "Laugh if you want to. But a conspiracy is in the making. And in time you'll find out. Just wait."

"We don't want to wait," they said. "We want to know now. So go on tell us what the conspiracy is."

"I can't tell you precisely what's going to happen. But I'm telling you that things are not what they seem. Behind the scenes, a scheme of some kind is in the works. They had a reason for making Bill Brown the Postmaster. And it wasn't just to keep the peace. Believe me, fellows."

Mitchel was right. Indeed, a scheme was "in the works." Since its inception, the Metro City Post Office had been dominated by whites. Until recent years, instead of a 98% black workforce, there had been a 98% white workforce.

But now, whites had virtually deserted the city for the suburbs. They wanted to move their post office out there, too. And coming along with it, they surely wanted to see the 98% postal jobs that once were theirs. It was unrealistic to demand that the Metro City Main PO be shut down and relocated in the suburbs, and the 98% black workers be replaced with 98% white workers. Such an idea would be viewed as discriminatory, a charge which in no way whites could logically deny.

But, to white populated suburbia, the idea itself of having their own suburban PO and a 98% white workforce was not unrealistic at all. To achieve their goal, they needed only to come up with the right plan.

In order to put forth a convincing argument, white suburbia knew they had to establish the need for having their own PO and a 98% white workforce, and not let show only the naked appearance of harboring what very well could have been characterized as only discriminatory practices. And so they did.

Their plan was composed of only two steps. First, to appoint a black Postmaster at Metro City as a stabilizing force to prevent possible black worker unrest and a resulting backlash. This they had done. Or, as Mike Davis and Mitchell Wade claimed, Ed Riley had done it for them. In other words, "Front man" Bill Brown was already on the job.

The second step was not an easy task. White suburbia had to prove that the Metro Main Post Office was understaffed of personnel and short of floor space.

Overstaffing at the Main installation, not understaffing, was common knowledge among Metro postal workers, and so were the acres of daily unused floor space. Nevertheless, white suburbia pulled it off. One morning, out of the clear blue, came a mysterious volume of 10,000,000 pieces of backed up mail.

A taskforce from Washington came in and wrenched the power right out of Bill Brown's hands, and threw fear into the workers who wondered who was responsible for their coming in. But with pencils and pads, like jail house guards with guns and clubs swarming all over the place 24 hours a day, they slowly turned workers's fear into anger. After awhile, slumped on their individual seats, mean and recalcitrant, they didn't give a damn. Venting their mad dog feelings among themselves, and passing the word to give the taskforce the business, they dutifully went through their paces, but skillfully managed to produce little.

As one worker put it: "They come in here from Washington right out of Harvard reading them books about postal management. Now they think they know all about it. And, except to mail an occasional letter, they ain't never seen inside a post office before. So let's make 'em suffer. The bastards."

Although the school boys from Harvard, who "ain't never seen inside a post office before," were unaware that the workers weren't putting out a hundred percent, the work slowdown of the clever MMPO clerks backfired. Making the overflow appear larger that what it really was, it helped to make white suburbia a winner.

The taskforce concluded in their final report that the "Metro City PO was terribly understaffed, that it could not effectively handle the allotted workload, and that the main installation building suffered greatly because of a space problem." So they recommended the establishment of what they called a Sectional Center Facility (SCF). The function of this addendum, to be constructed in white suburbia, would be to ease what they deemed Metro City Main installation's excessive volume.

Although his worker friends did not believe him, Mitchel Wade was right. Indeed there was a conspiracy "in the works." He was wrong about one thing, though, the loser. White suburbia was truly a winner. But as Mitchel Wade had implied, blacks were not the losers. They maintained their full workforce.

And as Jimmie noted, when the construction of the Sectional Center Facility is completed, instead of having only one Post Office and only one 98% workforce, Metro City will have two of each. So the losers were not the blacks. They were the taxpayers.

The overflow fiasco was quite frustrating to freshman Postmaster Bill Brown. Now, however, the exasperation for him had begun coming from his own team. Jimmie Jones and Bill Brown were on the same wavelength. They both advocated increased efficiency and higher levels of productivity, aspirations of which his team was not necessarily inclined. One of their complaints was that Bill Brown had not chided Jimmie for having submitted his Blockbuster suggestion. They considered it a personal attack on black management.

There was no doubt. These were bad times for Bill Brown, proving to some evaluating Cassandras that he really wasn't qualified for the job, and to other envious Cassandras that he was truly only a front man. But Bill Brown could not blame the Washington taskforce and his fair weather management team for all of his problems. He made at least two crucial mistakes himself.

First, in 1967, the Metro City PO was a place of detachment, a meeting ground where people by the hundreds came in droves everyday and every night to work and laugh and talk and eat together; but a place where, indeed, there was little true and lasting community.

At the workplace, it was a must that they be together for eight hours. To attempt to remain detached would be crass and inhumane. They had no choice but to communicate with one another, no matter how awkward or insincere.

But away from the workplace, they quickly changed the tenor of their on-the-job brotherhood by literally avoiding each other. In supermarts, on L-trains, in downtown stores, their snobbish heads quickly flipped to one side giving attention to things that were not there.

There was something sinister about the MMPO building, the atmosphere, the breathing walls, its general ambience. It literally transformed people, seemingly changed them almost immediately, right there on the spot. There seemed all about, a mysterious aura, a cool chilling breeze that penetrated their bodies, and, like a carcinogenic substance, buried itself deep into their rapidly changing genes. Laced with invisible keys and buttons, mindlessly plodding through their monotonous daily routines, MMPO workers were zombies, human robots that the very atmosphere of the workplace had long since clandestinely programmed.

It was amazing. Blacks, through their long, faithful history, by all that was comfortable and acceptable to them, had always been a happy, outgoing people who proudly wore a permanently carved in smile that even the hardest of times could not erase.

But now, through the efforts of the only organization capable of doing so, this had all changed. The MMPO had achieved the impossible.

Like some painless, poisonous gas, this diabolical MMPO coldness had sieved its way through the sheath that for so many years had protected blacks from the insensitivity of the real world out there.

Like most Metro City black residents, most Metro City black postal workers were migrants from the Southland where a great blanket of kinship for several centuries had constantly nurtured and protected them. Perhaps it was asking too much of Bill Brown to try and spread that great blanket of sharecropping friendship over Metro City's vast dome of freezing apathy, but Jimmie thought that, at least, he should try.

He could have started out the day he was sworn in by speaking to the full complement of the Metro City postal workforce. He could have told them what he expected of them and what they could expect of him. In other words, as Jimmie noted in a letter to Postmaster Bill Brown, urging him to make a belated one, "It would have been very nice if you had made a 'Howdy Do' address that all workers could have heard."

True, installation ceremonies were held in the grand lobby of the Main Post Office building where, along with a selected group of local and Washington dignitaries, about 50 Metro postal workers were in attendance. But what about the 34,950 other workers? Should they not have heard and seen Bill Brown as he outlined to his listeners what his program was going to be? Through modern telecommunications, should he not have attempted to close some of the gaps among Metro black postal workers? Jimmie thought that this was Bill Brown's first basic mistake: not initially speaking to the full complement of people who were to serve him.

The second basic mistake Bill Brown made, according to Jimmie's reasoning, was to blame workers for the infamous overflow. When he took office, he outlined what he termed his 3 point program. At the top of the list was: to reduce absenteeism. The other two, to increase the use of modern postal machines, and to improve the operation of the ZIP Code program. As the ex-chief of personnel, Bill Brown knew that 2,000 Metro postal employes, ten percent of the main installation workforce, were absent from work each day. Absenteeism, over a long period, had been a challenge to him. He believed strongly that absenteeism was one of the greatest deterrents of productivity. So, accordingly, he thought that absenteeism at the MMPO was the main cause of the overflow. This got him into trouble with the unions.

In making the charge, Bill Brown said he did not hold workers totally responsible for the overflow, that there were other factors.

"The other factors that contributed to the overflow are receiving my personal attention, and corrective action is being taken to prevent their recurrence," he said. But he did not identify the "other factors." This meant only one thing to the accused workers: the Postmaster was lying; he blamed only them for the overflow.

The Star, Metro City's leading newspaper, reported in an article about Metro City getting its first black Postmaster that: "As a personnel expert, Bill Brown is sensitive to the charge of low morale." But the article said nothing about Bill Brown's ability to deal with the problem of low morale.

Taking into account his very early two basic errors: first, snubbing his full complement of workers by failing to present them with an introductory address, and second, by charging them with creating the worst crisis in Metro City Post Office history, one had no other recourse but to wonder about his ability to effectively communicate with a workforce such as that of the Metro City Post Office. Then, too, the question could have very well been asked: would any Postmaster have the ability to effectively communicate with the Metro City PO workforce?

Now, at any rate, in the light of these unfortunate blunders, reaching the Metro City postal worker anytime in the near future for Bill Brown would be highly improbable.

Many MMPO workers, the Dreamers, had viewed the coming of the black Postmaster as a great advantage for black MMPO workers. He would come in and free them of discipline, of rules and regulations, and from the indifference and cruelty of some insensitive MMPO white supervisors. To MMPO Dreamers, the coming of a black PM represented the arrival of a long awaited respite. "Whitey's 'been making this good money all these years sitting down doing nothing," they said. "Now it's our time to sit down and do nothing."

Not all black MMPO workers embraced the Dreamers's concept of a future of complete free-will for MMPO workers. Disagreeing voices, the Nay sayers, quickly cited the thrill that some black policemen get out of "beating up" blacks out on the street; how some black case workers relish holding up checks of welfare recipients; and how some black doctors enjoy ignobly brutalizing their black Medicaid-Medicare patients. To the Naysayers, the thoughts of free will hoped for by the Dreamers was pure and very simple wishful thinking.

Now, in the minds of the Dreamers, in the minds of the Nay sayers, and even in the minds of the Acquiescents, the whopping majority who took no stand before the overflow, at the end of the overflow, or anytime thereafter, Bill Brown was one great big disappointment.

But Jimmie thought it only fair to say that no matter what workers said about what they thought, or what they did not say about what they thought, in his opinion, what Bill Brown had done and was doing was not altogether wrong. In fact, it was right, just the kind of medicine needed to cure a very sick patient of a chronic illness. It's just that when issuing foul tasting medication, especially in large doses, it is sometimes wise to mix in sweeteners or to serve pop along with it to mitigate the bitter taste.

But despite Bill Brown's desires and Jimmie Jones' quasi-endorsement of those desires, MMPO workers had their desires, too. They wanted no rules, no discipline, no pressure. They wanted lots of colleagues on the job and little mail. Regarding their not wanting discipline, Jimmie had logged many examples in his little black book, such as this one: The clerk had just returned from a two month unauthorized leave. This was her first night back on the job. She was sitting on a stool at a sorting case. But before she started working, she decided to read the newspaper she had brought along with her out onto the workroom floor. She read the headlines and a couple of front page articles, then moved on to page two.

Her supervisor approached her. "No newspapers on the workroom floor," he warned her. "No books, either. You know better. You came here to throw mail, not to read newspapers. So let's get rid of it. And come on and let's get this mail out," he demanded and walked away.

"Supervisors always messing with people," the clerk complained. "I was just reading the headlines." She looked to the center of the aisle, at the 5 trays of mail left on the storage truck. Then, she viewed the other 30 clerks in the unit who, in a very short time, would have finished their first tray of mail and would be looking fruitlessly for a second. And she fumed out loudly, making sure everybody, but especially the supervisor, heard what she said: "Talking about let's get the mail out, you ain't got no mail in here to get out."

To combat the great problem of absenteeism at the MMPO, the Postmaster buttoned down his seatbelt and took a hard line approach. Suspensions for habituals and dismissals for incorrigibles became the order of the day.

The Letter Clerks Union called a news conference. And following it, the Star newspaper ran a front page article in its City Edition expressing union dismay at the turn of events. "The Metro City Postal Union complained today that employe grievances have caused an all time low in morale and an all time high in turnover at the Metro City Post Office," the article began. "Sonny Bowen, Union President, charged that many workers have been fired for being absent three times, even though the absences were justifiable. 'These workers were dismissed even with a doctor's statement,' Bowen further charged. 'It seems that some doctor's statements just aren't acceptable to the Post Office,'" the Star reported Bowen having said, and added that the Union wants the AWOL policy abolished because they think it has become a punitive weapon in the hands of supervisory personnel.

The Star quoted Charlie Smith, Union Secretary, as revealing that some sixty cases in the past year had been reported to the union of employes being dismissed for absences the Post Office refused to okay.

Union President Sonny Bowen released to the Star a letter from the Postmaster informing employes that supervisors had been instructed to recommend dismissal of those charged with three AWOLs. Bowen also charged that black workers, especially black women, were constantly abused by white supervisors; that substitute employes were being docked an hour's pay when only six minutes late for work; and that employes were not allowed to take sick and annual leave when they wanted to, even in cases of emergency.

The Postmaster flatly denied the Union charges. To the charge that white supervisors were abusive toward black women workers, he retorted that: "To the contrary, if anything, white supervisors go out of their way to avoid being abusive toward black women workers." In answer to the charge that substitute workers were being docked a full hour for being six minutes late for work, he quoted the Five Minute Grace Period Rule in which an employe late for work five minutes or less is permitted to punch in, and loses no time. "An employe arriving for work later than five minutes," he explained, " is not allowed to hit in. He must wait for the beginning of the next hour. Those hitting in on their own after the expiration of the five minute grace period, refusing to wait out the remaining of the tardy hour, and working without permission, will not be paid for that time."

And about his treatment of sick leave abusers, the Postmaster said he thought he was quite lenient in that area. "All a worker has to do is call and request sick leave for a legitimate encapacitation and it is granted," he informed. "But, in the case of habituals, those who have gone a dozen times to the funeral of the one and same grandparent, a doctor's statement may be required. True, some doctor's statements are turned down. We maintain a list here of doctors who, for a fee, issue slips to our employes without even examining them. Those slips, we do not honor."

Letter Clerk Union Officials didn't buy Bill Brown's argument, especially the part justifying his sick leave policy. That contrivance was a cold, calculated measure designed for one reason only, they said, to get people off the rolls, to take jobs away from blacks. So, they called more news conferences and went out into the black community: to civil rights gatherings, and to regular church meetings informing black people about what they termed Postmaster Bill Brown's horrible sick leave policy. And they solicited their support to get Bill Brown to back away from it.

But Bill Brown's eating desire to effectively reduce the horrendous absenteeism abuse was not daunted. As a result, suspensions and dismissals abounded. Accordingly, though, the Letter Clerks (LC) Union dug in, too. They contacted radio and TV talk shows to make arrangements for spot appearances. And they got them.

The LC Union came up with the idea that the semblance of growing public sympathy to their cause had become an overwhelming ground swell. And they brought out their most galling resistance to date. They sent out letters to their members to not deliberately defy Bill Brown's sick leave edict, but not to fear it, either. "If by chance you receive from the Postmaster a letter of suspension or dismissal because of three unauthorized absencies," the Union advised, "bring that letter in to Union headquarters and we will deal with it for you. Do not fear. We are here. Here to protect your interest."

By word of mouth, and in secrecy, the LC Union sent out the word for clerks to create a slowdown. In defiance of the Washington taskforce presence during the infamous overflow, MMPO clerks had successfully pulled off such a scheme. (Their victory was a pyrrhic one, though. It inadvertently supported the taskforce report that the Metro PO was understaffed which, unfortunately, led to the establishment of the superfluous suburban Sectional Center Facility.) Now, months later, in defiance of Bill Brown's sick leave policy, they would dutifully go through their paces, but, again, skillfully manage to produce little.

As the workers had punished the Washington taskforce with a sharp curtailment of production for holding them hostage during their several snooping weeks here at the Metro PO, so would they make Postmaster Bill Brown pay for the Draconian sick leave policy he threateningly dangled over their heads.

Some workers had charged that Bill Brown was responsible for the Washington Taskforce coming in. It was never really clear who was actually responsible. But there was no doubt about who called in the teaskforce to counteract this second worker slowdown. For sure, this time, it was Bill Brown. With 37 years of service, and having come up through the ranks, all the way from mailhandler to Postmaster, Bill Browm had a pretty good idea about who was working and who was fluffing off. And so did members of the taskforce he put together.

Unlike the Washington taskforce, which was made up of theory based "school boys from Harvard," Bill Brown's taskforce was made up of knowledgeable local boys right off the production line. They reported the fluff offs to Bill Brown; and Bill Brown directly sent the fluff offs home without pay.

But this turn of events would not be the end of the struggle. The determined black workers weren't going to let this black proselyte of a Postmaster slap them down so easily. At the Metro Main PO, there were one dozen separate unions. The most powerful of them was the Mailhandlers Union. The Letter Clerks (LC) Union sought their support first and got it. Then, they sought and got the full support of Metro unions across the board.

The one dozen unions declared an all out war against Bill Brown's sick leave policy. They called daily joint meetings of the Unions' top officials to map strategy. They regularly supplied union stewards with certain worker procedual information to pass on to rank and file members. And they periodically circulated among the emoloyes a printed pamphlet announcing special elements of progress being made. Also, included in the printed pamphlet, which they named Joint Leaflet, were hints that a strike would be called if found absolutely necessary, although strikes by postal workers were illegal.

If the speculation by those who had claimed that mayor Ed Riley had insisted a black man be appointed to the Postmastership at the Metro City PO in order to ward off a riot by black workers against the alleged coercive white management was true, Riley's scheme to spare his city such a calamity seemingly was about to backfire. His city was going to experience not only a calamity but a ridiculous calamity: black workers rioting against what they considered a coercive black management.

But it did not come to that. The opposition built up so greatly against Bill Brown that he had no other option but to give ground. Joining the unions in favor of the workers was a group which called itself The Protectors. Although the identities of its members were kept secret, it was believed that the five men were top level members of Bill Brown's own staff. "If not top level, they surely are an important part of his management team," an issue of the Joint Leaflet carefully implied. One thing for sure, they had the clout necessary to rein in considerable attention as to what they were about. The word got around that it was true the workers were unaware of whom The Protectors were, but that Bill Brown certainly knew who they were. They wrote him a red hot letter signed by all five members, the workers said, a letter that clearly outlined to Bill Brown that he had gone too far, and must now, without hesitation, back off.

At first, Jimmie thought the rumor by the workers was just plain wishful thinking, that there definitely would not be any letting up by Bill Brown. He thought that, at least for the workers, things would remain about the same. But contrary to Jimmie's calculations, there was a let up in Bill Browns policies, in several very noticeable ways. First, Bill Brown immediately recalled his personally assigned taskforce. Second, workers coming up with convincing arguments to justify their three unauthorized absences were instructed by the joint unions to bring their suspension and dismissal letters to Union headquarters, report for duty, hit in and go to work. They did. And in each case, Bill Brown withdrew the charges.

The next encouraging news to the workers was the rumor that Postmaster Bill Brown, with his thirty seven years of service, was being forced to retire. A conflicting, companion rumor, though, noted that Bill Brown was not being forced to retire but was being kicked upstairs, possibly to the job of Postmaster General in Washington, D.C.

Chapter 5

Jimmie walked into GS-48P and took a seat. This was the section where first class letters addressed to Metro City Postal Zone 48 got its first sorting. Jimmie was assigned to GS-48S where first class letters addressed to Metro City Postal Zone 48 got its second and last sorting before it was shipped out to Zone 48 Carrier Station.

Assigned to GS-48P were three of the Hatchet Ladies: Mamie Smith, the Unlearned One; Blanche Mims, the Late Set Sweetheart; and Bible Toting Dolly Jean, the Confused One.

"There he is, the traitor," Bessie Black, the leader of the Hatchet Ladies, said. She was there, too. But she didn't belong there. GS-48P was a section for clerks. Bessie Black was a mailhandler. "What is you doing in here?" she asked Jimmie.

"The real question is, what are you doing in here," he quickly responded.

"Ain't none uh your damn business what I'm doing in here," she scowled. Then, as if on second thought, looking down at the sheet of paper she held in her hand, she smiled and said: "But if you jes gotta know, me and my lady friends here got some business to take care of."

"Hey, Jimmie, what's up, man," Ronnie asked. Among the 31 GS-48P workers, he and Oscar were the only two men. "I'd like to know, too," he said. "Why did they send you up here?"

"Don't ask me," Jimmie answered. "All I know is they sent me up here to work in Lois Flowers's place and sent her back to GS-48S to work in my place."

"Why did they do that?"

"Who knows," Oscar said, joining in. "Don't even ask. Crazy

people 'round here do anything."

"Is Lois suppose to help with the Man's Work (heavy and dirty work) back there," Ronnie asked, smiling.

"You know better than that," Jimmie answered in a mild scolding tone.

"Well you said she was going back to GS-48S to work in your place..."

"You know I didn't mean she was going to do Man's Work, though."

"What I can't figure out is why they sent her back there at all," Ronnie said, scratching his head, "and you up here. What does it mean...?"

"Nothing," Oscar interrupted. "It ain't got nothing to do with nothing. Them dummies over there at that detail desk jes done messed up again, that's all. They do it all the time. The other night, they sent two women down to the dock by mistake, down there where they loading and unloading them big trailer tractors. So don't worry 'bout it, Jimmie. They'll be over here in a few minutes asking what you doing in here."

Jimmie motioned his head in the direction of Bessie Black. "Speaking of the wrong people being in here, what is she doing in here? And what is it she has to discuss with her 'close lady friends' that's seems so important?" he asked, mimicking Bessie Black.

"Ah, man, women," Oscar said in disgust. "They ain't never satisfied. They don't have to do no heavy and dirty work 'round here. They can set up on their cases and do their nails and stuff and boss you 'round while you do they work for 'em. But that ain't enough. They wants to be supervisors, too."

"That's what the sheet of paper Bessie Black has in her hand is about," Ronnie said. "It's a petition..."

"A petition? What for?" Jimmie asked. "What does it say?"

"Yeah," Oscar joined in. "It's from that broad EEO Geneva upstairs there. She's always talking 'bout sex discrimination, 'women getting the short end,' as she calls it. She say 'cause women is 98% of the workforce here, that the Postmaster ought to be a woman. Can you believe that? They wants to take over everything."

The workers nicknamed Geneva EEO Geneva because she was the head of the local Equal Employment Opportunity Unit.

From across the aisle, Bessie Black gave Oscar an evil look.

"What's that woman hater talking 'bout over there?" she asked.

"None uh your business, woman!" Oscar shouted back.

"It's strange how EEO Geneva, as head of the Equal Employment Opportunity Unit here, would dare campaign so publicly in an effort to get women up the management ladder," Jimmie said. "The way conditions are here, you'd think she'd assume a low profile on that issue."

"What do you mean, Jimmie?" Ronnie asked.

Jimmie hesitated for a moment, then he came right out with it. "Sex discrimination, that's what I mean. You have some older men here with back problems who have to get younger men to help them do their Man's Work. Suppose they were as vocal about their plight as EEO Geneva is about what she considers the women's plight here. And suppose one day these men grouped themselves together, as the women do about their problems, and refused to do the women's share of Man's Work. And just suppose they got support from the rest of the men. Where would that leave the MMPO women?"

"You're right, Jimmie," Ronnie agreed. "The women here don't know how lucky they are..."

"But back to the petition Bessie has," Jimmie interrupted. "What does it say?"

And Ronnie answered, "At the top of the sheet of paper, there is a single, simple sentence which asks: 'Do you think we should have lady supervisors here?' And all the way down the rest of the page are yes and no boxes for workers to put their x's in."

"If that's to be considered a survey," Jimmie questioned "a few x's marked on a single sheet of paper, it isn't going to tell EEO Geneva very much."

"Oh no," Ronnie explained. "That's not all. EEO Geneva has worked out an extensive program. And Bessie Black and her Hatchet Ladies are in charge of it. Armed with bundles of petition sheets, they will be making the rounds throughout the building. Bessie is just using the one sheet she has there to explain to her group how the procedure works."

"How the scam works you mean," Oscar said. "Them old broads ain't gonna be making all them rounds you talking 'bout. Maybe a few. But that's all. You ain't suppose to put no names on them sheets, just x's. So I'm gonna tell you exactly what Bessie Black and them three broads that hangs 'round with her is gonna do. They going off somewhere in a secret corner and fill up every one of them yes boxes on every one of them sheets."

Reconsidering, Oscar said, "Well, maybe not all of 'em. They too smart for that. They'll mark a few no's to make it look good. But it ain't gonna be too many. And you can believe that. Then they gonna take 'em back up there and give 'em back to EEO Geneva, the slick broad who cooked up that whole tricky deal.

A clerk from the adjoining section JS-17P walked into GS-48P. "Hey, Blanche," he called out, "I hear that we're going to get some lady supervisors. Is that right?"

"You better believe it, Nab," she assured him. "And real soon. A list is all made up."

"Are you on the list?" Nab asked Blanche.

"I sure am," she said, and got up from her seat. She strolled to the center of the aisle, clasped her hands against her slender hips, twitched her rounded buttocks and dug her right heel into the hard parquet floor. She rocked her legs back and forth and winked her large brown eyes at Nab and asked, "Any objections?"

"No, not from me," Nab quickly said. Then, with an anxious smile on his face, he added: "You can be my supervisor any day, baby."

"Right on," she said, taunting him with twisting hips. "Just you and me in the section all by ourselves. How about that, huh?"

Blanche considered herself a beautiful girl. And for good reason. Everybody told her so. That's how she got the title: The Late Set Sweetheart. But to Jimmie, the attention and flattery she received from fellow workers made a braggart out of Blanche, sometimes disgustingly so. Especially on those occasions when she stood exuding her pride to the tune of: "My great-great grandfather on my mother's side was Irish, and my great-great grandfather on my father's side was a full blooded Cherokee."

Blanche went on taunting Nab, with him enjoying every minute of it. She squeezed her hand more tightly about her waistline, and her gray plaid mini skirt crawled a little higher up, making the viewing even more revealing. She twitched her buttocks more torridly and said, "What you see is what you get."

Nab wheeled around, turned his back to everyone, quickly rammed his hands into his pocket as if trying to hide something and dashed to the front of GS-48P, and back over into JS-17P.

Blanche returned to her case and started sorting mail again. Later, when she had run out, she asked Oscar to bring a tray of mail to her case from the storage flat truck situated in the middle of the aisle about 20 feet away. It was a game the female clerks played with Oscar whom they considered a hardened woman hater.

Blanche's motive was to liven up GS-48P by provoking from Oscar his stock answer to such a request which was: "Not me, baby. You make the same money I do. That try of mail don't weigh but 18 pounds. If you wants it, you better get up off your black butt and go get it yourself." That direct no nonsense response from Oscar usually brought upon him a crushing tongue lashing from the women working in the section. And that's what Late Set Sweetheart Blanche Mims had in mind, getting something started.

But before Oscar could get his response oiled up and ready for delivery, Nab, with his energy now under control, dashed back over to GS-48P and down the aisle to the storage truck. "How many do you want, baby?" he asked Blanche, flexing his muscles.

"Look at that damn silly ass," Oscar said, slammimg the mail he held in his hand back down on the ledge.

"Just one will do, goodlooking," Blanche said, turning and doing a spread eagle. Then she stretched her knees far apart and pressed them against the ledge of the sorting case, zipping her abbreviated skirt up to where it covered almost nothing.

Nab took a tray of mail from the storage truck, walked over and set it on the ledge to the left of Blanche. Watching her come-on sitting position, he stood there tightly clutching the tray of mail, unable to release it.

"Over here," Blanche said, motioning her head to the right Deciding that her skirt was not yet quite high enough, with slow calculated speed, she reached down and pulled it well up above the top rim of her hose.

Nab, seeing the naked flesh of her thigh, yanked up the tray and said, "Yeah, baby, yeah, anything you say," then placed it directly in front of her.

"No, no, over there," she said, pointing to the right side. Nab picked the tray of mail up and started walking around to the back of Blanche. She turned and placed her hand on top of the tray and pushed it back down to the ledge "Why walk around when you can reach it right across?" she questioned him.

Except for Blanche's exposed thigh, Nab had not noticed anything else different about her unusual sitting position. He reached the tray of mail across her lap without looking to see where he was placing it. He was still looking at her naked thigh.

But when he decided to look to see if the tray was sitting okay on the ledge, he stopped his looking half way across. Blanche's naked thigh never looked this good, Nab must have thought. There was nothing better than this. "Oh my God!!" he gasped, "Blanche! What are you doing to me?"

Oscar was visibly disgusted with the whole affair. Nab racing over from the next section to lug around an 18 pound tray of mail for Blanche. And now creaming at the mouth all over her like a sick stud horse. It was too much. He side glanced the situation, ripped an awful frown across his face and squirmed uncomfortably on his stool. "What's wrong with that fool anyhow!" he shouted "Ain't he never seen a woman's naked thigh before?"

"Maybe he sees more than just a naked thigh," Ronnie said.

"More than a naked thigh!" Jimmie excitedly repeated. "You don't mean...?"

"Yeah, that's exactly what I mean. See the goofy look on that dude's face?"

"Could be," Oscar agreed. "I don't put nothing past these black bitches 'round here."

Jimmie winced from Oscar's words. He was a woman hater. Jimmie knew that. And it was a time in history when women all over, black ones too, were becoming more competitive, even aggressive. On occasions, the antics of the rising new female breed had caused him great anxiety. For example, Mary Belle, his own wife. She stayed on his case constantly. But, to Jimmie, black women were no different from any other women. In all races, there was good and bad. For Oscar to put all black women in the same ugly bag, Jimmie didn't like it. Not one damn bit.

"Oscar, how many times have I told you, man. You know I don't like that kind of talk about our women. If no one else respects our women, at least we should."

"Yeah, I know," Oscar said. "I'm sorry, but damn, man. Look at that. Ain't no way in hell for that whore to get her legs to open up no wider. Right in that silly ass's face, too. And she calls herself a lady. Oh yeah, speaking of ladies, Jimmie. You give me hell for low rating these broads 'round here. But you yourself say they ain't

"Well, what I mean, Oscar, as I understand it, a decent woman and a lady are not necessarily the same things. A lady is the queen of England, the wife of a president, of a governor, or of a mayor. A rich woman with servants, expensive jewels, one who doesn't have to work. I certainly don't see anyone around here who fits any of those descriptions.

"Nab finally released his hold on the tray of mail he had reached across to the other side of Blanche and had straightened his body back up again. But he was still looking at the object that had now practically hypnotized him. "You and I could make some beautiful music together, baby," he told Blanche.

Jimmie winced again, not from what Nab was proposing to Blanche, and not from something derisive that he thought Oscar might say about it, but from what he was afraid Blanche's response would probably be. Jimmie was thinking of something Slick, his 7:12 station mate back in GS-48S told him the first night he had walked into that section, six years before. Slick was not necessarily a woman hater as 10.12 Oscar was, but he harbored some scandalous opinions about the women who worked at the MMPO. One of those opinions he had revealed to newcomer Jimmie Jones right away: "If the price is right, man, any of these broads 'round here will go," he had told Jimmie.

This was one item of Jimmie's indoctrination into the MMPO family that he had never forgotten. On that occasion, he had not outright called Slick a lie, but he had strenuously protested in disbelief. But Slick bragged that he could prove it. And Jimmie challenged him to do just that. As bold as he pleased, in an attempt to show Jimmie the light, Slick approached MMPO female workers almost across the board, and at random. Taking his wallet out of his pocket and showing it to the female worker, he'd say, "How about a private party tonight, Baby, just you and me?"

As the deal went down, true, Jimmie made a liar out of Slick. All MMPO women would not go if the price was right. But those who said no to Slick were far too few in number for Jimmie. That created in him feelings of shame and embarrassment, not so much for himself, but for those involved in the smutty little game, especially the black women. That's why cold chills ran up and down Jimmie's spine when Nab suggested to Blanche that they could make sweet

88

music together.

Though not overly convincing, Jimmie told himself that, just maybe, this time there would be no cause for shame and embarrassment. Slick had won too many times before. He couldn't win this time, too. The odds were against him. In any game of chance, numbers, lottery, one arm bandits, craps, whatever, a guy could win just so many times. Then he'd lose. In fact, in most games of chance, one loses more times than one wins. For Slick, he vowed, one of his rare times of losing had come.

Besides the odds being against Slick, Jimmie thought of another possible reason why Slick would lose this time. Blanche was not that kind of woman, he'd like to believe. Oh, she was flip, coquettish and glib, but she wasn't for sale. Beneath that brusque, care free outer crust was restraint and decency. There had to be.

"Well, Blanche, what about it, baby?" Nab pressed her. "You and me making beautiful music together, huh?"

Blanche took the two middle fingers of her left hand and ran them ever so slowly, across the naked part of her thigh and winked at Nab. Then, as schizophrenic patients do, she quickly changed her mood.

She snapped her limbs together at an uncommonly fast rate of speed, and gave Nab an "Ah no you don't, it ain't like that" kind of a look. Then, in a cunning and challenging voice, to the sad disappointment of Jimmie, she said in clear tones: "If the price is right, baby, then, everything else will be right."

As Bessie Black fingered a second sheet of paper up on top of the first sheet she held in her hand, Nab, with obvious feelings of disappointment and dejection, left section GS-48P and quickly headed back to his own section.

"Now let me see who's on here," Bessie said. It was a list of names of women who were eligible for supervisory consideration. EEO Geneva from the Equal Employment Opportunity Unit had given her the list and asked her to look it over and make some recommendations. "Lois Flowers!" she gasped. "Who put her name on here? Hey, Mamie? You think Lois Flowers is qualified to be a supervisor?"

"You mean Mrs. High and Holy Lois Flowers?" Unlearned Mamie Smith asked, making a fist of her hands. "Naw, she ain't qualified."

"What about you, Blanche? You think Lois is qualified to be a supervisor?"

"No, I don't," Blanche said with certainty. "She's not qualified. What about you? Do you think she's qualified?"

"Hell naw!" Bessie snapped. "You know damn well I don't think she qualified."

"So what are you going to do?" Blanche asked. "Some people around here think she's pretty hot stuff."

"Yeah, look," Mamie Smith said, pointing to the sheet of paper Bessie was holding, "They got her name up there at the top uh the list."

The opinion Bessie, Mamie and Blanche shared about Lois Flowers had nothing to do with qualification. It was all about dislike. Although she worked right there in section GS-48P with Mamie Smith, Blanche Mims and Dolly Jean, Lois Flowers was not one of them.

Unlearned Mamie Smith disliked Lois because Lois was her direct opposite. Not only was she intelligent. But, by day, she was a school teacher. With a PH.D., she was the Principal of the Southside High School. Lois didn't use foul language. She didn't think all black men were mean and evil. And, like all four Hatchet Ladies, she was divorced, but she spoke kindly of her ex-husband.

("I still love him," Lois would say. "And he still loves me. It's just that he believes the man should be the top bread-winner in the home. My earnings were greater than his. We tried hard to make a go of it. But it was a part of his upbringing that he just could not forget. I understood.")

Late Set Sweetheart Blanche Mims disliked Lois mainly because, although Lois was a few years older, she was a woman that men took a second look at. She wore smart suits, nice dresses and form fitting slacks that caught the eye of most men, young and old. And, unlike Blanche Mims, although she was divorced and unattached, Lois was not a flirt.

Mailhandler Bessie Black, the fiery leader of the Hatchet Ladies, disliked Lois for the same reasons unlearned Mamie Smith disliked her. She also disliked Lois for other reasons.

Lois was a dedicated postal employe. Despite being on duty at her school job each day, she came to work at the MMPO every night, and on time. She was a hard worker. She did not make unauthorized visits to other work sections while on duty. She did not overstay her break time. And she did not approve of the Man's Work philosophy.

She especially opposed the department policy of forcing men to do work women were legally required to do

So, Bessie Black disliked Lois Flowers because she surely knew that, as a supervisor, Lois would bring some kind of order to the place, that she would require employes to become more efficient and productive. And Bessie knew that Lois would not permit her to roam freely all about the building spreading her low life philosophy.

Jimmie often wondered why MMPO workers permitted brash, abrasive, unlearned people to rise above the rest and become their leaders. He frequently asked himself why were such people as mailhandler Bessie Black and ex-mailhandler EEO Geneva so charismatic to MMPO workers. ("'Cause they got big mouths and smell bad," Slick often put it.)

Delighted with the quick and clearly stated rejections of Mamie Smith and Blanche Mims, Bessie Black moved on to the last member of the Hatchet Ladies, Bible Toting Dolly Jean. "Okay, Dolly Jean,' she barked. "How about you? Do you think Lois is qualified to be a supervisor?"

Dolly Jean said, "Well, she's, uh, I don't know." She refused to lie. But, as most MMPO workers probably did, Dolly Jean thought that Lois was an excellent choice. She didn't want to lie, yet she couldn't afford to tell the truth. Bessie Black and her Hatchet Lady colleagues surely would censor her.

Unlike the other members of the Hatchet Lady Gang, Dolly Jean obviously did not hate Lois. But she must have envied her. She certainly had reason to.

Some women who can't handle a divorce, become alcoholics. Bible Toting Dolly Jean became a confused, religious zealot. But the divorce didn't do the full job on her. It had help. Dolly Jean had an unfortunate episode to happen in her life that no one on the job knew about, not even Bessie Black and the Hatchet Ladies.

During the time between the divorce from her husband and getting a job at the Post Office, financially, things got a bit rough for Dolly Jean. To make ends meet, she did a little prostituting.

Now her teenage daughter was doing the same thing. It was different with the daughter, however, that is, from the start it was. She didn't go looking as her mother has done. She was a beautiful girl, as Dolly Jean was. And every time she walked down the street men in cars blew their horns at her.

One day she crawled into a man's car just to see what would happen. He was a nice honest looking man, she thought. And he offered her twenty dollars. It was a lot of money for just a few minutes work, more than her mother had ever given her in a lump sum. So she said yes. She quickly developed a taste for expensive clothes, and lots of them, far more than her mother could afford to buy for her. So she went out again and again looking for tricks as her mother did before her.

Dolly Jean found out about it and approached the girl.

"You are a good one to try and tell me what not to do!" the girl exploded. "You've been in and out of more cars than I ever have."

The girl's reaction was a real shocker to Dolly Jean. She had been out there only a brief period. And she thought that she had well covered her tracks. But she hadn't. The girl knew about it, so there was nothing to do but admit it. And she did.

"But I did it for you, baby" she told the girl. "When your father left us, I didn't have a dime in my pocket and no job to go to. And it took too long to get aid. We needed food and a place to stay. There was no other way. I had to do it. But now we've got food and a place to stay, and I got a job. You don't need to do that anymore.

But Dolly Jean's words fell on deaf ears. An early grade school dropout with her good looks, the girl made money fast and easy. She needed money now, too, and lots of it. She had to feed her growing desire for expensive clothes, and she had to satisfy her developing daily habit of shooting up dope. So she refused to stop.

That brief, unfortunate episode of prostitution in Dolly Jean's life that caused her daughter to become a prostitute, a grade school dropout and a dope addict was why she envied Lois Flowers. Lois Flowers's had two children, a boy and a girl. Her son was in medical school and her daughter was a law student.

Turning away from the EEO Geneva female supervisory campaign, Jimmie recalled the scene with Blanche Mims and Nab. He was displeased with Blanche and her "If the price is right" response. But he was more displeased with the actions of Nab.

The MMPO black male was a freak of nature, he thought. Seemingly, unlike all other males and unlike all other humans, his central nervous system was not located in his head, but in his groin. He seemed endowed with one engulfing mission: to go to bed with somebody.

Information entering the body of the MMPO black male may have first gone to the brain, but not before it reached the head of his penis did he react to it. With women and sex constantly in his thinking, he was a crazed defenceless soul. Like a confused runaway youth trapped on a big city street corner by a glib mercenary hawking an exotic cult, he was the willing prey of the MMPO black female.

Feigning affection for these philandering black males, the deceptive MMPO black females wooed them easily into their camp, leaving the few non-flirting MMPO black males to fight alone a losing battle.

Oscar was concerned, too. "What happened to that Nab dude," he asked.

"He finally got the message that his proposal to Blanche Mims had fallen on deaf ears," Jimmie answered.

"He should have known that She wasn't going to bed down with him tonight or any other night," Ronnie interjected, "unless, as she says, the price is right. Her wide wing spread and her exposed naked thigh were all a come-on to get him to do her work."

"Man, these broads 'round here really come on strong," Oscar said. "They's making the same money you making. Back in secondary, while you hangs all them old dirty sacks and pulls 'em off the racks, some of 'em weighing a 100 pounds or more, they's sett'n there on their fat asses doing they nails and laughing at you. But that ain't enough. They comes out here in primary where they don't have nothing but a eighteen pound tray uh mail to lift and they wants you to do that for 'em, too. 'course long as there's uh old funny style dude lak Nab around, they gonna get away with it..."

Bessie Black cut in. "He's a nice man," she said, "a gentleman like them men mailhandlers over there in my section. He don't believe in setting 'round watching us ladies strain ourselves lifting all this old heavy mail."

Oscar stopped throwing mail and took a good long look at Bessie Black's 250 pound frame; at her coal black ashey face that pimpled of an acne she never had; he looked at her unkept hair, the coarse, short black-gray strands that quickly turned back to the scalp forming individual clusters of tiny beads; and he looked at the long ugly scar that split open her left ear.

Watching Oscar's gesturing lips, Ronnie cautioned: "Don't say it, man."

"Naw, I ain't gonna say nothing. I was just trying to figure out something."

"Trying to figure out what?'

"What the difference is between MMPO black women and Southern white men."

Jimmie and Ronnie gave each other a look of surprise. Then they gave Oscar an accusing one. They were facial expressions that yelled out loudly: ("He's comparing our women with the race-bating southern white man!")

Oscar motioned his head toward Bessie. "That old black ass ugly broad say black mens is dumb, ain't got no education. And we acts like a child. That ain't no different than what that white man boss down there in Mississipi think about us."

Jimmie and Ronnie listened patiently to Oscar's argument, but said nothing.

"Well, how about it?" Oscar prodded them. "You tell me, what's the difference?"

"Ah, man, get up," Ronnie said. "What are you talking about?' Then he quickly changed the subject. "Hey, Jimmie, who is that little fine chick I saw you with in the cafeteria the other night?"

"Oh, that's my new station mate "

"I thought she was new. That's the first time I had seen her. How long has she been working here?"

"Just a few months."

"You don't waste no time, do you?" Oscar asked, in a prying tone.

And Jimmie became defensive. Had he done something to make Goldie look cheap? he wondered. "What do you mean I don't waste any time? We were only sitting there having coffee."

"I mean the way yall was looking at each other," Oscar explained. "That's what I'm talking 'bout. I can see a dude lak you getting hung up on a fine broad lak that in a few months, but she looked lak she was hung up on you too."

Jimmie shaved off a bit of his tension. He remembered how it once was when he and Goldie could never seem to get enough of each other. Whenever they were together, for the whole time, in reality or imagined, they were having sex. Whether in bed at the Lakeland Hotel, walking down city streets, or shopping in downtown stores, they were constantly touching each other and staring right through their clothes at their stark naked bodies.

Sitting there in the cafeteria with Goldie, after not seeing her for seven years, I don't know about her, he admitted but, although I was sitting on one side of the table and she was sitting on the other side, I probably did put on a pretty good show for Oscar to see.

"I'm sorry, Oscar," he apologized. "I didn't mean to snapped you up like that." Then he simply said, "Goldie is new here on the job, but I didn't just meet her. I've known her for a long time."

"Oh, so that's Goldie Greer, huh," Ronnie asked Jimmie.

"Yes, but how did you know her name?"

"Slick was talking about her."

Jimmie got edgy again. Like a nervous father who's overly concerned about the vulnerability of his teenage daughter, he had always been protective of Goldie. "What did Slick say about her?" he asked sharply.

Ronnie must have noticed Jimmie's face that was beginning to cloud with anger. He spoke with caution. "Nothing to get uptight about, he said, then added, "anyway, what he said was really more about you than about Goldie."

"And what's that?"

"He thinks you are afraid of something."

"Afraid of something? What did he mean by that?"

"Well, he says he knows you are crazy about the babe because he can see it in your eyes. So, he thinks you are holding back for some reason."

Jimmie truly was holding back. He took the position that it was different now. Seven years before, he was not a married man. Not that he owed anything to his nagging wife Mary Belle with whom having sex was like taking a great big fat dose of castor oil, but he owed it to the institution of marriage.

That's probably what Jimmie was trying to make himself believe. But for him to declare, now, this great respect for the institution of marriage, didn't hold water. What about all those years he chased around after Goldie? She was married, and always had been, for as long as he had known her.

Slick was right. For some reason, one he could not readily explain, Jimmie really was afraid.

"Look who's coming," Oscar drolled out.

"Who?" Ronnie asked, looking back over his shoulder.

"That dummy from the detail desk."

"I wonder what he wants," Ronnie joked.

"Take one big guess," Oscar challenged him. "I told you uh long time ago they'd be coming in here after 'em."

The detail clerk walked up to Jimmie and asked: "Mr. Jones? What are you doing in here? You're supposed to be back in GS-48S, your own section."

Chapter 6

Jimmie and Goldie have planned to meet at twelve noon, as Jimmie puts it: "Just to talk." But the meeting place is the Lakeland Hotel in Room 33 where they have experienced some of the most satisfying moments of their lives. Who is Jimmie kidding?

She has prepared breakfast for her husband Paul and left the kitchen to take her morning shower before retiring. She closes the blinds, turns on the lights in the bedroom and bathroom and begins. When she finishes, she steps out of the shower, towels off and stands before the mirror staring at her stark naked body. She looks at her yellowish golden skin, her medium shoulders, her square hip line and at her flat, dimpled abdomen. She notes the hollowed out calves that make her well rounded legs look bowed.

And she sees how full and firm her breasts still are. How, in Jimmie's words, the constrasting bronze nipples make them so luciously appealing. At 29 her body looks eighteen. She is proud of it. And she is happy that the only man she has ever loved will take her in his arms at noon and make long lasting love to her. He was never a minute man, she remembers.

She removes a tall bottle from the vanity table that stands beside her bed and pours the emollient oil from it into her hands. She sits down on the tiny metal cushioned chair and begins massaging her thighs and legs with it. For a moment it is already twelve noon. They are at the Lakeland Hotel in their favorite Room 33. And the hands that are carefully massaging her body are Jimmie's hands. She feels the warm wetness of his lips kissing hers and she sees her body weaving beneath his body, crying out for him to give her more. And to last.

She is overcome with excitement. It has been seven long years since she has had sex with Jimmie, seven long years since she has really had sex with anyone. Occasionally Paul gets the notion, she's regretfully reminded. But generally that's all it is, a notion. They hardly ever really get started anymore. It doesn't matter anyway. In their twelve years of marriage, she has never reached completion with Paul, not even during the earlier years when he did have a little fire left in him.

Still naked, with her smooth golden body fully oiled, she leaps up from the tiny metal cushioned chair and starts humming and skipping in circles about the room. She taps the bedpost lightly with her hands, the chest of drawers, the vanity table and everything in the room as she passes by them.

Finally, still in the nude, she turns off the lights, tries to close the blinds even tighter and hops into her big fluffy bed. She lies there with folded arms in a simulated embrace. Obviously, her heart pounds of expectation. She has finally got to Jimmie. He has told her that he can't fight it any longer. That at twelve noon today he'd like to meet with her and talk. "And where are we meeting?" she asks out loud of herself. "The Lakeland Hotel, where else? In room 33." It's 9:30. She'll rest for two hours, then start for the Lakeland. She closes her eyes and awaits sleep. Sleep does not come.

But a loud, excitable banging on her bedroom door does come. It's Paul. Why is he here? she wonders. He should have left for work at nine. Her heart, that has been pounding of expectation, now begins pounding of panging apprehension.

"Goldie! Goldie!" Paul screams through the closed door. "Are you awake? Open the door. Are you awake? Open up," he says again and again continuing to bang loudly on the door.

Goldie's pounding heart beats Faster and faster. This time with fear. She throws both hands over her mouth and presses down hard. In low audible tones she prays: "Oh, God, no. Please. Not this morning."

The banging continues. It grows louder and more frenzied. And Paul's voice grows louder and more anxious. "Open the door, Goldie. Open up!" he yells.

Goldie tries to compose herself. She sits up in bed and attempts to blink the terror from her face. And she says in a small, weak voice: "It's open, Paul. Come on in."

Paul swishes the door open and clicks on the light. He is a handsomely odd looking man, in that he is tall, almost six feet, but has the outstanding features of a small, short Oriental. He is a dissipated relic who married Goldie for her good looks, to show her off to his friends. He has long black wavy hair and yellowish skin. His upper and lower eyelids overlap to almost hide his eyelashes. His eyes are brown and set apart. They are oblique and slanted downward. The skin above them looks fat and puffy. His cheekbones flare to the front. His nose is round and depressed. And beneath his sparse mustache, his square chin recedes.

At fifty one, Paul Greer has lived through several lifetimes. He is a man of a thousand escapades. And he has told Goldie about each one of them a thousand times. He brags about the number and types of women he has been to bed with: young and old, rich and poor, white and black, single and married, sinners and Christians "You name them and I have had them."

He has gone into clinical details, telling Goldie, on occasions, how he has had trouble because, "I was too big for some of them, but they wanted me anyway. So, what could I do? They'd get lubricants or vaseline and stuff, and we'd go on with it. They'd scream and yell, but then they'd put a bear hug on me so I couldn't get up. Some of them just couldn't take it, but they'd hang on in there anyway. They just loved that big joint of mine."

Goldie stares up at Paul in sheer fright. Her terror stricken body shakes with such intensity that the quiet bedsprings beneath her squeak out loud. But Paul Greer, standing in the doorway, just sticks out his chest. With pride and sheer joy, he starts grinning. "Look!" he says and points to his monstrous erection. "How about that fellow, huh?"

It is apparent that Goldie sees the twelve noon ecstasy with Jimmie swiftly fleeting away. She grabs a section of the bedding with both of her hands, gathers it up in a ball and crushes it between her fingers. For a flash, her face that constantly smiles, looks criminal.

Paul Greer rushes over to the bed and says, "Move over, baby. Move over."

Goldie's teeth rattle as if she's having a chill. Her eyes grow large and they dance about.

Paul has always been rough, she vividly recalls. Even before he lost his potency, he'd sometimes plunge wildly into her, tear skin and cause excessive bleeding. Terribly bruised and tender on occasions, it would be weeks before her vagina would completely heel. But, at times like this, with his great fear that nature will fail him before penetration, Paul is like a wild man, the experience for Goldie is one of pain and horror.

"Move over, baby. Move over," Paul cries out again. "Quick." He reaches for the covers to pull them back from over her. His hand brushes against her violently, trembling shoulder. To Paul Greer's satisfaction, but to Goldie's repulsion, that brush on the shoulder pounces her flat on her back, fast to the far side of the bed. He hops into the bed with Goldie, throws his arms around her, pulls her to him and squeezes her tightly.

Goldie's body still trembles. Through her tightly closed lips, comes an odd kind of fluttering noise.

Paul gives her a smothering kiss on her fluttering lips. He cups her face in one of his hands. And he gouges the fingers of the other hand into the upper part of her neck, unaware that he is choking her.

Goldie pants and gasps several times, trying to catch her breath. She pleads for him to release the choking grip. "Please, Paul, please," she says faintly.

Misunderstanding her meaning, Paul says: "I know, baby. I feel the same way, too. It's been so long." Then, fortunately, he lets go of her neck, turns his body over and crawls into position.

Goldie breaks out into a nervous sweat. Her blood pressure goes violently up. Her body stiffens. Her eyes seem hollow sockets. She screams down deep inside. And she prays. She hates Paul Greer for what he is about to do to her. She cannot see Jimmie now. And she asks Jimmie to forgive her. Not that Paul Greer can take anything of Jimmie's away from her. For he cannot.

During their twelve years of marriage, she has never had an orgasm with Paul, and she knows she will not this time, either. As far as that goes, though, she could meet Jimmie at twelve noon in a condition as good as new. It's the tearing, the bleeding and the lingering pain that will force her not to see Jimmie, which will deny her the long awaited pleasure.

In the midst of Goldie's fright and frustration, a thought comes to her. Maybe if she could just relax there would be no tearing, no bleeding, no lingering pain. Her date with Jimmie could still be on. But then, she says no to that. A very definite no. It would not be fair to Jimmɪe. With Paul this morning and him this afternoon, no. She can't do it.

Paul Greer hovers heavily over Goldie. He snorts and growls and claws like a predatory animal about to consume its prey.

She reluctantly resigns herself to the fact that she is his wife and not Jimmie's wife. This is her duty, come what may. So she braces herself and waits for the tearing, the bleeding, the unbearable pain.

But now, Paul just hovers above her. He isn't lowering his body. He isn't clawing at her. And he isn't snorting anymore. Goldie, seemingly, isn't sure that Paul is even breathing anymore. The bed and the room are quiet. There's no movement. No noise.

Suddenly Paul breaks the silence. He cries out in more pain and hurt than Goldie had anticipated for herself. And rightfully so. What Paul Greer is feeling now is the kind of pain and hurt that can rip open and bash about the very soul of the toughest kinds of human males

"What the hell," he screams. "Goddam, sonofabitch. Motherfucking bastard." And with those few blasphemous words, like a hand launched flying kite, he flips up off the bed and soars swiftly through the air. And because he uses no hands to break his fall, like a thrown hunk of beef, out on the highly polished hardwood floor, he clumps flat on his back. His monstrous erection plops limp between his rage trembling legs. And he just lies there for a moment breathing hard and pounding his chest. Finally, he says: "I'm sorry, baby. Goddammit, I'm sorry."

Goldie whispers through gushing tears of joy. "That's all right, Paul," she says. "Don't worry about it. There'll be other times. Maybe tomorrow."

"Yeah, maybe so," Paul says, reaching for the bedpost to pull himself up off the floor with. Then, with head lowered not facing Goldie, he starts for the door, mumbling to himself. "Motherfucking bastard."

Goldie ɪs at home with her husband Paul. She has just had a narrow escape. Jimmie is at home with his wife Mary Belle. He is having a bad experience, too. It all started on his initial arrival.

The old aging Grove apartment building where Jimmie lives, is a three story yellow brick structure that's located at 7002 South Grove Street. With three spacious courtways, but no longer graced with beautiful flowers and picture green grass, the Grove building is a complex of 105 apartments. Jimmie parks his car on the vacant lot in the rear, makes it around to the front and climbs the stairs up to his 3rd floor, three room apartment.

He puts his key into the door's keyhole, but, before he can trip the lock, the door swings open. Greeting him, with a watch on her wrist and a clock in her hand, and eyeing them both at the same time, is Mary Belle. "Come on in, Mr. Postmaster," she says, "I been waiting for you." The sound of her voice is normal, but the derisive intent is certainly an eardrum blaster. Then, immediately accompanying the intent, she loudly screams out: "Where in the hell you been? Thought I was gone to work, huh? Been out ho-fucking somewhere, I know."

Mary Belle is an olive complexioned woman, almost six feet tall. She has a long face, high cheekbones, a small head, narrow shoulders, and a long steepled neck. She steps aside and presses her high overblown buttocks against the open door.

Jimmie walks in. "I'm only 30 minutes later than usual," he says. "It's only eight o'clock.

Like the pitch of a flute in the hands of a novice, Mary Belle's voice quite often becomes terribly uncontrollable. In times of stress, which she has often, her voice shoots up to high strange levels and shrieks out ear panging sounds that do more dammage to the listener than the words themselves.

"I know what time it is, Goddamit," she says and slams the door shut behind her. "You always telling somebody something. You think don't nobody know nothing but you..."

"It's only because you were trying to make something out of nothing," Jimmie tries to explain. "That's why I mentioned the time." He takes off his coat and hat and walks out into the kitchen. Mary Belle follows him.

The kitchen's furnishings include a small black and white porcelain stove that has no broiler nor pot-storage facilities, a refrigerator with no freezer compartment, and an undersize four chair dinette set. Jimmie pulls out one of the chairs and sits down. So does Mary Belle. They sit for a moment face to face without saying a word. Jimmie eyes cigarette butts and ashes on the table and the floor, too, but says nothing. It will do no good. It will only become the basis for an argument. He'll have Bobbie, his step-son, clean it up before he leaves for school.

Mary Belle makes puffing noises while ringing her hands.

"Where are the children," Jimmie asks.

"They's in our bedroom," Mary Belle answers, "all except Kathy. You know where she is. In the bathroom primping. Ain't twelve years old yet and got boys on her mind. Po little ole thing, if she only knowed like I do..."

"What are the others doing in our bedroom?" Jimmie cuts her off. Normally, Jimmie's five step kids all sleep in the living room, two in a wall pull out bed, two on a convertible sofa, and Kathy, the oldest, sleeps on a roll away bed.

"I sent them in there. I told them I wanted to talk to you."

"Why didn't you go to work? Today is Tuesday not Wednesday. Tomorrow is your day off."

"I can stay home if I wants to!" she yells at him, then smiles and tries to put coo in her voice to create a sexy atmosphere. "I can stay home with my husband if I wants to, cain't I?" she oozes out. But her upper lip rolls back into a snarl. Her voice, although softer than her original blast, is still loud and screechy. It has no warmth. And for sure, there certainly is nothing sexy about it.

Jimmie drums the middle finger of his right hand several times on the small table's wooden top. "I'm touched," he says.

Mary Belle's face clouds with anger. "I stayed home 'cause I wanted to be with you!" she shouts. "You don't appreciate it?"

"Well uh... " he starts to say but she cuts him off.

"We ain't together enough no more," she says. "You working nights and me working days. When I'm coming, you's going. And when I'm going, you's coming. It ain't right. We just don't see enough uh each other no more."

"Well, that's the way you wanted it," Jimmie reminds her. "I was perfectly satisfied carrying mail, working days and being at home at night with you and the kids... "

Jimmie was not all wrong. He had told her back in 1961 that MidSouth carrier station management was uptight about all the suggestions he was making. He told her that he would change over to a clerk and go downtown for that reason; he should go down there to get in out of the weather because of the hints he'd had of arthritis and he should go because by working nights he'd make more money, too. Mary Belle asked: "Why don't you?" "I will," Jimmie said.

"Leave those unprogressive people out there in the sticks all by themselves where they belong." Mary Belle hounded him until, finally, he did.

"You mean being at home with the kids. Not me," Mary Belle complains. "Yall didn't pay me no 'tention."

"That's because you'd leave us and go off into the bedroom all by yourself."

"I didn't want to watch no T V every night. You and them kids used to drive me crazy with that thing going all the time. Half the time yall wasn't watching it no how. Kids down on the floor screaming and playing all them old silly games you bought 'em. And you right down there with 'em."

"I knew it would be this way," Jimmie says. "By working nights I make a little more money, and we save a bit more money by eliminating some baby sitting time. But the price we pay for it, is far too great. This is what I tried so very hard to explain to you. If a couple wants to make a marriage go, working different shifts is not the way to do it. It can create too many problems."

Mary Belle's lips droop, her shoulders slump. "Yeah, I guess you right," she agrees. Then she quickly squares her shoulders and curls up her lips again and fires. "But if you'd come on home like you suppose to do, we'd have more time together..."

Jimmie cuts her off again. "But you are not here mornings when I get home," he corrected her, "except on Wednesday mornings, your day off."

"I'm here this morning," she snaps.

"How was I suppose to know?"

"You'd uh knowed if you'd uh come on home like you suppose to. But okay, then. What about in the evening when I comes home from work?"

"I'm right here, Mary Belle, everyday."

Mary Belle gets up from the table, walks over near the open back door and stares down the empty exterior wooden stairs. Two medium size rats, racing about the yard, are playing a I bet you can't catch me game. "so what," she snaps. "What are you trying to say? Quit signifying. If you got something to say, go on, say it."

Jimmie begins to come a bit unfurled. "What do you mean signifying?" he shoots back. "All I said was that I'm here everyday when you get home from work."

"Yeah, but the way you said it. That's what I mean. Like you got something on your mind. I knows you. So why don't you jes out and say it?"

"I don't have to say it. You know what I mean. If and when you decide to come home from work, all we do is what we are doing right now. Argue. As soon as you hit the house, you find something to start an argument about."

Mary Belle swings her tall not so slender body around and faces Jimmie. "You jes a dam lie. I don't do no such damn thing. Any argument we ever had, you started it. And anyway!" she shouts. "What cha mean 'bout if and when I decides to come home from work?"

Kathy comes out of the bathroom and into the kitchen. At eleven, she has her mother's smooth olive complexion, her long coal black hair. And she has a smile and a warm outgoing personality that, too, must have once been an attribute of her mother's. She brushes wrinkles from her blue dress with white trimming and says, "Hello, daddy." Then she walks over and hugs and kisses him.

He squeezes her little fluffy cheeks and says, "Hi, baby."

"God, you finally come out uh there," Mary Belle marvels and sits back down. "All that girl do is primp. Her and Bobbie. Them two couldn't be no more lak you, 'less you was they daddy. So particular 'bout what they wears and how it looks."

"I am their daddy," Jimmie says smiling and patting Kathy on the head.

"You ain't they daddy," Mary Belle snaps. "And don't you be telling 'em that."

Kathy puts her arms around Jimmie's shoulder and nestles up to him.

"Go on in the bedroom there with the rest of the kids," Mary Belle says to her. "I wants to talk to Jimmie. Go on now."

Kathy is slow about pulling away from Jimmie, But she finally does.

"And shut the door behind you," Mary Belle says as Kathy enters the bedroom. "And now," she says to Jimmie. "You didn't answer my question yet."

"What question?"

"What you said about if and when I comes home. What did you mean by that? I comes home everyday."

"What about last Friday?"

"Last Friday I was at the hairdresser's."

"From five thirty until nine?"

"What cha mean, 'til nine?"

"That's what time it was when you got home."

"You jes a bare faced, black ass ugly lie."

"I leave for work at nine o'clock. When you came in I was walking out the door."

"Aw shit. You gonna tell me what time I comes home jes 'cause you was leaving for work? Hell, you ain't no time clock. You jes left early, that's all." Mary Belle swallows several times and blinks her eyes rapidly, inadvertently revealing that she is lying. But she goes on with it anyway. "I was home long before that, and you knows it."

Jimmie gives her a kind of smirk smile, drops that subject and comes up with another one. "You are giving me the business about being thirty minutes late. I have never said anything about you going out into the street at night while I'm at work."

Mary Belle's face quickly clouds in anger. And she yells, "About me doing what!"

"Mary Belle, you go out two or three nights every week. Especially every Friday night, you go out. And about your not coming home last Friday night until nine o'clock, as you say from the hairdresser's, as soon as I left for work, you went right back out again. And you beat me home the next morning only by minutes."

"Well I'll be damned," Mary Belle says. "That's the biggest damn lie I ever did hear. What cha been doing anyhow, checking up on me? Calling up here hoping to find me gone, huh? I hear the phone ringing every night 'round your lunch time," she obviously lies, "I knows it's you. I jes don't answer it. I'm in bed trying to get my rest."

Jimmie replies in a calm, even tone. "No, I haven't called here," he says. "You know I don't call here anymore. I don't want to know that you are not here."

"Well, who been telling you all them lies, then!" she screams, "Saying I'm out in the streets to two or three...?"

One of the kids in the bedroom coughs, clears his throat and accidentally knocks an ashtray off the dresser. It's Bobbie.

Mary Belle cocks her small, round head over to one side and pushes her giraffe like neck out toward the bedroom door. "Little sonofabitch," she says. "My own damn child. So, that's where you gets all them lies from, huh?"

"Now don't go jumping the gun," Jimmie warns, "placing blame when you don't really know where to place it."

"But I do know where to place the damn blame," Mary Belle says. "Oh, hell yes, I know." She hops up from the kitchen table and races for the bedroom.

"Mary Belle!" Jimmie shouts. "Mary! Come back here! Where are you going?"

With a queen size bed, a seventy two inch dresser, a five drawer chest, and a vanity table in a nine by ten bedroom, and four kids besides himself, and only one door, there is no place for Bobbie to run to. But he tries anyway. He is quite an agile boy. Nine years old, he loves sports, especially track. Outside around the building, he is frequently running and leaping over things.

But now, in such small quarters with an angry, fiendish, woman streaking after him, will that agility help him out any?

He hops up onto the big queen size bed and, as if on a trampoline, starts pumping the bed's crying springs. He will get a good bounce from the springs, leap over his mother's head and run out the door.

Bobbie is not a bad boy. He has good manners. He is soft hearted, gentle and obedient. Jimmie thinks Bobbie is worthy of a mother with a warm and even temper, like Goldie. He is that kind of boy. Even a role model of sorts for other boys his own age. Then why is his reaction to his mother's approach so unusual?

Bobbie knows too well about Mary belle's crazy fits. He is also painfully aware that, since he's the only boy of five children, whether he is directly involved in her frustration or not, he usually suffers the brunt of her frequent crazy fits. Bobbie has a high sense of morals, and he has an intense love for Jimmie, more than for his biological father. Mary Belle hates Bobbie more for his high sense of morals than for his intense love for Jimmie.

She furiously yanks open the bedroom door. Seeing Bobbie bouncing up and down on the big queen size bed, her nostrils flare open and her breathing comes out in snorts. "Come here, you little sonofabitch," she says and starts toward the bed. "Yall get out of here!" she screams at the other children. And they scamper out of the room. Bobbie, obviously, thinks he sees enough space between Mary Belle and the door behind her to successfully make his get away. He takes a deep breath, crouches and pumped the crying springs of the big queen bed several more frenetic times. But what Bobbie has not taken into account is the low ceiling that hangs only inches above his bouncing head. With his last deeply, accented pump, he sails up and off the huge bed like a rocket from its launching pad.

Mary Belle, a smooth operator, surely is calculating, too. She, obviously, senses what Bobbie intends doing. She begins backing up, fast, toward the door behind her.

Bobbie crashes up against the ceiling and bounces back squarely into Mary Belle's arms. There is an animal like grimace on her face, and a seething rage in her eyes. When Bobbie looks up at her, he lets out an earth shattering yelp, and his eyes sprout water hydrant tears.

Mary Belle, as if tossing a toy football, quickly and violently throws Bobbie back up onto the big high bed. With her long oversize legs and her high hanging behind, she straddles him. "I told you same as I told the rest of these kids, not to tell!" she screams, "didn't I?" Then she makes two fists. Not the kind of fists a normal woman would make, but like those a prizefighter would make.

The boy cries out, Mamma, don't hit me. Please, mamma. Don't hit me with your fists."

But Mary Belle doesn't pay the boy any mind. Maybe she doesn't even hear him. She raises her long right arm high in the air and brings her fist down with a hard crashing blow to the left side of the boy's head.

Bobbie is stunned, seemingly senseless, but he cries out for his mother to, "Quit beating me" and tries deaparately to wriggle free of her grasp.

But Mary Belle's 200 pounds has pinned the boy's small body hopelessly down onto the big sagging bed. "Goddamit, I talks to you. And I talks to you" she puffs out. "But it don't do no good." She pounds at Bobbie with her fast falling left fist. But more alert this time, Bobbie sees it coming and, with a quick flick of his arms, manages to ward off the blow.

"I'm your mamma Goddammit. I'm your mamma," she blurts out. "That black sonofabitch out there in the kitchen ain't a Goddamn thing to you. Nothing. you understand? Nothing." She throws another blow at Bobbie, but he manages to ward that one off, too. She throws another one. Bobbie rolls his head to one side. She misses again.

Mary Belle's eyes grow large and glassy. Her breath comes out in snorts again. She snarls her top lip back. And in a feminine fitful flurry, she starts pounding the boy with both hands as hard and as fast as she possibly can. This time she finds waiting targets in his chest and ribs.

Bobbie quickly moves his guard down to protect the lower part of his body.

Now, as a highly trained professional prizefighter would proceed, Mary Belle immediately drops her awkward, feminine tactics and, with a fast flicking right hand, she skillfully aims for the boy's head. "Goddammit, I'm your mamma," she screams again and comes down with another fast flicking right that again catches the boy on the head. "Ain't I been good to you?" she yells and comes down hard with her left fist against the other side of the boy's head. "Ain't I been good to you?"

Bobbie screams in terror as he sees large spouts of blood shooting out from his nose. He brings his guard back up.

Mary Belle snorts. And she grits her teeth hard together. One can hear the grinding crackling noise as if they are literally being shattered. Her face is an animalistic mask. She grabs the boy by the neck with both hands and begins choking him.

Bobbie makes gulping sounds in an effort to breathe. And he tugs at his mother's hands. But he cannot break her death like grip.

"Whatever I do, I'm doing it for you," she says. "I'm doing it for you. You hear me?" Suddenly, she releases her hold on Bobbie's neck and starts pounding him again, first, in the ribs and chest, then the head, wherever there is no guard warding off her blows.

Bobbie gives up. In ways as if to say: "What's the use? I can't stop her. She's crazy. She's gonna beat me anyway. So just let her." He drops his guard and gives completely of himself. He quits pleading with her to stop. And he refrains from crying out of pain. With blood streamimg rapidly from his nose, with his battered ribs pulsing abnormally, and with his swollen face puffing to close up his eyes, he just lies there, absorbing his mother's violent, uncontrollable beating.

Nevertheless, Mary Belle continues beating the boy, and yelling and screaming at him. Suddenly, she stops.

Witnessing the deafening silence, Jimmie wonders what the matter might be. He quickly hops up from the kitchen table and dashes out into the bedroom. "Oh my God!", he exclaims. "Woman? What have you done?"

Slumped under the weight of her own sagging shoulders, Mary Belle, with her long fleshy legs, and her big high hanging buttocks, still straddles the small boy. Her arms hang limp from their sockets. A snow white foamy substance flushes from her mouth. And with deep, sunken vacant eyes, she stares blankly at the room's walls.

Bobbie's face is puffed and swollen. His eyes are all but shut. And he lies in a puddle of thick, crimson blood.

Jimmie yanks Mary Belle off Bobbie and off the bed onto the floor. He slaps her face several times to try and bring her out of her apparent stupor, and he pushes her out into the kitchen. She flops into a chair, and just stares as if she doesn't know where she is, or if she even knows what she has done.

Jimmie picks Bobbie up from the bed and rushes out of the apartment with the boy in his arms, and takes him to the nearest doctor.

Jimmie and Mary Belle sit at the kitchen table talking. The small three room apartment consists of a living room, but, unless entertaining company, they use the kitchen. The kids have all gone to school, including Bobbie. Jimmie had wanted him to stay home. But he said he felt okay. And since the doctor's report revealed several very bad bruises but no broken bones, fractures or serious lacerations, Jimmie agreed to let him go.

'I don't suppose you are sorry." Jimmie says and looks deep into Mary Belle's eyes.

She squares her unusually narrow shoulders, straightens her long skinny neck and tries to appear unruffled. "Sorry about what?" she asks.

'Sorry about what you did to your own son."

'Hell naw, I ain't sorry," she snaps. "He needed a good whipping for telling you all of them lies."

I'm not going to argue the point of whether or not he told me about your escapades," Jimmie says, "because you listen only to what you yourself have to say. But I'm going to tell you this: one day you are really going to hurt that boy, and bad. You say he needed a whipping. What you gave him was a beating. There is a difference you know."

"Ah hell, there ain't nothing wrong with 'em. The doctor said so, didn't he?

"Physically? No," Jimmie agrees. "But inside his head. His mind. And inside his heart, what he thinks about some of the things you do. And in his feelings for you. There's plenty wrong. Believe me, Mary Belle, there's plenty wrong."

"Aw shut up. I didn't stay home to hear no damn preaching, 'specially from you. If I wanted to hear some preaching, I'd go to church and hear it. So jes keep your damn advice to yourself."

"Another thing, Mary Belle," Jimmie says, "Bobbie doesn't have to tell me when you go out. No one has to. I know when you go out."

Mary Belle frowns and snarls out: "You don't know shit. That's your whole trouble. You thinks you knows every damn thing. And everybody else is a damn fool. Two weeks down to that damn Main Post Office and you knows more than everybody down there, how it ought to be run. (Six years and it's still only two weeks to Mary Belle, he notes, and recalls a previous occurrence: "Two weeks and you got a drawer full uh shit that you say is wrong down there."

"I've told you to stay out of my drawer. I know everything in there is all messed up.")

Jimmie is wrong in the statement that no one has to tell him when Mary Belle goes out. However, that is not exactly what he means. What he really means is that, he knows when she has had sex. About that, he is not lying. And he doesn't have to attempt to have sex with her or to resort to any bizarre tactics such as examining her panties or the like to reach that conclusion.

The guilt in her face will stare out at him, for hours, sometimes for days. Not because Jimmie is so smart that he can read or interpret the psychological expression on her face. But because something physically strange happens to Mary Belle each time she has sex with someone, even with him. A hazy milk like film forms overs her right eye. The film seemingly pushes her upper eyelid outward to form a kind of canopy that casts additional shadows.

Jimmie looks at his watch. It's nine thirty. "How about some breakfast," he asks Mary Belle.

"I ain't fixing you shit!" she yells. "If you wants some breakfast, you better get up off your dead ass and fix it yourself."

Jimmie gets up and fries four strips of bacon and two eggs, and sits back down to have his breakfast. "Oh, the ketchup," He says. He likes a little ketchup spilled over his eggs. He walks over to the refrigerator, opens the door and picks the ketchup bottle up by the neck. He doesn't dare pick it up by the cap. Too many times he has spilled ketchup, mustard, pickles and the like all over the refrigerator, himself and the floor. Mary Belle does not believe in screwing caps back on bottles after serving from them.

"Why don't you set down and eat that shit before it gets cold," Mary Belle asks. "Piddling 'roud here like some old lady in her change of life."

He sits down, then, pops his fingers and looks toward the oven. "Oh! the biscuits," he says. He had opened a refrigerated can and put them in there a few minutes earlier. "Hey, baby, take the biscuits out of the oven for me and hand me a couple. Okay?"

"Get 'em yourself," she says, folding her arms and leaning back in her chair. "I didn't stay home to wait on you."

Jimmie gets up from the table, retrieves the biscuits from the oven, puts several on his plate, and sits back down and starts eating. He studies Mary Belle for a moment and thinks about their marriage. It's a crime, he reasons, one for which he is as much to blame as she. Mary Belle had married him because she wanted security for her five kids. He had married her because, living alone, he was lonely. Nowhere along the way. Not at any time could he remember having heard the words: "I love you." Not from Mary Belle's lips to him. Nor from his lips to her.

Mary Belle seems uncomfortable. She unfolds her arms and starts squirming in her seat. "What the hell you sett'n there looking at me lak that for?" she shouts. "Better go on and eat your breakfast."

Jimmie knows that Mary Belle is not inherently a bad person. At least he tries hard to make himself believe that. Again and again he has tried. It's the environment, he tells himself. The rotten environment that she has been exposed to has made her that way.

He has almost finished his breakfast, and he asks Mary Belle, "Why did you stay home today? You didn't ever tell me." The dark cloud of dread and disgust has already come over him. He knows the answer. However, he doesn't expect it to come out the way it does.

Mary Belle sounds off loud and clear. "I wants you to fuck me,

Goddammit, that's why I stayed home. And if you don't, I'm gonna want to know why."

Jimmie knows he can't embarrass Mary Belle, but he never fails to occasionally try. "You sound like a lady who really wants to get it on with her husband," he says and smiles wryly. "Your warm personality and the choisey, sexy language you use. It goes all through me, baby." Then he wrinkles his face and slants his eyes downward. "It moves me just like a dose of castor oil would. Damn, why didn't you go to work? Why don't you go to work everyday, including Wednesday, your day off, and Sunday, too?"

Mary Belle's face flushes as she tries deperately to look the part she is playing. "I don't care what you say," she says. "I'm your wife. I can stay home with you whenever I gets ready. And you gonna fuck me, too, when I gets ready. You black sonofabitch. You fucking everybody else. You gonna fuck me, too. I ain't yellow and I ain't white, neither. Maybe that's why you don't care nothing about me. But you's my husband. And you gonna fuck me whether you like it or not."

Jimmie is puzzled. The skin below his eyelids wrinkles. "What are you talking about," he asks.

"You know what I'm talking about," Mary Belle blasts at him. "That yellow whore you was going with before we got married. The one that used to ring your doorbell everytime I used to talk to you on the telephone. I ain't never seen her, but I knows who she is. Little old yellow bitch who thinks she's cute and high society. 'course when I used to ask you who that was ringing your doorbell, you said it was the cleaning woman. That's the shit you laid on me. A nigger with one room, and a cleaning woman? Ain't that some shit.?"

For, at least, the first four years of their marriage, Jimmie thinks, only a few days passed that Mary Belle didn't bring up the cleaning woman. Even before leaving the MidSouth Station and coming downtown to the Main PO, he recalls that some days when he was only ten minutes or so late coming in off the mail route, Mary Belle blamed it on the cleaning woman. Now, for the first time in seven years, Mary Belle is right. He has been out with the cleaning woman this time, for sure. In fact, he was out with Goldie all night, but on the job. And he was with her this morning, too, he happily recalls. It was just a little more than an hour ago. And as soon as he can find a way to get out of the house, he's going to see her again today.

Mary Belle goes on with her tirade. "And that little skinny, scare crow, white bitch you plays cello with in the orchestra. I know you fucking her, too. I can tell from the way yall looks at each other."

"She's my stand mate," Jimmie says. "I have to be cordial. What else can I do?"

"Ah, don't give me that stand mate shit. I knows all about how yall black boys like to kiss on them high yellows, and them white bitches."

"I don't know what you are arguing so strenuously about. You are not really a black woman yourself."

"Yeah, but I ain't yellow enough for you. Niggers black as you, likes 'em yellow as they come. Anyhow, you don't never kiss on me."

Jimmie could say that he doesn't ever have a chance, because she's always kissing on him, but he doesn't. He doesn't even want to think about it. Some of the things Mary Belle does to him in the name of making love are sexless, forceful, and without warmth or meaning. They are bizarre exercises that many times do not affect him even physically.

However, Mary Belle's cold, coarse, indifferent attitude about him, about sex and about life in general, is something she has acquired later in life, Jimmie continues to try and drive home to himself. He is hopeful that one day she will change, revert to the warm, loving person he is sure she once was. But how long must he wait? Seeing Goldie again, with her considerate, altruistic personality, how long will he wait?

Mary Belle leans across the table and takes a folded sheet of paper from Jimmie's shirt pocket. "What's this?" she asks.

"It wouldn't interest you," Jimmie says, and tries to take it back.

But she quickly swishes it out of his reach. "How do you know it wouldn't interest me?"

"Because I can't think of a single thing I like that you like. You don't like the movies, you don't like television, you don't like good books, and you don't like music."

"You just a damn lie. I do lak music. I just don't like that old sad ass classical music you play."

"No, not unless you are trying to impress someone, let them know how informed you are. I heard you at the last concert, naming off instruments to your sister and her husband."

Mary Belle opens up the sheet of paper she has taken from

Jimmie's pocket. With a wry smile and a sarcastic tone, she says. "Ah, suggestions. My husband. The Postmaster hisself. Two weeks on the job, and he knows it all." She takes on a demeaning pose and places one hand on her cheek. "Now let me see," she says, thoughtfully. "What do we have here? Pivot Distribution. 'I, Jimmie E. Jones,'" she starts reading, then stops to say: "What do you mean Jimmie E. Jones? Jimmie Elijah Jones, that's your name..."

"You are really a blood thirsty woman," Jimmie says, cutting in. "A little sick, though. You like to prick at the wound just to see if it will bleed again. When we first got married, I related some of my quirks to you, that is, a few of the things that irritate me, including my middle name, Elijah. You said you wanted me to tell you in order that you'd know what not to say and do to bug me. I Believed you. Instead, that very day, you started on a wound pricking campaign that has never ended.

"But I've got news for you, baby You have virtually benumbed my wounds. They don't bleed anymore. So prick your evil, pernicious heart away. Put the Elijah in my name as much as you like. Do and say anything else, or everything else you please. Knock yourself out. Believe me, baby. It just doesn't hurt anymore."

Mary Belle starts reading again. She looks up over the sheet of paper with eyes that are seemingly searching for Jimmie's "Doesn't hurt anymore" expression. "'I, Jimmie Elijah Jones,'" she reads on, inserting his middle name, and giggling, "'suggest that a Pivot Distribution method be adopted. The Pivot Distribution method would improve production in two ways. First...' ah shit," she says and stops reading. "I don't want to hear none of your dry ass explanations."

"It's only a rough draft, anyway," Jimmie says, and reaches out his hand. "Will you please give it back?"

"Ah, here's another one," Mary Belle exclaims. "And it says 'An Introductory Training Program for Secondary.' Now, what you really ought to have here," Mary Belle instructs Jimmie, giggling again, "ain't no training program for secondary. Not for them folks that's been working down there for years, but a training program for the ass who jes went down there two weeks ago, you: Jim-mie E-li-jah Jones," she says, stretching out his name and breaking out into hysterical laughter.

"You are a real comedian," Jimmie says "A natural."

Mary Belle stops laughing and quickly clouds up her face. "Ah naw, baby. Not me," she retorts, and points a finger at him. "You's the comedian. I bet they gets back up in them fine offices down there, leans back in them big soft chairs and reads this shit you write, and cracks up way more than I do." Mary Belle calms down a bit and asks Jimmie in a sneaky, grinning voice a question that she has asked him far too many times before.

Sensing it coming, he moans of boredom.

"Why don't you jes go on down there and work lak everybody else? Why you got to try to run everything everywhere you go?"

Jimmie blinks open his half closed eyes, yawns and pecks the table top with the ends of his fingers. "Well, it's getting pretty close to that time," he says.

But, like a broken record, Mary Belle clanks on. "Think you smart," she says. "But you ain't nobody. With your cello and poetry and stories and stuff, trying to make people think you important. And I'm getting tired of cleaning up after the professor, too," she giggles. "Leaving your mess all over the house all the time."

"Ah, come off it, Mary Belle," he shoots back. "That's a lie and you know it. I write here in the kitchen on the table because..."

Mary Belle lights a cigarette and takes a deep lung choking puff as if it is the first she has had all morning. "Ah, I don't want to hear all that shit," she snaps him off. "Heard it a thousand times. Let's talk about something else. Anyhow, ain't you sleepy? You say you is. Come on, let's get it on, baby. I'm for it. Ain't you? How 'bout it? She reaches under the table and tries to fondle him.

Her hand is colder than even the words she speaks. He pushes it away. If he doesn't get out of here, and fast, he will not see Goldie, and this will be his painful experience for the rest of the day. Mary Belle will paw over him, cry for sex, orally pump him up for the occasion, and cry for more sex. She will curse and rave and bang him with her fists each time he tries to fall asleep.

Mary Belle is an odd breed, Jimmie thinks, strange, a woman possessed. She isn't an alcoholic. She'll have lots and lots of beer some nights when she has trouble dropping off to sleep. But that's it. And she isn't on drugs. Yet, on occasions, she bares all the symptoms of an addict or of someone terribly crazed. Medicine has it, he remembers having read somewhere, that the liver produces alcohol. Her liver, obviously, manufactures cocaine, too, he thinks.

He wrinkles his brow, pops his finger and says: "Ah, stupid me..."

Mary Belle interrupts with: "I'll buy that."

"I forgot to get some gas," Jimmie continues, "and the hand is sitting on empty." He gets up from the table and heads for the door. On the way out, he places his hand over his mouth and forces himself to yawn loudly several times. "Well, there's only one thing to do, and that's to go back out and get some. Right now. Can't take chances on waiting until tonight. Just be my luck to forget it again and run out of gas out there on the drive half way to work."

"See? I tells you all the time, you ain't nothing but a dummy," Mary Belle depraves him. "Can't even remember to put gas in your own car. Think it's gonna run on air?"

He deliberately yawns again. It's a loud and long one. And he thinks it sounds pretty convincing. "Damn, and as tired and sleepy as I am, too," he puffs out. "But it's got to be done"

Mary Belle follows him to the door and yells after him to: "Hurry back here, now." Then she pulls her dress up high, the only garment she is wearing, and exposes her overblown lumpy thighs, and grins at him and adds. "'Cause I got some work for you to do."

Jimmie has successfully schemed his way out of the house and out of reach of the pawing claws of Mary Belle. Now, sitting in his car in nearby Carver Park, he patiently awaits twelve noon, the time he is to meet Goldie at the Lakeland Hotel. But for some inexplainable reason he is now having second thoughts.

I'll make this marriage go, he vows. I'll get it off the rocks. I'll show Goldie that I can live without her, even if it kills me. I've done it for seven years. So I'll continue to do it. I'll let her know that she has no permanent hold on me. If she can live without me, I can live without her. Why can't I marry if I want to? She's married, and has been all the time. As long as I have known her, she's been married. She took up with me only because I was single. She wanted someone whose time she could fully monopolize.

When I first met her she said that she didn't love her husband, Paul. She lied then and she's lying now. She's at home with him this very minute locked up in an intimate embrace, showing him how much she loves him. She also said he could not satisfy her sexually, and that he had not made love to her in months. She lied about that, too. Now she says she hasn't had a man in seven years, "not really," as she puts it. Not since I quit seeing her and married Mary Belle has she really had a man, she says. Boy, what a line.

She's there with him right now. Every night, every day. They share the same room, the same bed, the same side of the bed. She disrobes before him, shows him everything she's got. She makes him want her. She taunts him, dares him. If he's a man, any kind of man at all, how can he resist? Someone else perhaps, but not Goldie.

Something is going on over there at that house. All these years, no sex? She couldn't last that long without it. Not Goldie. Sex is an important part of her life. It's what makes her tick, the way she maintains her sanity. Without that kind of attention she is incapable of intelligently functioning. Sex is like food to her. It's a mega-vitamin that keeps her healthy and strong. It's a life giving substance which she has to have three or 4 times a week.

Jimmie remembers the first day he met Goldie. He was a cab driver at the time. Hauling multitudes of people around Metro City all day everyday, he became adept at reading in their faces their varying states of mind. Although Goldie showed no alarming outer signs that she was suffering from stress, he could tell that, inside, she was deeply troubled. It was carefully covered over by the radiant smile she constantly wore. Nevertheless, to Jimmie, the fury, the turbulence and the burning desire all were definitely there.

In contrast, the first night Jimmie saw Goldie after not seeing her for seven years, he didn't sense any real stress in her, nor has he since. In fact, to Jimmie, she seemed more in control than ever before. What is she trying to pull off here? he wonders. Did Paul get a fix? In some remote corner of the city, did he find a doctor with a miracle hormone that gave him back his virility? Or did she find somebody else? Hey, maybe that's it, she found somebody else, younger perhaps. But if that's the case. What does she still want with me? he asks himself.

The Ultimate Commitment, that's what she wants, for me to kiss on her the way Mary Belle kisses on me. That's what she's always wanted. To be, not only admired and adored but idolized, loved beyond the periphery of normalcy. She is selfish. She was then. She is now, perhaps unconsciously so, but no less selfish. Unless a man in the act of sex wholly commits himself to her, she thinks he doesn't really love her, Jimmie says, but then corrects himself. In all honesty, though, I can't say that. Before she met me, she knew nothing at all about the Ultimate Commitment.

Goldie was not a materialist, he remembers. Although it might have seemed so to many, money and things meant little to her. She lived in a kind of subliminal world, not necessarily in a world of fantasy, yet out of touch with the real world.

To her, respect, appreciation and love were not objects of the world of things that one could see, hear and touch. They were not merchandise to be bought and sold, used up, discarded and thrown away. One of the things she valued most in life was thoughtfullness, to be remembered, or as she put it," the little things."

Where most girls fancied motor cars, mink coats, jewels and expensive perfumes, a girl who did not drink, Goldie flipped over the package of gum, or the pint of ice cream he thought to have at his place when she came over, or remembered to bring along to wherever they met.

Since she was one who believed in the person and not the gift, and since she claimed to love only him, he thought of nothing less than his soul to give in return. That's why he made love to Goldie in a special way.

The act of love, the physical expression—having sex—Jimmie believed seven years before and still does, is but a manifestation. It is a system of actions representing something else. It is a language in which one speaks out in definite tones to express to his mate the warmth, intensity and duration that gives a clear account of the extent of that love.

Love making is a time for the grandest of language, he thought then. It is a time for eloquence, inflection, rhapsody, a time for one to speak out in language best known to him or her—in language placed on a level that directly complements the intrinsic qualities of the listener.

Language itself is only a symbol that attempts to depict the thought we wish to express. If through the symbolism of language we fail to communicate, how else can we hope to break through? To bring home the message of love to those whom we devoutly dedicate ourselves? But there are many languages, and there are many ways of expressing love. Even within a single language, there are many ways.

Yet, most important, perhaps, Jimmie thought way back then, is to know the function of language, why we use it. A musical instrument is not music. It is only a means of making music. Another way of singing your song of love. Motor cars, mink coats, jewels, and rare perfumes are not wealth. They are but symbols of wealth.

But then, symbols must have some kind of value, too, Jimmie pointed out. For, when we attempt to show appreciation for an act of kindness, or of love, we try to make the symbol match the deed. That's what I attempted to do in the case of Goldie, he now remembers sitting there in his car in nearby Carver Park. She was a special kind of girl. The expression of my love for her had to be a special kind of symbol. So, to her, I made the Ultimate Commitment.

Jimmie, suddenly, leaves the ecstasy of the past and comes back to the hard reality of the present. Mary Belle's physical manifestation of her love for me simulates my love for Goldie, he admits, but it is not the same. Her physical expression of her love for me is cold, estranged and inhuman. It is a sacrilege. It bears no warmth, love or affection. Having sex with Mary Belle is a show. It's a burlesque of butt shakers and belly dancers. It's a brothel revue where anything-you-want girls work overtime using special techniques to revive the virility in old and decrepit men. Mary Belle is a whore, and I am a paying customer.

Twelve noon with Goldie will be a glorious reunion. God bless this relationship. Goldie, baby!!! Here I come.

Chapter 7

When Jimmie reported to section GS-48S for work each night at 10:12, he and his 7:12 station mate Slick were responsible for rounding up the equipment needed to dispatch the mail processed in GS-48S from the Main Installation out to the zone 48 Carrier Station.

MMPO men workers disdainfully referred to such duties as Man's Work. Among other things, it entailed getting a tying machine which was used to tie letters in bundles, bags in which to transport the bundles, racks on which to hang bags while they were being filled with the bundles, and hand trucks on which bags were loaded.

One of the worst aspects about Man's Work was the rounding up of these items. Section GS-48S was located on the fourth floor. The tying machines were stored on the ninth floor; the bags were stored on the sixth floor; the racks were stored on the fifth floor and the hand trucks were stored in the second sub-basement.

Jimmie and Slick had finished the Man's Work chores and were now sitting at their respective sorting cases along with the female clerks ready to start sorting mail. There were many things about operations at the MMPO that Jimmie disliked. Man's Work was definitely one of them. He disliked it immensely.

Unlike Slick and his locker room buddy Oscar, though, he usually did not outwardly express that dislike. Just the same, his general approach in performing those chores, though subtle and restrained, usually spoke out quite loudly regarding how he felt inside about doing them.

But tonight, it was a different story. He looked over at Goldie.

She puckered up and pointed kissing lips at him.

"It was wonderful," he lipped back at her.

They had been to the Lakeland Hotel again that day. The high was still with Jimmie. He looked about the section, at the big heavy trucks, at the hanging sacks, and at all the other items of Man's Work. They were all in place. He tried to recall when he and Slick had rounded them up and brought them in. He couldn't.

He was still trying to recall when Supervisor Willie Moses strolled down the aisle to his case. "Mr. Jones? General Foreman Brim wants to see you in his office," he said.

Jimmie swiveled around on the restbar he sat on and looked up at him. "What does he want, Mr. Moses?" he asked.

Willie Moses was a big man with broad shoulders, a wide trunk and narrow hips. He had well proportioned limbs, a broad head and a wide face that appeared swollen. His neck was thick and his arms were long and fleshy. They hung almost to his knees. He had been a white button (a relief supervisor) for several years under the white administration. Now, under the black administration, he had been promoted to red top (regular supervisor). Clerks, especially women clerks, spoke of him as a "nice supervisor." He gave them a free hand. They also called him a fool for doing so.

"I don't know what he wants," supervisor Moses said to Jimmie.

Jimmie had an idea that he was lying. He looked at him squarely, face to face.

Willie Moses twitched his lips and rapidly blinked his eyes.

Jimmie smiled with the assurance that Willie Moses actually did know, and got up from his restbar and started for Brim's office. He walked a short distance to the south end of the main center aisle and made a right turn. He noted that the big hole, gaping up from the parquet floor for the past three weeks, was now repaired. Passing workers would no longer stub their toes in it.

Jimmie should have been pleased that the floor was now repaired. Several times in route to the freight elevators with the GS-48S dispatch, the heavily loaded truck had stalled in the hole. Two nights before, he was forced to walk back to the station and get Slick to help him push it out.

On each occasion, he had reported the incident to Supervisor Moses who told him that he had reported it to the maintenance department. Maybe he had, maybe he hadn't, Jimmie figured. Anyway, weeks and weeks later, the maintenance people had finally taken care of it. The old loose, scattered blocks and squares of the torn up parquet floor had all been cleared away and replaced by new ones. The floor looked smooth and normal again. Jimmie was looking at it, but not really seeing it.

What he saw was a mental recall of the front page of the MMPO monthly newsletter. It was a photo of Postmaster Bill Brown presenting a young woman with an award. The caption below the photo said that she had "been instrumental in preventing possible injury to employes, and damage to equipment by reporting the serious condition of the fourth floor work room area." It nauseated Jimmie. To think that the PO would disapprove the many money saving suggestions he had made and shell out $250 for information the maintenance department had had on its files for weeks. It was shameful, he thought.

The whole thing was ironic. For weeks, the hole in the floor had been in plain view of every clerk, mailhandler and supervisor on the floor. It was even in plain view of the maintenance people who were being paid salaries to check daily for such irregularities.

He passed the central mail dumping area operation where mailhandler Bessie Black, leader of the Hatchet Ladies, was supervising a group of men clerks who were yanking heavy sacks of mail from a pile of some 100 and dumping them down chutes. A mailhandler supervising clerks who were doing mailhandler work was also shameful, Jimmie thought, a private telling a sergeant what to do.

The GS-48S office complex, located in the southwest corner of the building reminded Jimmie of the candy counter that was situated off the corridor in the northwest end of the building. Like an added growth slowly forming on human skin, from out of the west wall, it unexpectedly came crawling onto the workroom floor. Jimmie walked into the entrance area and was directed by the receptionist to General Foreman Brim's office.

G.F. Brim reared back in his massive mahogany, leathered chair and said: "Come on in, Mr. Jones, have a seat."

Jimmie walked in and took a seat in a chair facing Brim. It was the first time he had gotten a real good look at his General Foreman.

G.F. Brim had a face that looked like apples, peaches, plums and grapes all rolled up in a lopsided ball. Painted of various colors, it was splotchy. He had a thin body that was tall and slightly hunched. And he had spindly limbs that appeared frail and unsteady. Sitting in the middle of that massive mahogany chair that accommodated him several times over, he was a ghostly sight.

"I have a copy of your suggestion here which you have titled, Conditions at the Metro Main Post Office," G.F. Brim informed Jimmie."

"I have later given it the title Blockbuster."

"Yes, so I have heard. Why so?"

"In the process of putting it together, the idea came to me that that would be the kind of impact it would make on the staff and workers here"

"And you were right. That's exactly what it has done. And that's why I have called you in here, to find out from you, why now."

"Why now? I'm not sure I know what you mean by why now."

"You've been down here at the Main Installation for six years, and you are only now discovering all these things that you say are wrong down here?"

"No, I didn't only now discover them," Jimmie explained. "I've known about them for some time."

"So, if you've known about them for some time, why did you wait until now to reveal your feelings about them?" Brim continued to press Jimmie.

Jimmie knew what his motivation was. The word being circulated, thanks to the Hatchet Ladies, was that Jimmie had deliberately branded MMPO black management incompetent. He wanted to tell Brim how it really happened, that he had actually started the Blockbuster before the black administration took over, and that he waited almost six years because he had vowed before leaving the MidSouth Carrier Station that: "Because the white man thinks me incapable of knowing how he can improve his inefficient, low producing Metro City Post Office, I'll never make another damn suggestion about it as long as I live."

He also wanted to tell him that the problems at the Main Installation were of a great magnitude when he came down there, and had continued to grow steadily. Finally, it reached a point where he could no longer restrain himself. He had to act. But Jimmie had a feeling that G. F. Brim would not buy his explanation, that if indeed he did, he would not admit it. So, he did not reveal it.

"You spoke of standardization in your Blockbuster," G.F. Brim called to Jimmie's attention. "What precisely do you mean by the term? How would such a program profit the service? And in what ways would it benefit the worker?"

"A standardization law would require customers to post letters in envelopes that did not exceed, larger or smaller, a prescribed size," Jimmie explained. "According to my observation, since there are no limitations, letters sent through the mails today come in all shapes and sizes. This reduces letter sorting machine usage by some fifty percent. Simply because non-machinable letter mail must be sorted by hand, which requires three times as long. So, it is quite clear to me that, especially in the processing of letter mail, standardization would profit the service in two significant ways: first, by improving efficiency, and second, by raising productivity levels.

"Okay, Brim interrupted. "Now, how does it benefit the worker?"

"Well, let me say, just this," Jimmie expounded but a bit cautiously. "Standardization may not immediately benefit the worker, but improved efficiency and higher productivity, over the long term, would benefit everyone, including the worker."

"What you're really saying," Brim questioned, "is that standardization will cause some workers to lose their jobs, right? Black people need these jobs."

"And one of the best ways to keep these jobs, I believe, is through efficiency and higher levels of productivity, doing the very best job that one can do."

"Yes," Brim partially agreed, "but try to sell that to a guy who is out of work, or to one who is about to be out of work. These people don't care about efficiency and productivity. Their great concern is jobs. In order to survive, they need work. They can't live off efficiency and productivity. And because of slavery of blacks in America, and years and years of discrimination in employment even after we were free, the United States government owes us a job. So, maybe blacks think of the Post Office as a kind of reparation agency..."

"The U.S. government is indebted to blacks for having held them in bondage, and for past job discrimination," Jimmie admitted. "And we should be paid. I don't dispute that. But I don't want to get off on that subject because I have a whole different theory about reparation..."

"You are a man who's just full of ideas, aren't you?" Brim interrupted.

Jimmie wasn't sure if Brim's comment was a demeaning quip or a friendly compliment. "Well, I'm basically no different to anyone else,

I guess," he said. "Everybody has ideas about things that go on around them, I would think."

"I would like to hear your ideas about reparation," Brim invited Jimmie.

But Jimmie tried to back away. "As I said, I'd like not to go into that. Because it takes a bit of explaining."

"You don't have to go into deep details. Just give me a brief outline of what your theory is."

"Reparation is not a simple matter. And brief outlines might turn out inadequate."

"I understand. But go on try it anyway. Make it short and sweet. If I don't get it. I don't get it."

"Okay," Jimmie capitulated. "In defining reparation, my dictionary uses terms that indicate that one should pay for the damage he inflicts on another. In other words, the perpetrator pays for the damage already done. The damaged person is not required to sustain a second dose of damage in order to receive compensation for the first dose. As enslaved partners in the building of America who never received their fair share of the benefits, blacks have already been damaged. The clandestine scheme of using the Postal Service as a form of reparation for blacks by hiring blacks to work there, is a travesty. It is a modern form of slavery, and it is an out and out denial that the United States has ever wronged American blacks."

"So, you advocate that the United States government pay us off in cash, huh?"

"Right. I have proposed a plan which I call Lump Sum Cash Reparation. I suggest that the United States government award each qualifying decendant of an American slave one hundred thousand dollars, which, in these times will buy only a decent home for one's family, nothing much else."

"How do you suggest this be handled?"

"You asked for a brief outline," Jimmie remimded Brim. "I've given you that. So now, let's go on with the initial reason you called me into your office."

"Okay," Brim conceded. "Let's go on with it then. But until the government starts paying off this Lump Sum Cash Reparation, as you call it, what do blacks do in the meantime?"

"There are many things we can do," Jimmie assured Brim. "But, as I said, I don't want to get into that now."

"No," Brim scolded Jimmie. "You'd rather spring RIF (reduction in force) on these people who are educationally disadvantaged and can't get a job out there in the private sector which pays what they make here."

"It is amazing how you agree with the basic premise of my Blockbuster. Yet, in the same voice, you violently disagree with the primary method for resolving the problems we have here. And that seems to be the hold-back down here, on all levels. People agreeing but disagreeing, refusing to own up to the real living facts of the matter," he said, remembering Mamie Smith's words: "To hell with education, efficiency and productivity and all that bull shit. What black folks needs is jobs."

"And in that regard," Jimmie continued, "here are two important factors I'd like to point out. First, the government has spent considerable sums of money in installing letter sorting machines (LSMs) in most large city post offices. Eventually, a call for full usage of those machines will undoubtedly be forthcoming.

Second, as a result of the overflow, the taskforce recommended the establishment in the Metro City suburbs its first Sectional Center Facility (SCF). Washington thought it was such a good idea that now 552 are to be scattered across the country. They are supposedly to be designed to relieve some of the processing and transportation pressures on big city post offices by absorbing some of their workload. They will be located in suburbs where less than one percent of blacks live and work. These facilities will be fast growing bureaucracies that will dig deep into big city workloads that are now guaranteed to blacks."

"Yes, yes, Mr. Jones," Brim interrupted. "You don't need to tell me all this? I'm a General Foreman here. I know all about the LSM machines here, and about the 552 SCFs which are to be constructed out there in the suburbs. And I know what they will do to our workload here. They will take jobs away from blacks. So, what is your point?"

"My point is the same as I told you before," Jimmie hammered at Brim, "improved efficiency and higher levels of productivity."

"You're talking RIF," Brim told Jimmie. "laying people off, taking jobs away from blacks. I have tried to get the point over to you that I am against that kind of procedure..."

"You just agreed with me that SCFs scattered across the country will dig deep into big city workloads. Did you, or did you not?" Jimmie probed G.F. Brim.

"Yes, I did," he admitted. "And that's why I oppose your standardization idea. This efficiency-productivity scheme of yours, in a sense, would serve only to reduce our workload that much more."

"That's where you're wrong," Jimmie argued. "The SCFs will grow. And they will continue to grow. But we here at the main can control that growth, simply because they will grow only at our expense. Frankly speaking, the kind of thinking I am referring to could have very well prevented their origin. But that's neither here nor there, now. They are coming. The question now is, will we stand defenselessly by and watch them banish us?

"So, the only thing I am saying is, yes, I'm talking RIF. But what kind of RIF am I talking? I Don't have any figures on this, being only a clerk. As a General Foreman, you are more into that than I am. The Metro City Post Office, in the latest proposal, will be surrounded by two sectional centers," Jimmie said, then quipped, "of course I call them interceptors, but we won't go into that, either, now. We'll have one on the north and one on the south. I don't know what percentage of mail they will ciphon off from the Metro City PO, but I know Metro hires about 35,000 workers. I also know that, as the metro workload will diminish, so will the Metro workforce diminish.

"So, what's my point? Simply this: the more productive we are here at Metro, the less our workload will diminish, the less our workload diminishes, the less our workforce will diminish. Putting it another way, if we can considerably slow, or even halt the drainage, we will lose, perhaps, only 5,000 workers. But if we don't start plugging up the holes now, all the jobs you say you are trying to save for black people could very well go down the drain, excuse the pun."

"I can't see it that way," Brim objected. "No way the government is going to put all these people out of work."

"What has to happen for you to see it that way?" Jimmie hammered at Brim. "What is the picture here now? Lots of people, little mail. Do you think that's going to last forever, even in government service? I understand that certain adjustments in that regard are being discussed now."

"Yes, I know," Brim admitted. "But we are going to fight it."

"You're going to fight it with what?" Jimmie challenged him.

"With our records," Brim shot back. "Facts and figures, that's what."

Jimmie smiled in amusement. He wanted tell Brim that the only resemblance between what happens at MMPO and what is put down on paper describing what happens is that they both occur under the same roof. One hundred pounds of mail collected and processed at MMPO, after numerous countings and weighings, could wind up in the written records totaling anywhere from 500 to several thousands of pounds. So he said to Brim, "Before the occasion arises in which we must try and stand on our written record, I hope standardization has come and saved us from potential embarrassment."

Seemingly, it was apparent to Brim, now, that Jimmie wasn't about to change his mind. He had not insisted that Jimmie call back parts of his Blockbuster, especially with the Hatchet Lady kind of zeal, but he had certainly suggested to Jimmie that that was what he wanted. "I truly thought you'd understand," he beseeched Jimmie.

"You thought I'd understand what?" Jimmie asked, as if he didn't know.

"About your standardization suggestion and how it would take jobs away from blacks."

In pigmentation, Jimmie was about as black as any man could get. But, in logical reasoning, and certainly in plain old home spun honesty, he was nowhere near that black. And he made it known to Brim. "Maintaining jobs for blacks by turning down the opportunity for greater efficiency and improved productivity, is wrong," he said. "It just isn't good management. And good management is what this country and everybody in it needs, especially black people," he emphasized, "that is, if we ever hope to intelligently and effectively compete. Letter sorting machines should be allowed to operate at full capacity. Standardization in letter mailings would make that possible."

There was no question that Jimmie was a determined man. And there was no question that Brim was, too. Jimmie could see it in his eyes. "Mr. Jones?" Brim called out, changing the subject. "There's a supervisor's exam coming up very soon. The service needs thinking men like yourself. Why don't you try and qualify?"

Now they will change their tactics, Jimmie surmised, try and buy me off, dangle a carrot in front of my eyes. That won't work, either, he vowed. "I took the exam once before," he informed Brim, "back in 1958."

"Don't give up because you failed it once," Brim advised him. "Try again, and keep on trying until you finally make it. And you will, because I can see that you've got what it takes."

"I didn't fail it. I didn't make a great score, only 70, but I didn't fail it."

"So, what happened? That was 9 years ago, long before you left the carrier station."

"Yes, it was," Jimmie confirmed. "Well, I really wasn't interested in a supervisory position in the first place."

"So, why'd you take it?"

"A clerk out at the MidSouth Carrier Station had taken the exam, oh, I don't know," Jimmie pondered, "eight or ten times, I guess, and had failed each time. Carriers kidded him about it because clerks considered themselves smarter than carriers. And we black carriers, including me, got a real big kick out of kidding this guy because he was white, and white boys think they are smarter than black boys, no matter what position they hold, or what position you hold. Well, one day when I was kidding him, I told him I could pass the exam with my eyes closed. He said he'd bet me ten dollars I couldn't. I called his bet, took the exam and qualified."

"That's quite a story Mr. Jones," Brim remarked.

"I didn't think anymore about it," Jimmie went on, "until I changed over to clerk and came down here in 1961."

"What happened, then?"

"Well, a couple of clerks I know had planned to take the 1961 exam and suggested to me that I should take it, too. I related the 1958 incident to them and they informed me that the 1958 exam was being thrown out and the only way to remain on the list of eligibles was to either take the exam again or to go somewhere, but no one I contacted knew just where, and sign up for retention."

Certifying only a portion of eligibles from a supervisory exam list and dropping those remaining before conducting another exam was really a violation of Postal Law.

The "Zone of Consideration" provision was created to guard against such unfair practices. It said that the top ten percent of candidates on a supervisory exam list of eligibles would be first considered for certification, then the next ten percent and so on until the list was exhausted. Then and only then would another exam be conducted, it said. But Metro City Post Office took great pride in violating the Zone of Consideration law.

"I remember that mix up," Brim recalled. "There was a notice printed in the General Orders about that. So, did you sign up?"

"No".

"Why not?"

"I just told you," Jimmie said, inflecting his voice. "I couldn't find out just where to go and sign up. But it wouldn't have made any difference. As I eventually discovered, the fellows informed me too late, anyway."

"Too bad," Brim allowed. "But why don't you check with personnel just for the heck of it. You never can tell. Your name may still be on the eligibles' list. If not, my advice to you is to take it again."

"Oh, I don't know," Jimmie floundered. "I'm still not sure I want to become a supervisor."

And Brim added: "In the meantime, refrain from submitting such wide sweeping suggestions that are going to affect the lives of vast numbers of people. Make suggestions that pertain particularly to your own work section."

The next day Jimmie was having second thoughts about not wanting to become a supervisor. And just "for the heck of it," as Brim had suggested, he went down to personnel to check about his rating. But not only was his name not on the list of eligibles, personnel had no record that he had ever qualified on any supervisor's exam at all. So, whether he was interested in becomimg a supervisor or not, this act of apparent ineptitude on the part of personnel piqued his appetite. Standardization, efficiency, productivity, the Hatchet Ladies, Brim, black management, the overflow, and 552 proposed sectional center facilities, all at once, crowded into his brain. And he thought, this place is really messed up.

"What do you suppose happened to those records?" Jimmie asked the personnel clerk (P-C).

And the P-C gave Jimmie an accusing look. "What records?" he snapped.

"Records about me passing the 1958 supervisor's exam," Jimmie snapped back, "that's what records."

"How am I supposed to know what happened to them?"

"If you people here in personnel don't know what happened to my records, who does?" Jimmie continued to question him.

"Maybe nobody knows what happened to them, because maybe

they don't even exist," the P-C said, and looked Jimmie squarely in the eye. "Are you absolutely sure you qualified on that exam?"

"Sure, I'm sure," Jimmie pummeled back at the P-C. "Why else would I be here insisting that it should be mentioned in my folder?"

"Workers are consistently coming in here with wild stories about things that don't exist," he lectured Jimmie. "And this sounds like another one." He held up Jimmie's folder and waved it through the air. "There is absolutely nothing here in your records indicating that you ever qualified on any supervisor's examination at anytime. So, friend," he said quietly, "it didn't happen. So now, if you'll excuse me, I have other people here that I must wait on who don't have fairy tales to tell me, okay?"

Jimmie quickly rammed his hand down into his pocket and came up with two business size official envelopes and pointed to one of them. "I don't know what you have or don't have there in my folder," he told the P-C. "But here's what I have in this envelope."

It was a notice of rating from the 1958 supervisor's examination. If only by the skin of his teeth, Jimmie had indeed qualified on it, answering correctly, 105 of a total of 150 questions. It was a 70 rating right on the head. "And what about this?" Jimmie asked the P-C, taking a letter from the second envelope. By adding points for written evaluation and career service, Jimmie's rating had jumped to 85.39.

The P-C checked the two documents, but insisted that since there was no such evidence in Jimmie's folder there was nothing he could do about it.

Jimmie demanded the personnel clerk call his supervisor. The personnel supervisor came and suggested Jimmie write a letter to the Employment Placement Officer. He did this and waited for a whole month for a reply that did not come. Then, on instructions from the grapevine, he sat down and wrote a letter to the Director Of Operations. "With that dude on the case, I bet you get some action," he was guaranteed. "And if he can't help you, you're out of it, man. Can't nobody help you. Forget it."

But Jimmie waited a month this time, too. And no answer. He began questioning the grapevine advice. "With that dude on the case," if he really was on the case, Jimmie still wasn't getting any action. He wondered if indeed he could be helped, if he truly was out of it. He thought that, as Brim had suggested, perhaps he should forget about the 1958 thing and just go on and take the exam again. But a few days following the one month mark, "With that dude on the case," Jimmie finally got an answer. But the answer did not come from the Director of Operations, neither did it come from the Employment Placement Officer. It came from the guy the personnel supervisor should have referred Jimmie to in the first place, the supervisor's boss, Bob Bell, Chief of Personnel.

Jimmie went to Bob Bell's office, walked in and introduced himself. Bob Bell was a black xanthochroid. With light hair and fair skin, he appeared more white than black. He was sitting at his desk pawing over some papers spread out before him. "Come on in and have a seat, Mr. Jones. What can I do for you?" he asked Jimmie.

"I have come in answer to your letter," Jimmie told Bob Bell, reaching it out to him. Referring to it as a letter, though, was a kind of patronizing gesture on Jimmie's part. He had branded it a cryptic note. And under critical analysis, that's just what it was. Excluding the address of the Metro City Main Post Office, and the room number, the one sentence communication only said: "Kindly report to the personnel department between the hours of 8:30 AM and 5:00 PM, in regards to your request of March 8, 1967." This was the date of the letter addressed to "that dude," the Director of Operations.

Bob Bell took the note, glanced at it, gave it back to Jimmie, got up from his desk and strutted back and forth across the floor several times. He was a young black man dressed up in a suit and tie. From head to foot, he seemed drenched in some kind of dime store cologne. And with both hands rammed deep into his pockets, much like a small time conjurer leaving an alley crap game, he continually jangled with his right hand what sounded like large pieces of silver.

As far back as Jimmie could remember, he had been extremely leery of strutters, especially those who paraded about clanking pocketed silver coins together. For some reason, he thought most were not to be trusted, that they were devious, sadistic and cynical, and that many floated around precariously mounted on a false sense of power. Jimmie took the cryptic note back and waited for his response.

"Oh yeah, I remember," Bob Bell said. "Now, what was this all about?"

As he had done with General Foreman G. F. Brim, Jimmie

related to Personnel Chief Bob Bell the 1958 incident from beginning to end.

Bell leaned against his desk and continued jangling the large silver coins in his pocket. He claimed that he could not recall the 1958 supervisor's exam. "But you shouldn't worry too much about it," he attempted to comfort Jimmie. "We haven't certified anybody from any previous exam that did not score 92 percent or better. We want only the best qualified people as supervisors here. But you should have signed the list to be retained anyway," he admonished Jimmie.

Jimmie viewed Bell scornfully. Not even a devious, or a very specious person, would make such a dastardly inaccurate statement. It was the biggest lie of the year. Bob Bell was truly living up to the reputation of the strutter Jimmie had thought him to be. Across the board at MMPO, the supervisory force was composed of about 75% unqualified people, clerks off the case. In the City Letter Section where Jimmie worked, the percentage was even higher: 80 percent.

These relief supervisors, white buttons, as they were generally referred to, were unqualified to perform supervisory duties because some had taken the exam numerous times and failed it. They were also unqualified because others had never taken it, and because many, with gross educational inadequacies, would never dare take it for fear of embarrassing themselves. One of those unqualified supervisors with gross educational disadvantages was none other than fiery Hatchet Lady leader Bessie Black herself.

"I can't understand, Mr. Bell," Jimmie said, "how it is that there is no record of my having qualified on the 1958 exam. I find that quite strange."

"No, it's not strange," Bob Bell disagreed. "In a big operation like we have here, it's very possible. Things like that happen all the time. It'll turn up." Then he proceeded to demean Jimmie. "But don't worry about it, with a score as low as you say yours was, as I said before, you would not have been considered anyway. We want the best qualified people," he said, repeating that lie.

Jimmie was sick to his stomach. Civil rights organizations all across the nation were charging whites of discriminating against blacks because they claimed certain examinations, such as police, fire etc. favored whites over blacks. They demanded the simplification of these exams, and, across the board they called for affirmative action and quotas in that regard. Blacks, his own people, were denying him his lawful rights to a job for which he had legally qualified, and on an exam that had not been simplified. It was a disgusting situation to Jimmie.

He felt somewhat like many whites must have felt who had strenuously complained that it was discriminatory and wrong for employers to hire or promote blacks making lesser scores on certain examinations, while refusing to hire or promote whites who had made substantially higher scores. They termed it reverse discrimination.

So, by hiring the services of a 75% unqualified supervisory workforce, instead of hiring him who was legally qualified, the MMPO black administration was also guilty of reverse discrimination, Jimmie thought. The black bastards are no better than Mississippi plantation bosses who overwork and cheat the hell out of their defenseless sharecroppers and beat up on them if and when they dare complain.

"So he questioned Bob Bell. "The best qualified? "You've got all those white buttons out there? They're not qualified, and they are supervising everyday. What about them?"

"Oh, they're only temporary."

"But white buttons have been so called temporary for the full six years I've been down here."

"Yeah, I know," Bob Bell agreed, walking behind his desk and sitting down again. "That was their game (the white administration). We're going to change all that."

"That's what they said, too," he reminded Bell.

"But we mean it," he tried to convince Jimmie, then changed the subject. "Why don't you take the upcoming exam and get back on the list? It could be to your advantage."

Jimmie sensed something odd in Bob Bell's question, and he asked himself: what was Bob Bell really saying, or perhaps more correctly, what was Bob Bell not saying. Slick had laid out for Jimmie how easy it was to land a supervisory job if a person really wanted one. "All you got to do is act lak you wants it," Slick had insisted, "and you don't mind paying for it, that's all. You won't bave to go looking for them. They'll come looking for you."

"Why should I have to take the exam again," Jimmie complained to Bell. "I qualified once. How many more times do I have to qualify to get on the list and stay there?"

"But the 1958 exam was thrown out," he reminded Jimmie.

"Yes, but why was it thrown out before they got around to certifying all the eligibles appearing on the list?" Jimmie pressed Bell.

"I just told you," Bell emphasized, putting his feet up on the desk and rearing back in his chair. "They certified only the best qualified."

"Anyway," Jimmie continued prying Bell, "if they were going to throw it out, why didn't they notify the eligibles remaining on the list?"

"They did," Bell replied. "You just said they did."

"No I didn't," Jimmie refuted. "I said I was informed by several employes that a notice was printed in the General Orders that it was being thrown out. I think those remaining on the 1958 list should have been notified by letter that it was being thrown out. And I think they should have been instructed as to what to to if they wanted their names retained on a new list." he explained, then added: "The General Orders, what a joke."

"What do you mean, what a joke?" Bell challenged Jimmie, taking his feet down off the desk and looking him straight in the eye.

"I mean the General Orders is a joke," Jimmie shot back at Bell, not wincing. "At least, the way it's handled, it's a joke. It was a joke when I came down here in 1961 and it's still a joke."

Bob Bell didn't like what Jimmie said about the General Orders, and he snapped back at him: "I think you'd better explain that."

"I did explain it, and in detail, in my Blockbuster."

"In your what?"

"In my suggestion: Conditions at the Metro Main Post Office," Jimmie informed him.

"Oh yeah," Bob Bell sighed, in a put down tone. "So you did, they say. But I haven't had a chance to read it, so tell me about it."

Jimmie had an idea that Bell was lying about that, too. I bet he read the Blockbuster from cover to cover, he thought to himself, but he said to Bell:

"Well, when I first came down here in 1961, I didn't even know that the Metro City Post Office printed such a publication. Not once during my eight years at the MidSouth Carrier Station did I hear the term General Orders. Down here, I didn't hear about it either until one night about six weeks after my arrival when I saw a group of workers gathered around the main bulletin board out in the main corridor. And I stopped to find out what all the curiosity was about. The whole slough, about 50 or so, were pushing and shoving each other.

They were trying to read what the copy of the General Orders was saying about coming adjustments in certain work schedules..."

"And that was a joke? People trying to find out how changes in the overall work schedule is going to affect them? I am sure that if you were smart, you did the same thing," Bob Bell sniped at Jimmie. "I can see you now, yelling: 'Hey, what about the 10:12s?' Right? Isn't that what you did?"

Jimmie sensed a bit of history in Bob Bell's attack and served up to him a disarming probe. "Yep, that's right. That's what I did."

"I have no doubt," Bell responded with confidence and much satisfaction. "I know you did. When I was a clerk, I did it, too. And you thought it was a joke, huh?"

"Well, yes, I thought then it was a joke, especially as I observed several workers at the front of the crowd reading the message loudly in unison for the benefit of those in the far back "

"What do you mean you thought it was a joke then? Your Blockbuster, as you call it, is now, today. And you are still calling the General Orders a joke."

"Well, actually, I don't really mean now that it's just a joke."

"Well, I should hope not. But if you don't mean it now, why do you say it now?"

"What I mean now is that it is not just a joke. It's a bad joke. That's what I'm saying."

"And what is that suppose to mean?" Bell snapped back.

"I got a chance to see a copy of the General Orders once. It was about four pages long, the one I saw. I held it in my hands; and I read it from cover to cover."

"How did you happen to manage that? Workers are not given copies of the General Orders, only members of management are."

"You're right. It wasn't my copy. It belonged to my supervisor. I saw it lying on his desk and him looking the other way, so I swiped it. When I finished, I caught him looking the other way again, and I sneaked it back."

"So, you held a copy of the General Orders in your hand," Bell berated Jimmie. "And you read it from cover to cover, so, what's the big deal?"

"The very first thing the General Orders says," Jimmie informed Bell, "is that: 'This publication is for the instruction and guidance of employes of the Metro City Post Office.' I'm an employe of the Metro

City Post Office. If it's issued for my intruction and guidance, why should I have to creep around like a thief in the night and steal it from my supervisor?

Second, as for the contents, a large part of the publication is spent in listing clerk and mailhandler jobs throughout the department, including carrier stations, which are available to clerks and mailhandlers wishing to transfer to different sections and locations. Considerable space is allotted to the names of workers who submitted suggestions. And quite a bit of the space is allotted to the listing of lost stamp meters and other such miscellany. At the very bottom of the fourth and final page, utilizing only about one twentiest of its total space, are three management proposals.

"So, it is safe to say that about 95% of the General Orders's message is aimed at the line worker, clerks and mailhandlers, not supervisors and managers. That's the bad joke: a newsletter designed and printed for the benefit of group two but withheld from group two and distributed solely to group one. Because of this limitation, I contend that those workers whose names appear on eligible lists be informed by letter of any changes made as crucial as eligible lists being thrown out."

"That's water down the drain," Bell pounded at Jimmie.

"There's nothing we can do about that, now. Your best bet is to take the exam again."

"But what about my having qualified on the 1958 exam? Whether the exam was thrown out or not, the fact that I qualified on it, is a part of my employment record. And it should show in my folder."

"That's water down the drain, too. There's nothing in your folder indicating that you did. So, there's nothing you can do about it."

Jimmie produced his two letters of evidence, first, the one confirming the initial rating of 70. And second, the adjustment letter which brought his rating up to 85.39. "But I have records," he told Bell.

"The department has to operate on the basis of its own records," he flatly informed Jimmie. Then, getting up from his desk again and strutting across the room, the black xanthochroid softly massaged his carotene face with one hand and gently ran the fingers of his other hand through his light colored hair. This odd, physical behavior of Bob Bell reminded Jimmie of Late Set Sweetheart Blanche Mims and how, at the drop of a hat, she'd brag about her Irish-Indian heritage.

But he thought that Bob Bell's admixture was not a result of some innocent, romantic sexual mishap of several generations back.

Neither did he think it was a case in which Bell's great grand mammy had been forced by the crack of the slave master's whip to unwillingly give of herself to him. Jimmie thought that this smart ass trick baby got here because his black slick grade school dropout mammy refused to earn money any other way but to sell exclusively to white boys whatever they thought they wanted to buy from her. If he and Bell were in South Africa, though, he bitterly thought, this shit colored nigger would be considered just that: colored, superior to Jimmie, and allowed certain public accommodations that would be strickly denied to him.

American admixed-blacks, which most American blacks mostly were, did not foster among themselves an overt structured caste system based on skin color. Yet, such a system in America did indeed exist. As South African coloreds thought themselves better than South African blacks, so did American admixed-blacks think themselves better than American pigment-blacks.

Bob Bell walked back to where Jimmie was sitting and stood looking down on him. "We have no record that you qualified on any supervisor's exam!" he told Jimmie again, shouting. "So, there's nothing you can do about it. Take the exam again. That is, if you ever did take it. That's your best bet."

A build up of anger flooded Jimmie's veins. It gave him a temporary vicious streak. He eyeballed Bob Bell hard and straight. And he tried desperately to restrain himself. The words he spoke came out like small squeaking columns of air that are allowed to slowly seep from a full blown balloon. "What do you mean if I ever did take it!" he shot back at Bob Bell, leaving unsaid: you shit colored bastard.

Bob Bell was a victim of the phenomenon Jimmie called the Lord Peasant Syndrome. Most blacks are tentative when responding to whites, he thought. Just any old white dude, they hesitate, pull punches, don't say what they mean, and scratch where they don't itch. But when responding to blacks, they are straightforward and blunt. This is especially true with most black bosses, and blacks in position, like this ass, he admitted. To them, the black worker is a true underling, an inferior, a kind of non person. He is someone to look down on, to abuse and ignore.

A philosophy equally incredible, is what Jimmie dubbed the

Infinite Peer Syndrome. This is the phenomenon where black ghetto grade school dropouts consider themselves equals with black lawyers and doctors. When it is pitted against the Lord Peasant Syndrome, the confrontation can sometimes become very ugly, even bloody.

Jimmie didn't consider himself a victim of the Infinite Peer Syndrome. But he did think of himself as somebody who was not exactly a run of the mill. He knew that he was only a clerk and that Bob Bell, Chief of Personnel, a black man, was his superior. But he also knew that, in his Blockbuster, he had submitted to the Postal Service his Standardization suggestion and many more such money saving ideas.

What has this affirmative action shit colored nigger contributed to the service besides his big mouth? Jimmie asked himself. What else besides his ability to lose vital records and have the gall to admit that it happens all the time? He's a big important executive working for a vital United States Government agency. But if he were trying to make it in private industry, Jimmie predicted, he'd last just about as long out there as a bowl of ice cream would in a sunny Nevada desert.

Jimmie really wanted to tell Bob Bell off. He also wanted to prove that he truly was not a victim of the Infinite Peer Syndrome. So he simply said, but firmly: "I passed the 1958 exam all right. How do you think I got these documents? Forged them?"

"The only thing I can tell you is what I've already told you," Bell said in a quiet patient voice. "If there's nothing in your folder to verify your claim, there's nothing we can do. That's regulations."

"What does an employe have to do, come down here and put stuff in his folder himself to make sure it gets in there?"

"I don't think that will be necessary, Mr. Jones."

Jimmie got up from his chair, stuffed his two letters back into his pocket and said: "That's the way it looks to me," and walked out of Bell's office without saying another word.

Reaching the decision to forget about the 1958 supervisory eligible list being thrown out and having to take the exam all over again wasn't easy for Jimmie to make, but he finally did. And it would not be a repeat of 1958, taking the exam without studying. This time he would study and study hard. It would not be another 70 rating for him. If a best qualified 92 score was what Bob Bell and the Metro City Post Office wanted, that was what they were going to get, even better. I'll show 'em, he vowed. Hell, I'll probably score a hundred.

And study hard Jimmie did. He went to the store that sold civil service exam books and bought the one titled: Preparing for Postal Supervisory Examinations. He also ordered the eight volume Postal Manual. He read all of them from cover to cover. Then, he went out and purchased a tape recorder and taped the bulk of the material he thought most pertinent. While taking a bath, shaving or whatever he was doing around the house, he had the tape recorder going. He had read somewhere that thoughts register quite well in the mind while one sleeps. So, he'd put a tape on the recorder when retiring, and wake up in the middle of the night to put on another one.

He bought a dozen little black three by five note books, which he filled with exam materials. And wherever he went, to work, to the grocery store, the movies, a baseball game, he took one of those little black books along with him and buried his face in it. So much would he become involved with the little black book that sometimes riding the train to work and home, he'd pass up the work and home stops several times before finally becoming aware and pushing the buzzer to get off.

When the day of the exam rolled around, Jimmie was confident that he would have no trouble at all coming away with a high score. He'd kick the hell out of Bob Bell's best qualified 92 score with a big fat one hundred. But he stopped concerning himself with his qualifying on the exam long enough to ponder the benefits of the exam. The material included in the 1958 exam on which he qualified, and the material in the 1967 exam book: Preparing for Postal Supervisory Examination, were one in the same. In both cases the material was almost exclusively about general education: vocabulary, math etc. Those pertinent things that one needed to know about supervising at the Post Office came up in terribly short supply.

So he promised his next suggestion, following his Blockbuster, would be one of revising supervisory examination materials. As soon as he gets the happy results from the examining board, and is certified and placed in a supervisory position, that will be his first priority. But Jimmie was planning too far ahead, at least, in 1967 he was. He didn't get certified and placed in a supervisory position, and he didn't kick the hell out of Bob Bell's best qualified 92 score with a big fat one hundred. In fact, after all that studying at home, at work and at ball parks, he didn't even qualify.

But not qualifying was not the worst. The really surprising thing about this whole episode was Jimmie's score. To him, not only was it shocking, it was demoralizing. Out of a possible one hundred, can anyone conceive of a person making a score of 14.40? He suspected that a grade school drop out could do better than that. In 1958, he bought no books to study. He taped no materials to listen to, and he carried no little black books around containing important notes to keep him sharp. Yet, he scored 70 on the exam. In 1967, there was something wrong with the computing system at the Metro City Post Office, he thought. They made a mistake.

But if they made a mistake in 1967, they also made a mistake in 1968, and again in 1969. It was ridiculous what they did with his scores. These goddamned black ass niggers are a bunch of back street, carnival comedians, Jimmie said. It was a sick joke the way they played around with him. In 1968, they plotted a vast improvement in his scoring. They pushed it up all the way from 14.40 to 31.88. And in 1969, albeit slight, they gave it another nudge upward, awarding him a score of 35.68.

Jimmie thought that no white administration nowhere in the whole world could be as sadistic as these no good black bastards here at the Metro City Post Office. They were a bunch of barbarians. Not only did they cavort about in daylight pricking the wounds of the injured, they skulked about graveyards on dark nights smashing the bones of the dead.

He hadn't wanted to become a supervisor anyway, not even from the beginning, back in 1958. Why then, year after year, was he inviting for himself this humiliation? It was because of General Foreman G. F. Brim and Personnel Chief Bob Bell. Each time he had failed, they encouraged him to take the exam again. And they were responsible for the recurring embarrassment he was suffering. He was sure of that.

It was because of his suggestions, Jimmie reasoned. The Blockbuster, that's why. They want to embarrass me in front of the workers, make me look like a dummy. He remembered the ultimatum of Bessie Black and the Hatchet Ladies, how they had insisted he recall his Blockbuster. They gave four reasons why they disliked it.

First, they opposed Jimmie's Standardization idea requiring postal customers to mail their letters in a certain size envelope in order to increase letter sorting machine usage. It would cause a drastic reduction in force, they said. "It will take jobs away from blacks."

Second, they objected to Jimmie's idea that the dispatcher job be upgraded and put up for bid to anyone meeting the qualifications, man or woman. They claimed that Jimmie just wanted to see black women doing heavy and dirty work.

Third, they bitterly expressed their objections to Jimmie's claim that, because of their low educational level, most Metro City postal workers could not find work in the private sector making the same pay. And fourth, they thought that the whole idea of the Blockbuster was meant to prove that "blacks cain't run nothing."

Brim certainly agreed with the Hatchet Ladies, especially on the first and fourth points. Although Jimmie and Bell did not discuss these items, he was sure that Bell, too, was in agreement. In fact, he thought that, except for Postmaster Bill Brown himself, black Metro Post Office Management, across the board, agreed with the Hatchet Ladies.

Jimmie began to wonder if Bessie Black and the Hatchet Ladies had been hired by black management to harass him, make him look stupid. Maybe not from the start, he reasoned, but black management, now, was certainly encouraging them to continue. That is, black management wasn't forcing them to stop. He was sure of that, too.

In 1970, Jimmie had not recalled the Blockbuster nor any of its entries, but, obviously, black management thought that he had had enough and was about ready to come over to their side. So, they changed their tactics. They stopped antagonizing him with ridiculously low exam scores and gave him a passing one. Although black management had now qualified him, they had not completely refrained from embarrassing him. The passing score black management gave him in 1970, after all the comprehensive studying he had done, was identical to the 70 passing score the white management had given him in 1958 after doing no studying at all.

There was something about the 70 score that didn't quite ring true, Jimmie thought. He recalled a response Slick had made to him when he first came down to the Main Post Office nine years before. ("But you have to make 70 in order to qualify," Jimmie had said.

"That's the shit they tells you, man," Slick disagreed. "But all you have to do is have some bread and know the right people.")

Was Slick right? Did white management, back in 1958, try to get suggestion man Jimmie Jones off their backs by covertly putting him in a position whereby he could come over to their side by buying a supervisor job? Was that the significance of the 70 score? Was it the signal to start looking around for the guy to give the pay off money to?

If that was the case in 1958 with the white administration, did it still hold true in 1970 with the black administration? Would Jimmie really have to buy his supervisor job? That seemed an odd way to win over an honest, naive guy like Jimmie. Not only was it a long way around, it was risky. Jimmie was an above board and reproach kind of guy. Although he had not been inside a church in some 25 years, all his life he had been, truly, a sunday school boy.

Jimmie was a law and order kind of guy. He couldn't tell a lie if his life depended on it. And if he tried, everyone seeing his blinking, glaring eyes would immediately know he was lying. He didn't particularly want the supervisor job anyway.

To make him pay for a job he didn't really want in order to shut him up seemed a silly way to handle the situation. With naive law abiding Jimmie, instead of removing the obstacle, they would be creating one. He'd probably get a bull horn, go down on main street and yell it out to the whole town.

Chapter 8

Jimmie received a notice that he was to start attending supervisory training classes July 6, 1971. This would be the first time ever that such classes were conducted at the Metro City Post Office. It was unbelievable to him, both the inception of the classes, and that he had been chosen to attend.

Did this mean that he would not have to buy his supervisory job? Why did they not throw out the 1970 eligible list before calling him as they had done with the 1958 eligible list? Why were they obeying postal law by calling all eligibles before conducting another exam? Was it because they wanted him, along with his numerous suggestions, off their backs? Were they trying to buy him off? If that was the case, though, he was the buyer, for sure, not them. Without a doubt, he was buying his supervisory job, not with good old American currency, nonetheless, he was buying it.

How were the supervisory classes conducted at Metro City PO? Jimmie was not a Jazz musician. He played the cello. But, as an ardent jazz fan, he had caught many jazz sessions and knew how they functioned. Along with the rhythm background, soloists without a script, one after the other, paraded out on stage and improvised their offerings to the listener. This is how the 7/6/71 supervisory training classes were conducted at the Metro City Post Office.

The rhythm section was composed of the same kind of combination one sees on the evening televised newscasts, a white anchor dude in charge with his faithful black "Girl Friday" by his side.

At the MMPO, the number ten printed on a time card and the number ten stamped on slot ten on the time card rack meant nothing to the timekeeper. He'd put card number one in slot nine today and in slot 15 tomorrow. Likewise, numbers on the faces of wristwatches and clocks and the scheduled jam session time meant nothing to the Jazz musician, especially to the horn man, the star of the show. He came to the set when he got good and ready. So did the stars at the supervisory training classes. They came when they got good and ready.

Waiting for the first celebrity to arrive, the white anchor dude killed time by just talking a little about a lot of things while his black Girl Friday passed out copies (hand-outs) of the basic tune the first performer would improvise on. To get the full message of what these shrewd, parading play-it-by-ear postal lecturers were going to say, it was up to the student supervisors to sift through the tricky, syncopated rhythms, highly unorthodox phrasings and the terribly complex harmonizations and come up with the real thematic inter-pretation of what the performer was trying to say. The basic song: (hand-outs) the black Girl Friday was passing about was meant to help them accomplish that feat.

But it didn't quite work out that way. Most late reporting, im-provising jazz musicians are thoroughly skilled in their craft. But out of ten of these lecturing guys that paraded out on stage, only one knew what he was doing. Jimmie thought the remaining nine had not heard anything at all about the subjects they were trying to teach until that day. And to think they had the gall to attempt doing it by ear. But even with a script, he added, there is no doubt in my mind that it still would have been a disaster. "Where did they find these guys anyway?" he asked the rhythm section, "down on the dock?" Then he proceeded to tell them what he thought about the group of lecturers, and what he thought about the training classes in general.

The next morning when Jimmie got home at 7:30, Mary Belle was sitting at the kitchen table drinking a cup of coffee. It was Wednes-day, her day off. But she didn't seem happy about it. "Come on in, Mr. Super Star," she said with a wry smirk. "Your secretary got some messages for you."

"Somebody call?" Jimmie asked. Then he walked out into the kitchen and sat down at the table with her. "When?"

"Last night, after you went to work," she snapped. "You don't think it was this morning, do you?"

"Sometimes we get calls early in the morning," Jimmie reminded her. "You do, at least."

"Well, this was last night."

Jimmie did not want an argument. They were on the verge of one and he knew it. So he changed the course of the conversation. "Okay," he said, "who called?"

Mary Belle looked at Jimmie out of the corners of her eyes and pushed out a mischievous smile. "Your yellow ass cleaning woman for one," she said.

Jimmie felt sick to the stomach for a second. Had Goldie really called? He hadn't given her his number. But that was no real problem. It was listed in the telephone book. He didn't believe it, though. Goldie had told him in jest that she should call Mary Belle and introduce herself. She was kidding. He knew that. Yet, their relationship was rapidly working its way back to what it had once been. So far, the restraint on both sides had been remarkable. Had Goldie weakened? He didn't think so.

Yet, why would Mary Belle make such a crack if it wasn't true? Until only a few weeks before, he had not seen or heard from Goldie in seven years, not since he and Mary Belle got married. And Mary Belle had not mentioned the cleaning woman in almost three years. Why now? Did she really know that he was in contact with Goldie again? That she worked at the Post Office in the very same section with him? That several mornings he had brought her home? That they had made frantic love, like old times, at the Lakeland Hotel? Had she, or someone she hired, been following him?

Jimmie's mind quickly raced back seven years. It was as if Mary Belle had psychic power, he remembered. When she and Jimmie first started courting, she would call him on the phone from work only minutes before Goldie was to arrive at his place. Not only once, but almost everytime. When Goldie, a married woman whom he had been seeing for several years, would ring the doorbell and Mary Belle would ask who it was, he would reply that it was the cleaning woman.

What does this woman, my wife Mary Belle, know about my reborn relationship with Goldie? Jimmie asked himself, then answered. Nothing. Absolutely nothing. Then he recalled how scary it was seven years before when a video screen seemed to periodically pop up before her eyes revealing that Goldie was leaving her house and heading for his. But, at any rate, now, he'd play the nut role.

And he asked in a mock tone of surprise: "She did? What did the cleaning woman have to say?"

"Ah, your ass," Mary Belle said. "You think you so damn slick. That shit colored bitch better not call here."

Jimmie got himself a cup of coffee, took a couple of quick sips and set it on the table. "Well, I don't have any time to lose," he said. "Got that school job today. So, I'd better get with it." He headed for the bathroom to shave.

Jimmie was a cello player with the 35 piece Sanford concert orchestra which played music appreciation programs in Metro City public schools. Paid jointly by the musicians' union and Metro City community groups, the musicians received salaries well below scale. But it was worth it, Jimmie thought, Playing classical music for poor black ghetto kids who probably would never in their entire life have such a chance again.

"Don't you want to know who called your black ass?" Mary Belle asked.

"If you want to tell me," he answered. "Right now, I've got to get ready to get out of here. Burly school is on the far west side of town. It takes almost an hour to drive out there. I'm due there at nine. It's almost eight now.

Mary Belle yelled back to the bathroom at Jimmie, giggling. "How them supervisory training classes going, Mr. Postmaster?"

Ignoring her derision of him, Jimmie answered: "Like everything else at the Post Office. Disorganized, not planned and not thought out. They just up and do things," he complained, swishing the razor across his face, almost nicking himself. "And I told them about it, too."

"I know you did," Mary Belle railed back at him. "Why you got to try and run everything everywhere you go?"

Jimmie finished his shaving, left the bathroom for the bedroom where he put on his black suit, white shirt and black bow tie.

And Mary Belle continued to nag him. "Now you going out there and tell Mr. Sanford how to run his orchestra, huh?"

Jimmie took his black camel's hair overcoat off the rack, slipped into it, put his cello in the case, picked it up and started out the door.

"You coming straight home from the gig?" she queried him.

"What kind of question is that," he asked. "What else would I do after working all night, too?"

Mary Belle patted the vast inside area of one of her oversize loins "And you gonna work some more when you comes back here, too," she said.

Those words quickly jolted Jimmie into a notion of drastically changing his post concert plans. If he wasn't wearing a black suit, white shirt, black bow tie, and his black camel's hair overcoat; and if he didn't have his cello with him, having worked all night last night or not, he knew exactly what else he would do. He'd head straight for Carver Park. And there he'd rest in his car, undisturbed, for the rest of the day.

For Jimmie, having sex with Mary Belle right from the start, was pure torture. For seven long years, it had been torture. Not once during their marriage had he had a genuine desire to make love to her. He was living in a kind of hell. A hell that, through his own selfishness, he had wished upon himself.

Goldie had been one who slept with him during the day and had gone home to her husband at night. He felt that he was being used, locked up in an unnatural and irreversible situation. He was an enslaved stud. He had to free himself. He ran into Mary Belle. She was ready and willing. So they tied the knot. But now he realized that, for his freedom from Goldie, marriage to Mary Belle was a damnable price to pay.

But, he came back home, and, somehow, in bed with Mary Belle, he made it through the rest of the day. It wasn't easy. Sitting in the supervisory training classes listening to a string of inept, unprepared lecturers for two long weeks wasn't easy either. But he weathered that storm, too. At the end of the final session, the rhythm section white dude gave his rhythm section black Girl Friday a handful of small sheets of paper measuring three by five inches and instructed her to give one to each recruit. "There are four questions on the sheet of paper you hold in your hand," he said. "Please answer them and pass the sheet back in on your way out. Thank you and good luck."

Jimmie read the four questions: 1) What did you think of the class? 2) What did you like most about it? 3) What did you like least about it? 4) What suggestion do you have to offer? There was no way he could begin answering those four questions on a three by five sheet of paper. He knew that but he tried anyway. He ran out of room on the front side of the tiny sheet of paper, flipped it over and started writing on the opposite side. But it was simply no go. Still working on his answer to the first question, he soon found himself running off the back side, too.

He took an 8 1/2 by 11 sheet of paper, as an add-on, from his briefcase, clipped it to the scrawny three by five question sheet and started writing on it. The first question was what he thought about the class. They wanted to know, and he was telling them. He began to worry about his answer, though. He was now running out of space on the add-on sheet, and was reaching for another. As he did so, he made himself a promise: he would begin closing out his answer to the first question, and hit questions number two and three only lightly. For the question he really wanted to deal with, and the one for which he surely needed lots of space in which to effectively expound, was question number four: What suggestions do you have?" He added on an S to the word suggestion because he had many suggestions to offer.

He was sure that the other students had a lot of suggestions to make too. He looked around to see how much paper they were using on which to enter their answers. There was no one there. They all had turned in their tiny question sheets and gone. He was the only one left. He didn't care. So they were all gone. That was their business. They had to live their lives for themselves, and he had to live his life for himself. If he didn't do what he was doing, living with himself through long sleepless nights of regret would be no easy task. So he went on doing what he was doing.

He would now finish question number one, get his third sheet of add-on paper, make ready for a quick shot at questions two and three and, then, on to bonus question number four. But things weren't going to work out quite the way Jimmie was planning them. That is, if the rhythm section white dude was to have his say. And why should he not have his say? He was in charge of the classes.

"Mr. Jones?" he called out in an very impatient and demanding way. "The session has ended. The course has ended."

"Yes, I know," Jimmie responded. "But you wanted my opinion about..."

"So, hand it in, so we can all go home," he demanded, cutting Jimmie off.

"But I'm not through."

"Oh yes you are," the rhythm section white dude said. And thoroughly taking command, he waved a finger for the rhythm section black Girl Friday to pick up Jimmie's answers.

Jimmie reluctantly gave them to her, gathered up his belongings and walked out of the room. But that wasn't the end of it. When he got home, in the form of a very long and detailed letter addressed to the rhythm section white dude, to his satisfaction, he answered the questions but good, especially the fourth one.

As a relief supervisor, Jimmie was assigned to the zone section ZS-1, a processing unit originally designed to train new distribution clerks in the art of properly distributing letters into sorting cases. All mail processed in ZS-1 was city letter mail ZIP coded to a zone (carrier station) destination. For example, a letter addressed to the apartment building Jimmie lived in at 7002 Grove Street, Metro City, 00925 was destined for zone 25 and was sorted into pigeonhole number 25 on the sorting case.

Ordinarily, new clerks worked in ZS-1 until they learned the city scheme which enabled them to sort mail by address only, void of ZIP Code number. Then they would leave ZS-1 and work in the primary section (the line) which received both, mail that was ZIP coded and mail that was not.

ZS-1 was a section in the Main Post Office Building that time had caught up with. Maintaining it was no longer necessary for training new clerks, nor for any other purpose, as far as that mattered. In 1971, more than 80 percent of all letter mail was ZIP coded. Decode clerks (regular clerks) as well as code clerks (new clerks) worked coded mail. The physical separation of the two clerk types did not particularly enhance the mail processing procedure in any way. Because ZS-1 worked only ZIP coded mail in 1971, it was not only a non-essential entity but, for two reasons, it was a liability to American taxpayers.

The original United States mail coding system, or Zone as it was called, started in the early 1950s, was a two digit system. Those two digits represented only a zone (carrier station) within a city. In Metro City, there were 55 zones. ZIP Code, a five digit system, introduced about a decade later, was a money and time saving improvement over the two digit Zone system. For example, a letter bearing the zone number 25 simply meant that that letter should be sent to carrier station number 25 located in some city somewhere in the United States.

With the advent of the five digit ZIP Code number, it was a

different story. A distribution clerk in the New York City main post office, or any clerk in any American post office, processing a letter addressed to Jimmie Jones at 7002 Grove Street, Metro City, 00925 that bore no street number nor city name but only the name Jimmie Jones and the ZIP Code 00925, knew that the destination of that letter was Metro City. Why? Because, as the last two digits represented the zone destination, the first three digits represented the city destination.

The two reasons the ZS-1 section was a liability to American taxpayers was, first, 99 percent of all mail processed there was presorted mail. The mailer had packaged all mail going to, say, Chicago and to other cities in single separate containers, and all mail addressed to, say, zone 25 in Metro City, in single separate containers. The whole mail coding concept was designed to save taxpayers money by eliminating useless handlings of the mail. Because presorted mail had been sorted once, the time and labor spent in sorting it again compromised the money saving intentions of the U.S. Postal System.

Second, unnecessary time and labor costs, precipitated by the resorting of presorted mail was not the only financial loss; there was another one. The theory behind the presort concept was not unlike the theory behind the ZIP Code concept. It, too, was designed to cut down on mail handlings. Because the mailer sorted and packaged his own mail direct to city and/or zone destination, supposedly saving the Postal Service money, the mailer was granted a discount for his services. So, the costs for maintaining the ZS-1 section was a double edged sword: the discount costs in grants to mailers to sort their mail ahead of time, and the labor costs in payments to employes to sort the same mail again. Jimmie started a personal, verbal campaign in an effort to bring attention to the problem.

As Jimmie stood at his post serving the costly, duplicating activities of the ZS-1 section, he observed the swing supervisor approaching. He wondered why. Only minutes before, he had returned from his break. And it wasn't lunch time yet. Why was this guy coming to relieve him? Not being able to determine why he was being relieved, Jimmie threw it out of his mind. Obviously, he wasn't going to be relieved. The fellow coming his way was the same person who had just relieved him for his break. Maybe the guy laid his cigarettes or something down on his desk and walked off forgetting them. Now he was coming back to get them, Jimmie thought. He started rambling through the items strewned on his desk, looking for whatever the guy must have been coming back for.

But, as Jimmie proceeded into his search, the swing supervisor walked up and tapped him on the shoulder. "Hey, Jimmie," he said, "General Foreman Brim wants to see you in his office."

"About what?" Jimmie asked.

"I don't know,: he answered. "No one told me."

On his way to Brim's office, it came to Jimmie's mind that maybe Brim wanted to see him about his verbal expose of the wasteful ZS-1 activities. Yeah, that's it, he satisfied himself and started working on his defense, which of course wouldn't take much working. He'd simply tell Brim the truth, the way it was. But then the idea came to him that maybe it would not be about his lambasting of ZS-1 needless duplicating activities. It could very well be about his letter to the white rhythm section dude. He gave those supervisory training classes hell, too, he recalled.

So, then, he started working on his training letter defense. He remembered that he had tried to make three points in the letter. His first point was what he called The High Cost of Consensus. His second point was a charge that there was a Lack of Structured Universality. And his third was what he referred to as, Misplaced Individuality. By the time he reached Brim's office, he was pretty sure he had very well briefed himself on the two subjects, the ZS-1 expose, and the supervisory training letter. So, G.F. Brim, fire away, he said to himself as he entered.

"Come in, Mr. Jones. Have a seat," Brim said, greeting him. "How do you like being a supervisor?"

"It's a little early I guess for me to really tell," Jimmie responded, walking over to a chair to seat himself. "But I'm sure that once I get the hang of it, everything's gonna be okay."

"And what about your new assignment? What do you think of it?"

Oh, oh, here it comes, Jimmie told himself. He wants to discuss with me all those uncomplimentary things he's heard I said about ZS-1. "Well, I uh . . ." Jimmie started saying, wondering just how he should begin, whether with some circuitous conversation to soften the blow of how he really felt about the parasitic ZS-1 section, or if he should let it all hang out from the very start.

But Brim cut in with: "You can bring me up to date later on that, though. Because I know you like it. Anybody would. Nothing much to do over there with all that nice running mail (Running mail means mail that is sequentially and/or numerically presorted). But what I called you in here for, is something entirely different."

Oh, it's about the training letter, Jimmie thought. I can handle that, too, he told himself.

Brim didn't want to discuss that subject, either. "Did you hear any word yet from your Blockbuster suggestion," he asked, surprising him.

"Oh, uh, no, not yet," he finally stumbled out. "Don't know why it's taking so long." He recalled briefly his oversize flaps suggestion, in which he proposed the Postal Service make mail carrier satchel flaps larger and longer in order to protect mail from the inclement weather. Four years time had elapsed before they finally disapproved it, he remembered

"Do you have a carbon copy at home of the Blockbuster?" he asked Jimmie, "or did you submit your only copy? What has happened is, the Awards Committee reports to me that they have lost your suggestion."

"Lost it!" Jimmie exclaimed. "How could they! A one page suggestion getting lost, maybe I could see, but 98 pages. First, they lose my records about me qualifying on the 1958 supervisor's exam. Now they lose my master suggestion. Boy, have they got a bunch of dummies working at this place..."

"Now just take it easy; don't go getting all upset, calling names and placing blame," Brim scolded Jimmie. "Black people running this place now are no more dummies than the whites were that used to run it."

"I didn't say anything about black people running this place being dummies," Jimmie explained. "Where did you get that idea that I think they are dummies because they are black? I think they are dummies because they are not doing their jobs, not because they are black. And I think I have that right. Twice now, I am personally a victim of their ineptitude, ineptitude that could have a disastrous effect on my postal career, one that could change the entire course of my life "

"Now don't go getting overly dramatic about this thing," Brim said, trying to calm Jimmie down. "Nothing has happened to your

Blockbuster that can't be straightened out..."

"But you said they lost it, didn't you?" Jimmie asked, cutting in.

"Yes, that's what I said, but just keep still and listen to what I am saying now. What I want to tell you is, I'm going to do you a favor; that's why I called you in here. We can lick this thing, that is, if you are really sure that you have a carbon copy of your Blockbuster; now, do you?"

Brim's sudden parental approach put Jimmie on slight edge. "Sure, I have my carbon copy," he snapped. "I told you I did, didn't I?"

"Yes, but I want to be absolutely sure before I start the ball rolling," he warned Jimmie.

"Start the ball rolling? What do you mean?"

"I'm going to call down to the Awards Committe and alert them to what I am going to do so they will know. And now, here's what I want you to do," he instructed Jimmie. "Bring the carbon copy of your Blockbuster to me. I will personally take it down there myself. That way, you'll know it got there. Okay?"

Jimmie didn't quite know what to make of Brim's offer. Why was he being so cooperative and generous, he wondered. He couldn't give him his last and only copy. It was a rule he had made: not only never to relinquish his only copy, but to not ever take it out of the house. Yet, it seemed that that was what Brim wanted. He specifically asked for the carbon copy. Why did he not just say copy? Notwithstanding, the next night, Jimmie gave him his carbon copy, his carbon copy, but not his only copy. On a duplicating machine, at a library near his home, he had run off another copy for himself. "Here's the carbon copy of the Blockbuster," he told Brim the next night, as he handed it to him.

And seeing that the copy was indeed a carbon copy, like a small time conniver, Brim hurriedly took the document from Jimmie and started flipping through its pages. He, seemingly, wanted to make sure it was all there. "Now don't you worry," he gingerly consoled Jimmie. "This copy is going to get to the Awards Committe, because I am going to see to it that it does. I'm going to take it down there myself."

"Thank you, Mr. Brim," Jimmie said, and left his office.

He went back to his supervisory duties at ZS-1 somewhat a happy man, but not totally happy. He was pleased that Brim had promised to hand-carry his Blockbuster down to the Awards Committe, but the idea of Brim specifically requesting his carbon copy worried him. No matter what might happen, though, he told himself, I will still have a copy. Then, he vowed to himself that he was going back to his old way of doing things: making carbon copies in duplicate. That way, the home copy would surely never have to leave home.

Almost immediately, on his arrival back at ZS-1, his ambivalent happiness went afoul after what he found there. Woods department store out in Zone 50 was conducting a sale. Three trucks of the store's advertising circulars (circs), 40 trays each, were wheeled into ZS-1. Each and every one of those 120 trays were addressed to residents of Zone 50. Each and every circ in those 120 trays had been presorted in a location in Zone 50 and shipped from zone 50 down to the Main Post Office. Each and every circ in those 120 trays would now be resorted and sent back out to Zone 50.

Jimmie winced at the thought. What a waste. With great sympathy for American taxpayers, especially the poor, unemployed, and elderly taxpayers, he watched each of the 30 ZS-1 clerks casually stroll over and get a tray of circs from the storage truck, stuff pigeonhole 50 over and over again, retray the circs, and load them onto dispatch trucks to be shipped back out to zone 50 again.

Ticked off about such blatant waste, he could not wait until he got home. He immediately went to the office, got a suggestion blank, completed it and dropped it into the suggestion box.

When he walked up to take over his post at ZS-1 the next night, he was met by his swing supervisor. "I'm taking over," he told Jimmie. "General Foreman Brim wants to see you in his office."

"Again?" Jimmie exclaimed. He didn't ask the swing supervisor this time what G.F. Brim wanted. He knew the answer would be: "I don't know," whether he really did or not. It was a sick kind of game people played at MMPO. No matter who delivered the message to you, whether it be a supervisor, detail clerk, distribution clerk, or a mailhandler, if it was about reporting to the office, the message carrier clammed up when asked why. Such messengers, at once, became sadistic little animals who watched with giggling satisfaction as you stumbled on your way, wondering why you were being summoned.

As usual, Jimmie tried to come up with an answer of why G.F. Brim wanted to see him. It was about the Blockbuster, he thought.

Brim had received some news regarding it. He hoped it was good. But, then, he extrapolated that what Brim wanted to see him about was not news from the Blockbuster. It was too early. It was only yesterday that he had given him the carbon copy. No, there was something else on his mind.

It's got to be about the Training letter this time for sure, he calculated. Yeah, that's it, the Training letter. So, now let me prepare myself. My three primary points in that letter were, first, the High Cost of Consensus. The training classes began with a room full of participants asking questions and freely expressing themselves, he remembered. But after several days into the sessions, segments of students were rounded up and placed into groups.

Like tripping a gigantic damper to slow down the rapid growth of sparkling energy, the establishment of consensus groups immediately inflicted upon the class a case of acute conformity. Some group members became terribly confused. Some began losing confidence in what they were saying. And others, wanting only peace, accepted whatever decisions were forced upon them.

As Jimmie saw it, the goal of consensus was to destroy individuality. But, at the supervisory training sessions, it really did not. Consensus only displaced free will individuality with its own brand of individuality, Jimmie thought: consensus individuality. One member of the group Jimmie was assigned to, as did one member in every other group, sprang forward to become its leader. As Jimmie saw it, in almost every case, the group leader was either physically attractive, or a loud mouth like Hatchet Lady Bessie Black, characteristics that were far from being crucial elements in sound decision making. Yet, through that process, group leaders of the supervisory training classes were selected acquiescently. In his Training letter, Jimmie strenuously objected to this procedure.

Second, in his Training letter, Jimmie discussed the Lack of Structured Universality. At the MMPO, there were twelve floors of operations and three tours of duty. Because there was no direction from the top establishing standards, each of the 12 floor managers demanded his floor operate according to his personally outlined procedure. Each of the three tour directors demanded the same. And because no single method was adhered to, workers, especially when moving from floor to floor, and from tour to tour, were constantly confused as to just how to proceed at specific locations. This precipitated, across the board, great losses in man hours.

Third, Jimmie discussed Misplaced Individuality. As great latitude was afforded floor managers and tour directors, so was individuality granted to individual workers. "I don't do it that way; I do it like this" was the banal statement workers used when demonstrating what they deemed the only logical way to perform a particular job.

In summing up, as much as Jimmie detested consensus, he thought that perhaps if at the MMPO consensus was moved out of the class room into the board room, maybe there'd be some semblance of structured operational universality coming down from the top, and less rampant individuality coming up from the bottom. This would result in greater efficiency and improved productivity. So, consensus only in the class room, lack of universality in the board room, and rampant individuality in the work room were the three points of the Training letter Jimmie would discuss with Brim, so he thought.

On his arrival at Brim's office, Brim sternly said to Jimmie: "I tried to get the point over to you at our last meeting that black people need jobs. And I tried hard to impress upon you that that is what we try to do here, provide jobs for black people."

"And I thought all the time that what we were doing here was trying to get the mail out." Jimmie quipped back at Brim, not smiling but wanting to.

"This is not a laughing matter, Mr Jones," Brim reproached him.

Jimmie wasn't sure what Brim wanted. Although it was only yesterday he had given him his carbon copy of the Blockbuster, he thought that he might have some news about it.

But Brim took off in a different direction. "The Zone section was designed to teach recruit clerks the basics in the art of sorting mail," Brim told Jimmie, "to help them get started, to give them a chance in a simpler setting to learn their craft."

"Yes, you're right; that was the original purpose, I guess," Jimmie agreed. "But that was before the invention of the presort procedure where customers sort their own mail and package it prior to sending it to the Post Office. There is now, no longer any need for ZS-1."

"Oh yes there is," Brim disagreed. "That mail's got to be checked. Also, ZS-1 is a holding section, a pool in which these youngsters can function each night until such time they are called out to report to other assignments."

"You're right again," Jimmie conceded. "I agree. ZS-1 is truly a holding place. A holding back place, that is. It is a section where these youngsters just sit and watch the already sorted mail literally flow freely through their hands. Then they are called out to perform, in most cases, chores that are not necessarily a burden on the budget but are equally menial. And they are mindless and non-productive. Yes, it's a holding place all right."

"You're cute, Mr. Jones, real cute," Brim snarled back at Jimmie, then said. "Now, what I actually called you in here for is about the Woods department store mail. We had that mail brought in here because we have been receiving complaints that it is not being properly presorted."

"And if we find errors, then what?"

"We notify them."

"I'm glad you told me," Jimmie snidely remarked. "As a supervisor over there, I probably should know about that, wouldn't you think?"

As if a prizefighter engaged in the ring, feinting to dodge an opponent's blow, Brim flicked his head to one side. "Well, uh," he stumbled out. "Nobody told you?"

"If anyone did, I didn't hear it," Jimmie said. "And I've been listening pretty good, and seeing pretty good, too," he added, alluding to the number of ZS-1 workers and man hours required to needlessly resort presorted mail. "So we notify them," Jimmie continued prodding Brim, "then what?"

"Then what?" Brim asked, sounding like a broken record. "Nothing."

"You mean you do nothing?"

"What is there to do? Once we tell 'em, the ball is in their court. It's up to them, then, to get their act together."

Jimmie didn't go into details as to the several things he thought could be done, but he did say: "Woods presorted mail is not the only presorted mail we are resorting over there. Ninety nine percent of all the mail sorted in ZS-1 is presorted mail."

"It's necessary that we sort all mail coming into and leaving the facility," Brim instructed Jimmie. "We've got to cut down on our errors."

It was a weak argument. And from the feebly manner in which

Brim interjected it, he surely knew, as well as Jimmie, that it had no teeth. Of the 99% presorted mail resorted in ZS-1, perhaps less than one percent were errors.

"But resort presorted mail?" Jimmie earnestly asked. "Think of the unnecessary expense to taxpayers. Thirty people, 24 hours a day, eight hours on our tour and eight on each of the other two. Twenty four hours a day, marking time. I have two points to make about that..."

"Don't lecture me," Brim sharply cut Jimmie off. "I've got two points to make, too. One, too many black people are out of work. And two, they need jobs..."

"What do your two points have to do with my two points?" Jimmie asked, cutting back in. "I'm talking greater efficiency and improved productivity."

"You're talking cold facts and figures," Brim charged. "I'm talking morality. It's morally wrong, utterly shameful for so many black people to be out of work, while whites have more jobs available to them than they can shake a stick at. So, what do my two points have to do with your two points?" he asked Jimmie Back. "Nothing. Absolutely nothing. As I told you before, most black people don't care one iota about efficiency and productivity, especially when it's taking away their jobs. And that's what you are talking about, a reduction in force, taking jobs away from black people. The rights of black people must be respected," Brim pounded At Jimmie, sounding like a store front Baptist preacher.

"You speak of facts and figures, and the rights of black people," Jimmie challenged Brim. "Suppose we take a look at some facts and figures, and the rights of black people. First, some facts and figures. For example, 1) The 35,000 Metro City postal workerforce is ninety eight percent black. 2) Of the 20,000 main installation workers, 2,000 are absent from work each day. 3) Contrary to meeting the production standard of sorting three trays of mail an hour, many indolent distribution clerks sort less than one tray an hour. And 4), although the work standard is far from met, and notwithstanding the 2,000 daily absences, the mail still gets out, and the production sheets are balanced.

"Now, what do those figures tell us, Mr. Brim?" Jimmie asked, rhetorically. "In my opinion they say loud and clear that at this place, it's not efficiency and productivity. It's hanky panky."

"Where did you get those figures?" Brim harshly asked.

"Oh, I came by them," Jimmie responded with a smile, furtively confident.

"Well, there're not right," Brim disputed, but with little energy, and no follow up.

"I have given you some facts and figures about conditions here," Jimmie further challenged Brim. "Now, suppose you outline for me some of those rights for black people you so eloquently spoke about that must be respected. Also, tell me, on what grounds you demand those rights."

"Moral rights," Brim shot back. "That's what I'm talking about. Black people are human beings; they deserve certain rights. And a decent job with which they can make enough money to take care of their families, is one of those rights..."

"So, because black people are human beings, they should be taken care of, huh? Is that what I hear you saying?" Jimmie interjected. "We live in a world of qualification and performance, Mr. Brim. People are usually rewarded in accordance with their education and ability, not because of race..."

"I tell you again, Mr. Jones, don't lecture me," Brim interrupted angrily.

"I am not lecturing you," Jimmie objected. "I am only pointing out to you, as you are pointing out to me, what I believe to be the right thing."

"So you believe taking jobs away from blacks is the right thing, huh?" Brim asked Jimmie with a bit of reprehension in his voice. "Well, that's where you and I differ, my friend. I think it's morally wrong."

"You keep talking about morals, Mr. Brim, what about the facts and figures I just gave you? 2,000 employes are absent from work every day. Manual distribution clerks, instead of meeting the standard of sorting three trays of mail an hour, average less than one an hour. Mail is weighed and counted two, three and four times. And, as one of your supervisors, at the end of the tour, I am asked, as are all other supervisors here, to balance my production sheet whether it actually reflects what happened in my section or not. Are those the moral rights of black people you are talking about that must be respected, the big lie that you, I, and 35,000 other Metro City black postal workers are living everyday?"

Jimmie paused for a brief moment. He was reminded of the recurring argument between his two station mates Slick and Johnnie Mae, where Slick declares that: ("That ain't no special no more. I tells yall that all the time. It's coming back." And Johnnie retorts: "I don't care, you still hold it out.")

"And back to my two points, efficiency and productivity, what do you have to say about clerks working here, whom you say need these jobs, who don't know what to do with undeliverable airmail and special delivery letters? Who don't know what to do with a registered letter found in the regular mail? Who don't know what a philatelic letter looks like? You speak of the rights of black people, what about the rights of the Postal Service which is promised a knowledgeable worker? And the taxpayer who is entitled to a fair return for his dollar?"

Brim didn't concede the argument to Jimmie, but this battery of questions caused him, later, to approach Willie Moses, supervisor of Section GS-48S and ask: "Mr. Moses, what do you know about Section GS-48S?"

"What do you mean, what do I know about Section GS-48S?" Moses answered, set aback.

Brim took Moses by the arm and led him away from the podium, out into the center of the main aisle, beyond the hearing distance of clerks working in the section. They stood beneath conveyor belts over which 40 pound tubs of flat mail (large envelopes) were being transported. And because of the continuous noise the clanking tubs and bouncing belts were making, they had to talk louder there. Yet, clerks in GS-48S still could not hear them.

"This fellow, Jimmie Jones, made a suggestion that a training program be instituted for secondary manual clerks," Brim informed Moses. "He says these clerks don't know where return air-mail and return special delivery letters ought to be sorted. He says that they would not know what to do with a registered letter if they found one out there in the regular mail. Also, he says that some of them don't even know what a philatelic letter looks like. What about that, Mr. Moses, do they?"

Supervisor Moses was slow about answering.

"Speak up, man. Speak up," Brim scowled.

But the only thing Moses came out with was, "Well, uh, I, uh."

Brim scowled again. "Well, do they or don't they?"

"I, uh, I really haven't checked them out to that extent "

"To what extent?"

"To the extent you mentioned.'

"To what extent, then, have you checked them out?"

"Well, uh, things, uh. We're getting along." Moses said. Then he tried making a feeble attempt at flipping Brim over on the defense "We're getting the mail out, ain't we?"

Brim yelled out loudly, then quickly covered his mouth. "I'm not talking about getting the mail out. I'm talking about clerks not knowing what to do with undeliverable air-mail and specials, and registered letters found in the regular mail; and about not knowing what a philatelic letter looks like, that's what I'm talking about."

Moses rammed his hands down deep into his pockets, both of them, then took them out, scratched his head, lit a cigarette and just held it burning in his hand without taking one puff off it.

Brim continued to pump him. "Well, what about it, Mr. Moses?' he bellowed through gritted teeth. "Do the clerks know what to do with that mail?"

Moses's face flushed full red. And he lied. "Ah, yeah, sure. They know."

"How do you know they know?"

"I know."

"Okay. So you know they know. Is that right?"

"Oh, sure. I know they know," supervisor Moses said, but not convincingly.

"Okay," Brim said. "Now, I'm going to ask you the obvious question. Do you know?"

Moses danced a little nervous jig, turned his body from side to side, and asked in a voice that was unbelievably unsteady: "Do I know what?"

Before answering Moses's question, Brim's clouded up face revealed his intense impatience. Then, seemingly, at the very top of his voice, he screamed. "Where an undeliverable air-mail or an undeliverable special delivery letter goes, that's what!!"

The clanking of the heavy tubs of mail moving along the conveyor belts overhead could not contain the shattering sound of Brim's rising voice this time. Every clerk in GS-48S looked his way. They might not have understood his words, but they surely heard his shouting voice.

Moses backed away. It was obvious that anger was building up in him, too. He clinched his right hand into a fist and rammed it hard into his pocket to hide it from Brim. "What is this!" he shot back at Brim, his voice sounding shrill and strained. "What are you trying to do?"

Brim cupped a piece of paper in his hand that had been folded several times into a small square. On it, he had jotted down several of the things Jimmie had discussed in the suggestion about establishing a training program especially for secondary manual clerks. And he had the answers to the questions he was asking written down on that piece of paper. He glanced down at the piece of paper and asked Moses: "When a clerk finds a piece of registered mail in with the regular mail, what is he supposed to do with it?"

Moses stammered out, "Well, he's suppose to, uh . . ."

Brim fired a second question at him before he could answer the first one. "And what about clerks writing on the cover of philatelic mail?"

Moses looked puzzled. "On what?"

Brim yelled back: "Philatelic mail." This time his voice was like a trumpet sounding out revelry to the residents of a wilderness army camp. There was no question that not only did clerks in GS-48S section understand his words this time but so did people passing by and clerks in other sections, too. "You know what that is don't you?" Brim continued.

Moses's puzzled face suddenly lit up. "Oh, you mean the mail those stamp collectors get. Right?"

"Yeah, that's what I mean," Brim gruffly agreed. "So, what about writing on the cover?"

Moses gave Brim a slightly puzzled look again. "On the cover?" he asked, seemingly, stalling for time.

Brim briskly gave his boney thigh several good licks with his open palm and snorted out through tightly closed teeth. "Yes, the cover. The face of the letter. The envelope."

Moses face lit up again. "Oh, the envelope?"

"Yes, the envelope," Brim answered, sounding winded of breath. "Why were your clerks writing on philatelic envelopes?"

Moses raised his shoulders, pushed his chest out and made a couple steps toward Brim. "Oh, that," he said. "I know what you mean, now. The clerks know all the stamp collectors out in Galova

Township by name," he said, and hastened to add. "And they know the addresses, too, because they get so much mail from all over the world, with all kinds of attractive stamps and envelopes..."

Brim broke in. He spoke in a low, pleading voice that inflected as he went on. "Yes, yes, Mr. Moses. Why in hell were they writing on the damn letters?"

"Some mail came through here about three weeks ago for one of the stamp collectors," Moses explained. "It was in bundles, three or four big ones. When the clerks cracked open the bundles they found that half the letters had names written on them but no addresses. One clerk brought a hand full of them up to the desk, told me that she knew the address, and asked me if she should write it on the letters so the carrier would know where to deliver them. I looked at the letters. They were from France. The envelopes were fancy and so were the stamps. They were really exotic. I just knew the guy couldn't wait to get his hands on them. And I knew they could bounce around here in directory for weeks before the directory people would finally come up with the right address. And I knew that in the meantime, they'd get all dirtied up."

Moses stuck his chest out a little bit further and, in continuing, said with great pride: "It's our job to expedite the mail. So, I told her to go ahead and write the addresses on the letters and shoot them through." He looked at General Foreman Brim as if expecting a big pat on the back. Also, he glanced at the piece of paper cupped in Brim's hand. It must be a note from the philatelic guy thanking me, Moses, seemingly, thought.

Brim was surely all choked up, too, at hearing this news from Moses. Not with gratitude, though, but with rage. Like a kid's flabby balloon refusing to take air because it has a hole in it, the quickened breaths of anger from Brim's frail, hunched body made a series of short funny sounds. For a moment he said nothing. He just stood there.

Then, he yelled at the very top of his voice. "Don't you know you are not supposed to write on philatelic..." then quickly realizing that he was being heard near and far, he said in a quiet but definite tone: "Philatelic mail is mail that stamp collectors, ah what's the use," he snapped in disgust. "Get yourself a pencil and a piece of paper and come into my office," he ordered Moses. "I got some things here I want you to copy down. Things, dammit, I want you to remember."

Later that night Jimmie's swing supervisor told him that General Foreman Brim wanted to see him in Sonny Blake's office. Why did Brim want to see him in the Director of Operations' office, he wondered. He left the ZS-1 section and started on his way.

When he got there, Sonny Blake's secretary directed him to the conference room. He opened the conference room door with caution, and walked in. Five black men managers, one a monster of a man, sat in silence at a very long, wide table. Sonny Blake, came in from an ajoining office through a side door and sat at the head of the table.

And prancing about the room in a dither, was General Foreman Brim. "It looks like my last little talk with you didn't do much good," Brim said to Jimmie.

"How do you mean?" he asked.

Brim pointed to a group of papers stacked on the conference room table in front of Sonny Blake. "You are still making these wide sweeping suggestions," he said.

"And I told you that I don't know how else to make a suggestion, but to tell it as I see it . . ."

"Gentlemen! Gentlemen!" Sonny Blake interrupted. "Let's calm down. We aren't going to get very much of anything settled this way."

Short of build and carrying normal weight, Sonny Blake was commonly referred to as the Big Man simply because he had a big job. He was the Director of Operations. In the chain of command, he stood right next to the Postmaster himself.

Most MMPO workers did not consider Sonny Blake only a charismatic figure and a big boss, they considered him a saint. "He looks out for his peoples," Johnnie Mae had said proudly. "Ain't gonna let none uh these jive ass nigger supervisors get nobody fired. It hurts him to see black folks out of work and on relief and everything. If it wuz left to him, and baby I show wish it wuz, he would go and get every black lady and black man in Metro City that wants to work, and give 'em a job right here at Metro City Post Office."

And Slick had agreed with her. ("Specially all them pretty little young girls out there The cock hound.")

"Suppose we try to understand one another," Sonny Blake encouraged the two combatants. "First, Mr. Jones, do you know why you are here?"

"From what Mr. Brim says, it seems that I'm here because of my suggestions. He thinks they are too wide sweeping," Jimmie said as the seven black Lords continued to probed him for more than an hour.

On leaving the conference room, for a fleeting moment, Jimmie had thoughts of greed on his mind. If these guys really wanted to deal, why didn't they put something on the table? he wondered.

My suggestions are not $250 penny ante offerings of fixing holes in floors to prevent injury to employes and to avoid damage to equipment. To name only two, my suggestions are about 1) Standardization of letter mail to up the use of letter sorting machines from six hours a day to 24 hours a day and 2) to consolidate dispersed, generically related sections in order to cut in half the costs of the handlings of mail, and its transportation.

And there are two significant high stake elements about my efficiency-productivity suggestions: 1) not only will they save taxpayers millions of dollars, but 2) some day, they may very well be instrumental in determining whether the black Metro City postal administration will remain in power or be forced to give the reins of power back to whites.

If they had offered me a job of Tour Director or Floor Manager to stop making what they term "wide sweeping" suggestions, you never can tell, Jimmie thought, I might have listened. Who knows, I might have even listened, if for the same, they had offered me a General Foreman job.

But no, these seven black Lords are men of force. They didn't say it. But they didn't have to. It wreathed from their condemning stare and dripped from their accusing words: ("We gave you a supervisory job. Isn't that enough, buddy? If it isn't, we're sorry, because that's all you're going to get.") Well, I didn't capitulate. So what are they going to do, now, sic the Hatchet Ladies on me again? Or are they going to change their tactics this time and send a couple of hoods out to try and beat me into submission?

Suddenly, Jimmie got mean. Is that all they are willing to offer me to refrain from making million dollar suggestions, a crummy supervisory job? He bit his own lip as he made an obscene gesture and shouted out: They can shove it.

Then, crowding out the remembrance of what had happened in the conference room was the recall by Jimmie of these words that had been uttered by Hatchet Lady leader Bessie Black: ("To hell with efficiency and productivity, what black folks needs is jobs.") And for a moment, he warmly empathized. These people do need jobs, including even the non-intellectual. If the vacuous minds of some blacks don't earn them jobs today, the hard working, callous, bleeding hands of their forefathers 200 years ago certainly did earn it for them, if not the job, Jimmie thought, and preferably so, a reasonable cash facsimile.

Spokeswoman Bessie Black had branded Jimmie a traitor. Was he really a traitor? he wondered. What is a traitor anyway? he asked himself. He thought he knew. Just the same, he looked it up in his pocket dictionary: "One who betrays another's trust or is false to an obligation," it said.

In Jimmie's opinion, the dictionary pointed up a kind of paradox. Bessie Black and those opposing him and his Blockbuster concept of greater efficiency and improved productivity based their charges on what they thought was a breach of ethnic responsibility. Jimmie was a black man whom they claimed was initiating a plan to "take jobs away from blacks." They felt very secure in accusing him of being "false to an obligation."

On the contrary, Jimmie argued that a consciousness of efficiency and productivity by blacks would be considered an act of being "true to an obligation." Taxpayer money saved in the maintenance of a well managed Post Office would benefit everybody. The Metro City black populace had few major victories of any sort of which to be proud. Bringing the Post Office up out of the red into the black would be an immense psychological boost to them, he thought.

No, I'm not a traitor, he proudly announced. And, mentally he went back to the conference room again. He saw black Lord G.F. Brim still cavorting about the floor. And he looked over at black Lord Sonny Blake, attired in his expensive suit, imported shoes and tie sitting at the long, wide table with the other five black Lords and he said to Sonny Blake: I am their guardian angel. Not you. Me.

And he loudly proclaimed that: Tomorrow, the same people who hate my guts today, including some of you in this very room, may not declare in public that my efficiency productivity concept for Metro City black postal management was a good idea, but in your inner repenting souls, you'll know the truth.

Chapter 9

Goldie usually drove herself to work, but this April night in 1972 she didn't. Approaching Jimmie at his ZS-1 supervising post, she asked: "Will you take me home in the morning?"

And Jimmie responded with: "You didn't drive?"

"No."

"Why? Something wrong with your car?"

"No."

A shadow of wonderment partially veiled Jimmie's face as he asked: "Well why didn't you drive, then?"

Goldie gave him a goo goo side glance and said in a short inviting tone, "Because I didn't want to."

"You didn't want to?"

"No."

Jimmie's face became more veiled of wonderment. And he asked: "But why didn't you want to drive?"

Goldie was thoroughly familiar with Jimmie's naivete, and how he rarely ever probed beneath the smooth surface of things looking for jagged edges. This undying confidence he had in the honesty of human nature Goldie appreciated and admired. Although sometimes, it irked her.

But one didn't have to probe deeply to solve Goldie's little scam of not driving to work. Those hidden jagged edges were almost up on top of that smooth surface of things right there for even a disinterested bystander to figure out. But she knew by now that her straight thinking lover man wasn't going to figure out anything. It didn't appear that he was. So she let out with it: "I did not drive because I want you to take me home. Any objections?

"Jimmie's face quickly threw off its veil of wonderment and lit up with approval. "Objections?" he asked her back. "Yes, if you try to back out of it."

And Goldie did not try to back out of it. At 6:42 the next morning, they punched out together and headed straight for Pete's parking lot.

It had been several years since Bessie Black and the Hatchet Ladies, armed with switchblade knives, had attempted to ambush Jimmie in the parking lot. It was probably because of the star studded gun slinging defense he countered with that morning that they had not. However, Jimmie didn't think they'd ever try it again. They may surprise him by doing it somewhere else, but not down there in Pete's parking lot, he thought. But just in case, every morning on the way to get his car, he had his eyes open looking everywhere. And that April morning, with Goldie holding on to his arm, was no different.

"You still remember, don't you?" she asked with concern.

"You can tell, huh?" he responded, wondering how. But there were no Hatchet Ladies waiting for Jimmie, and when they reached his car, they found all four tires fully inflated.

"I don't want you to just take me home," Goldie said warmly, getting into the car. "I'd like for us to stop someplace and talk if only for a few minutes."

Jimmie knew exactly what Goldie meant by talk. She was not only a hyper-feminine person, she was an overly affectionate one. She wanted him to hold her, caress her, and tell her how much he loved her.

"I know I see you at work, and we do talk," she added. "But it's so careful, distant and impersonal. Also, I know you say that Mary Belle goes crazy if you are a few minutes late getting home from work. I know that I must fix Paul's breakfast before he leaves for work, And best of all, I know that we are going to meet later today at the Lakeland Hotel. But before I go home this morning, I just want to be near you, no matter how short the time might be."

As Jimmie pulled the car out of the parking lot, he thought to himself: And oh how short the time has got to be. It was Monday, not Wednesday, Mary Belle's day off. She should be gone to work when I get home, he calculated. But you never know about her. Of late, she surprises me quite frequently, staying home, not telling me in advance. Crazy chick, standing there with a watch on her wrist and a clock in her hand waiting to sling the door open as soon as I put my key in the lock so she can tell me I'm five minutes late. Stupid. So, regretfully, he said to Goldie: "As long as we get home by the usual time, just in case she decides to surprise me this morning."

"That's fine with me," Goldie agreed. "You know our time is always quality."

"How well do I know, baby," he told her and headed straight for Carver Park, to the spot where he regularly hid out to avoid having sex with Mary Belle on some of those days she surprisingly stayed home from work, and to the same spot where he and Goldie occasionally held their secret rendezvous.

Sitting in the car in Carver Park, now, after Jimmie had driven them there at an anxious rate of speed, Goldie cuddled up very closely to him. "You know, I'll never forget the Post Office," she said with great admiration. "I love that place."

At the sound of the term Post Office, a sad expression came over Jimmie's face. How putrid, he thought. The conference room scene quickly flashed before his eyes. He could plainly see the faces of the 7 black Lords, including play boy Sonny Blake and desiccated G.F. Brim. They wanted him to refrain from making what they termed wide sweeping suggestions, he remembered.

"If I had not come to work at the Post Office, I might not have ever seen you again," Goldie continued. "For that, to the Post Office, I'll always be grateful."

And so would Jimmie. They embraced for a few minutes and rededicated themselves and their infinite love to one another. Then they went home and met later that day at the Lakeland Hotel, where they made love well past the state of exhaustion.

When Jimmie woke up that evening, it was almost time for him to leave for work. The alarm of the clock had sounded, but he didn't hear it. In disbelief, he checked to make sure it really had.

"What cha looking at?" Mary Belle asked. She was sitting in a nearby chair. "Ain't nothing wrong with it," she informed Jimmie. "It 'larmed lak it suppose to; you jes didn't hear it, that's all. What cha been doing all day anyhow that makes you so sleepy you cain't hear the 'larm go off? Laying up with the Scrubwoman, huh? Right?"

Suddenly, Jimmie had the feeling that someone was clubbing him over the head with some kind of heavy object. But it was a colossal sense of guilt, that's what it really was, and of suspicion. Jimmie thought that there was only one chance in a million that Mary Belle could know that he was seeing Goldie again. Did she? What was it with this woman? he wondered. Was she really psychic? Seven years before when they first met, Mary Belle seemed to know the day of the week and the time of the day he was to see Goldie whom he had been courting long before meeting her.

After not mentioning her for about three years, several months before when he saw Goldie for the first time in seven years, Mary Belle promptly brought up her name. Now, again, on the very same day he had been at the Lakeland Hotel having sex with Goldie, she accused him of exactly that, having sex with Goldie.

"You had a bath yet?" Mary Belle asked Jimmie, getting up out of the chair and walking toward him. "Come here, let me check you out, see what cha been doing all day."

"Ah woman, what are you talking about?" he growled, pushing her to one side. "I don't have any time for your silly comedy; I've got to shave so I can get out of here to work. You sat there and listened to the alarm go off and didn't wake me up. Now I've got to rush in order to make it on time. So please dispense with the antics."

"Ah, don't be getting so uptight. You got plenty time. You ain't gonna be late going nowhere. But you go on and shave; I ain't gonna bother you. But if I really thought you been out with that yellow bitch, don't think for one minute I wouldn't check out your black ass. And if you ain't had no bath, you better believe it, baby, I would know. And even if you did have a bath, I bet cha I'd still know."

But whether Mary Belle believed or didn't believe, whether she knew or didn't know, the reality and the accuracy of her recurring psychic implications were a harrying experience for Jimmie. As proof, although he made no visible show of it, he was glad he had wisely taken a bath when he arrived home from the Lakeland Hotel. And, although Mary Belle had declared: "If I thought you really been out with that yellow bitch" that she would not hesitate to check out his "black ass," she continued accusing him. And non stop. The whole time, through his shaving and dressing, she heckled him about Goldie.

When he walked out the door for work and politely said to her: "See you later, baby," she was still at it

Giggling, she asked: "You mean you really going to work? You looks lak you needs to go back to bed. That little yellow whore sho must uh worked you over but good. How long yall do it anyhow? huh?"

All the way to work, Much like a lingering case of tinnitus, Mary Belle's heckling voice rang steadily in Jimmie's ears. Registering pointedly with him was her remarks about, what appeared to her, his weakened bodily condition. The first thing he did on entering the building, even before going to his locker, was to duck into the men's washroom and get a peek at himself in the broad mirror that covered the room's south wall. It was not a floor to ceiling mirror. It showed only his bust and face. Yet, he saw nothing wrong or weak appearing about the part of his body that came into view.

He knew when Mary Belle had had sex with someone, including with himself. It was that hazy milk like film he thought he saw formed over her right eye. It seemed to push her upper eyelid outward to form a kind of canopy that cast additional shadows. And it lingered there for several days. Was there some similar facial anomaly about him that revealed to her that he had had sex with Goldie earlier that day? He examined his face thoroughly, but saw nothing unusual about it. So, he threw it out of his mind, went to his locker and on to his post at ZS-1.

The Zone Section was a double section, composed of ZS-1, Jimmie's section, and ZS-2 which was located right in the next aisle. ZS-2 was more of an overflow aisle. During unusual heavy periods, such as the Christmas holiday season when additional clerks were needed to sort the increased volume of mail, a second supervisor would be called in, and ZS-2 would be pressed into use. Other times, it stood vacant.

It was a habit with Jimmie. Each night, once he got all set up, and ZS-1 was operating smoothly, he'd make a check of ZS-2. It wasn't a structured check, adhering to some specialized procedure where he'd walk down the aisle examining things. It wasn't even official. It was more of a personal curiosity check. He'd just walk over, take a quick look down the empty aisle and promptly return to his post back at ZS-1

But, on this April Monday night, he didn't take a quick look down the empty aisle and promptly return to ZS-1, because the ZS-2 aisle was not empty. And that night, his personal curiosity check turned immediately into a structured one. This time, he did walk down the aisle examining things. Or more correctly, he climbed down the aisle, as far as he went, examining things.

Jammed into ZS-2, from front to back, were 25 hand trucks fully loaded with Woods store advertising circulars (circs). And taped on to the front center truck, as well as on each of the remaining 24, was a three foot square sign hand printed in bold white and red letters. He read it. "Hold, do not sort," it said. As Jimmie stood there trying desperately to figure out what the sign really meant, the ZS Section telephone, attached to the post standing between the two aisles of the double section, started ringing. He walked over and picked up the receiver.

"Supervisor Jimmie Jones here," he said.

"Mr. Jones? This is General Foreman Brim," the voice coming through the line, said. "I'm calling you about the Woods mail stored in ZS-2. Did you see it there, yet?"

"Yes I did," Jimmie answered. He stopped short of telling Brim that he made a cursory check of ZS-2 every night he worked, but he did say: "How could I help but see 25 trucks of mail jammed into a single aisle designed to afford space for five, at most?"

"So you did," Brim said, sardonically. "So you did. You even counted the trucks, huh? What about the trays of mail? Did you count them, too?"

"Funny that you should ask," Jimmie answered in a not so smooth tone. Then, he responded to a ridiculous question with a ridiculous answer. "Yes I did."

"How many were there?" Brim asked in an angered tone. For he knew that Jimmie, according to usual procedure, had not counted each individual tray, but had counted trays on a single truck, and calculated from there the total number.

And Jimmie had done exactly that, except that he didn't precisely count any trays at all, not even those on the front center truck. The capacity for hand trucks was 40 trays of mail. When they were stacked properly, eight trays five tiers high, and the Woods trays of mail were, there was no need for counting. Only a general visual observation was necessary. "There were one thousand trays, sir," he told Brim. "One thousand."

Due to the derisively, comical mood Brim, seemingly, was in,

Jimmie thought he might ask the outrageously, ridiculous question of whether or not he counted each individual letter. And Jimmie was ready and waiting for him on that, too. But Brim did not accommodate him. He must have realized how utterly ridiculous it all must have seemed. Instead, he went on with the reason he had called. But as far as Jimmie was concerned, the next question Brim put before him was almost as silly as the others.

"Did you see the signs on the trucks," Brim asked, hesitating, as if he surely thought he shouldn't have.

How did this man ever become a General Foreman, Jimmie wondered. There's a three foot square glaring white and red sign on each of the 25 trucks, and he wants to know if I saw them. How stupid! Now, he'll probably ask if I read the signs, and if we're working any of the mail.

It was good for Jimmie that his boss was not psychic, as his wife Mary Belle seemed to be. Because the answer on his mind was: Hell naw, stupid. With 25 roadside signs lighting up the aisle, any dummy, even you, would know not to work that mail, But he simply said, even before he was asked: "We're not working any of this mail."

"That's good," Brim said, approving his actions. "Hold off until I give you the word to process it. In the meantime, we'll just leave it stored there, okay?"

This was the second time Brim had used the word stored, and Jimmie pried him to explain. "Stored?" he asked. "What do you mean by that?"

"Just what it sounds like," Brim shot back through the line. "That mail is not to be worked right away. It's in storage. You know what storage means, don't you?"

"Yes, I know what storage means," Jimmie curtly responded. "The point is, I didn't think we were in the storage business. I thought our business was not holding the mail but delivering it, and as expeditiously as possible," he emphasized. "Even junk mail, such as this."

"And that's what we're going to do," Brim promised Jimmie. "And, as you put it, as expeditiously as possible."

"With it standing over there not being worked, I don't know how you're going to do that."

"The Woods sale doesn't start for ten days yet," Brim told him. "If their circs are delivered now, when the sale date rolls around, people will have forgotten about it. So the Woods people asked us to hold them until the day before the sale begins, then deliver them."

"But if the sale doesn't begin for another ten days, why did they ship the mail in here now?"

"Somebody over at Woods goofed. They ordered the printing of the circs too early. Woods doesn't have sufficient storage space, so they made arrangements with the Post Office to accept the circs and hold them until the release date."

"But suppose we need that space, then what?"

"Suppose we need that space for what?"

"For working mail, that's what. I mean, suppose we get enough mail where we would have to open up ZS-2, what would we do then?"

"This is April, not December," Brim reminded him. "We aren't gonna get that much mail, and you know it."

In reality, Jimmie agreed. With the MMPO bloated workforce, and its minimum workload, it surely wasn't likely. Just the same, he told Brim: "You never know."

"Believe me, we won't," Brim guaranteed.

Now, Jimmie put to Brim the question he had wanted an answer to all along. "You asked me if I knew the meaning of the term storage, now I ask you: Does the Postal Service charge a fee for providing such service?"

"That's out of your league. You don't worry about that," Brim snapped back. "You just do your job of supervising and let management do its job of managing."

"I am not only a supervisor here. I am also a taxpayer. And as such, I'm entitled to worry about how my tax dollars are being spent, especially, for the benefit of millionaires."

"Mr. Jones, how many times must I tell you?" Brim asked with added force resounding in his voice. "Black people need jobs. Big customers like Woods, provide those jobs. For that specific reason, we've got to keep them happy. A little favor here and there, doesn't hurt anything."

"You call storing a thousand trays of mail for ten days, a little favor? What do you think he'd get charged outside in private industry for that kind of service?"

"Now you just butt out, Mr. Jones," Brim shouted back through the line at him. "I told you, this is no concern of yours. You just supervise. Let us do the managing, okay?"

"And I told you, that I am a taxpayer, helping to take up the slack of all this waste."

"Taxpayers don't run the Post Office," Brim informed Jimmie.

"No," he agreed. "But they pay for its running."

"But they don't run it," General Foreman kept pounding at Jimmie.

"Okay, then," Jimmie kept pounding back, "you say that, as a supervisor, I should let management handle it; you say that, as a taxpayer, I don't run the Post Office. Well, there's a third thing that I am that certainly grants me the privilege to speak out."

"Yeah?" Brim asked cavalierly. "And what's that?"

"A postal employe, that's what, one who is bound by the Code Of Ethical Conduct decree. And it says that I should not only 'give a full day's labor for a full day's pay,' but that I should seek to 'find and employ more efficient and economical ways of getting tasks accomplished.' And, on top of that," Jimmie added, " it says that I should 'expose corruption wherever discovered.'"

"Okay, Mr. Jones, you have made your point." Brim said in a half restrained voice. "And management has made its point. Now, if you will, please go back to your post."

Jimmie hung up the receiver and walked away from the phone. But before returning to his lecturn, he took another look at the 25 nutting trucks jammed into ZS-2, at the one thousand trays of mail stacked high upon them, and at the big white-red-lettered "hold, don't sort" sign that was tacked on to each one. Not only was Jimmie bound by the Code Of Ethical Conduct decree, but more precisely, he was a captive of his own haunting, critical convictions. The sight of waste and corruption, especially such as free storage granted to millionaire merchants, was like witnessing a screaming child in the street being run down by a drunken driver, he thought.

Now back to supervising his crew at ZS-1, his eyes were physically unable to penetrate the sorting cases and see what was going on over in ZS-2. The backs of the sorting cases were made of steel. But in his troubled, ambivalent mind he saw the one thousand trays of mail that were stored there free of charge, each one separately. He even saw each of the 567 letters in each tray, separately. It was waste and corruption of the highest degree.

Since the Woods mail had been addressed and presorted at a site located somewhere in Postal Zone 50 for sequential house to house delivery only to residents living in Postal Zone 50, there was no need to ship it to the Main Installation in the first place, so Jimmie thought. And he strongly questioned such a money losing practice.

In addition to giving Woods free storage, before the mail goes back out to Zone 50, it will be sorted again, Jimmie thought. He took his little black book out of his pocket and started figuring. He didn't really need to, though. He knew the answer. He remembered that he had made the calculation back when Brim was asking him all those silly questions about: if he counted the number of trays, and if he saw the big goofy overblown white and red signs the nut had placed on each and every truck.

But, just to make sure his answer was correct, he figured the count anyway. One thousand trays, 567 letters per tray, he said. Oh my God! That can't be right. 567,000 hands are going to be required to sort, needlessly again, the Woods mail. And that's just for only one sorting. We'll probably sort it at least two or three times more before it finally manages to get out of here.

Chapter 10

When Jimmie was asked by General Foreman Brim, in November 1972, to take over section 150, there was no hesitation on his part. He said yes immediately. He had longingly awaited for the chance to get away from the open and deliberate fraud of ZS-1. Ordering 30 people, over an eight hour period every night, to do work needlessly again that was already done, was sinful, he vowed. He went home every morning with the unsettling guilt of an unseasoned conjurer.

Not only were tax payers paying for double work. Because business customers were given discounts for presorting their own mail, taxpayers were unknowingly kicking back about one fourth of the initial postage these customers paid. The people out there in Metro City were paying back in labor and handling costs about $1.25 for every dollar collected in such a transaction. Jimmie didn't like it. Not one bit. So, having to leave ZS-1 was no great loss. It was an advantage.

Section 150 did not present Jimmie with the problem of resorting presorted mail, but it was certainly not free of problems. In fact, the problems he found there were far more numerous and far more serious. It was manned by official duty clerks (ODCs). They were detail clerks, desk clerks, assignment clerks, relief supervisor clerks and manager-bed-partner clerks (dainty young girls who wanted an easy life). These were privileged clerks, as Jimmie referred to them, and Section 150 was a place reserved for them to work when they were not attending to the duties of their regular assigned details.

And because they were given carte blanche while actually functioning in those detail capacities, most of them found it difficult to modulate back to the function of distribution clerk during that period of the night when they weren't working in those capacities. All thirty ODC clerks assigned to Section 150 were women. They were a recalcitrant group. There was constant chatter in the section. And they literally got up and walked out whenever they pleased. They returned when they got good and ready; and they argued loudly with the supervisor who dared to ask them why they stayed away so long. Needless to say, this kind of loose behavior greatly affected productivity. And this is where the rub with Brim came for Jimmie.

The only way Jimmie could come anywhere close to making production, three trays of mail an hour per clerk, in Section 150 was to pad the production sheet at the end of the tour, which he repeatedly refused to do. Only last night he refused to pad his sheet, he recalled. Tonight he realized that when G.F. Brim sees that production sheet, he won't like it, and will probably call him into his office. And a little later on, as he stood at the lecturn, someone from behind called out to him.

"Jimmie, your presence is wanted in..."

And Jimmie cut his informer off with: "What took you so long? I've been waiting for you. I knew he was going to send for me "

Jimmie headed for Brim's office, but was definitely not in a rush. In fact, he was dragging a bit. Not only from having to go to Brim's office. That, too, but also, his pace was slowed by the effects of a kind of jet lag. When G.F. Brim moved him from the ZS-1 section to the 150 section, he also moved him from the 10:12 PM set to the 7 PM set. Adjusting to the new time change had not been easy for him.

He had worked the new shift two weeks now, but still had not completely settled into it. He wasn't complaining too much, though. There was one especially good point about starting at 7 o'clock. Giving himself an hour to get to the job and out onto the work room floor meant that he had to leave home at six in the evening, only a half hour after Mary Belle arrived home at 5:30. And when he got home at 4:30 in the morning she was usually asleep. That cuts down considerably on our arguing time, he happily thought.

But, walking into Brim's office, he started questioning himself about that one especially good point. There was something about this General Foreman Brim and his wife Mary Belle, that was strikingly similar. They both had big, loud mouths, and neither one was happy unless he was briskly flapping it open in recriminatory attacks on someone. So, on closer examination, Jimmie conceded that that one especially good point wasn't so good after all. What recriminatory time he lost at home with Mary Belle, he quickly gained back, on the job with G.F. Brim.

When Jimmie entered General Foreman Brim's office, Brim said, pointing to a chair for him to take a seat in: "In viewing your sheet from last night, I see you failed to make production. Is that right, or am I seeing wrong?"

"No, you're not wrong. I guess I didn't," he said as he strolled casually and sat down in the chair.

"Supervisors must see to it that their sections make production," he instructed Jimmie. "That is their prime responsibility."

"I'd like to know how," Jimmie responded, more in the form of a statement than a question.

"Well, you are new on the job," Brim comforted him. "You,ve got a lot to learn."

Jimmie thought to himself, yeah, how to use a pencil. I know all about that. But he said to Brim: "I work with what I have."

"But you are not working with what you have. If you were, you'd make production. Every other supervisor on the floor makes production. Every night. You are the only one who doesn't. Why? What makes you so special?

Jimmie did not verbally call Brim a liar. But the highly illuminated expression of doubt on his face surely told Brim what he was thinking. It prompted him to come up with documented evidence that the other supervisors were actually getting a day's work for a day's pay out of the employes working under their supervision.

He picked up a handful of production sheets from his desk which dated back several weeks, and disseminated them about his desk top. Fingering through a number of them, one after the other, he pointed to supervisor names. "See?" he said. "Everybody but you."

"As I said before," Jimmie calmly addressed Brim, "I work with what I have."

"And what do you mean by that?" he asked, with a voice of uneven edges.

"You assigned me to 150," Jimmie pointed out. "You know what I"ve got over there..."

"Maybe I don't know," Brim cut him off. "So, suppose you tell me."

"For one thing, little or no mail. For another, a lot of indolent, intractable petticoats who think they come down here, not to work, but to party all night."

' 'That's part of the supervisor's job, too," Brim instructed Jimmie, "to see to it that his subordinates do a full day's work for a full day's pay."

Jimmie recalled that in Section 150 the night before, he received only 3,000 pounds of mail. To equal the number of man-hours used, he needed 9,000 pounds, proving that the MMPO workforce was simply too large for the workload. "Yeah? And how do you do that?" he asked.

Someone knocked on Brim's office door. "Come in," he yelled.

It was his receptionist. "Mr. Blake wants to see you in his office right away," she said.

"Well, I'm sorry that we must end our little meeting so soon, Mr. Jones," Brim said. He got up from his desk and headed for the door to show Jimmie out. "But I think we covered the main points, don't you? I want to see a better sheet tonight, okay?"

But, at the end of the night, when the time came for Jimmie to total the pounds of mail received, processed and left over, and the number of man hours used, he did nothing different to what he had done the night before. He called the shots as he saw them. He added nothing and subtracted nothing. Therefore, he signed the sheet with a clear conscience. Lying was just not his thing.

Arriving the next night out on the workroom floor at his Section 150 post, he braced himself for what he was sure was going to happen. Brim was going to send for him to come into his office. He yawned of boredom. But the time started peeling off. 8:30-, 9-, 10-, 11, not even by 12 midnight did Brim send for Jimmie. It was strange, he thought, really out of character. More strange, though, was that, at 3:30 the next morning, time for Jimmie to hit out for home, Brim still had not sent for him.

The remainder of the 1972 month of November had come and gone. So had the Christmas holidays, and the remainder of the month of December. It was now mid-January of 1973. Icy reminders of the severe cold weather outside were sneaking in through the tightly closed car doors.

Working the 7 o'clock shift, now, and not the 10:12, put Jimmie home at 4:30 in the morning instead of 7:30. It was dark in the vacant lot out behind the old aging Grove building. Driving his car onto the lot and walking back out, avoiding empty beer cans, broken wine bottles, frozen dog droppings and human feces, would not be easy. Also, he could get mugged. So, as he currently did other mornings now, he parked his car on the street. Although a half block away from the courtway entrance leading up to his three room apartment, it was still better.

Oh how good that soft, warm bed is going to feel, he said to himself, walking back toward the entrance. Working with minimum amounts of mail and maximum amounts of people, tolerating their bold laziness and shameless recrimination, made his supervising nights hard and long. In those hard and long supervising nights, though, currently at least, there was one bright spot. For about two months now, there had been no irritating summons to Brim's office, neither had there been any death threatening visits from Bessie Black and her Hatchet Ladies. Boy what a relief, he said, smiling his approval. The thought was almost as comforting as he supposed his soft, warm bed upstairs was soon going to be.

He walked with a quickening stride; it was cold outside, around zero, he guessed. Only a few short steps from his car and his whole body was chilled through. January nights in Metro City were as cold as January nights in Alaska, he thought.

As he approached the door of the first entrance, fingering through the keys on his key-ring looking for the one that unlocked his front door, he heard foot steps following behind him. At 4:30 on a still, frigid morning, with people off the streets in bed, and traffic on Grove Street all but non-existent, the sound of footsteps crackling up from the crisp, frozen walkway jammed Jimmie with uncontrollable fright.

The foot steps sounded as if the person was getting closer to him, and they seemed anxious and deliberately rushed. They belong to a mugger, he first thought. Then, it occurred to him that just maybe the one bright spot in his life for the past two months of not being heckled by his General Foreman Jerome Brim and by Bessie Black and her Hatchet Ladies was now a very big, black hole in his life. But it can't be, he disputed. He was at home, not at the Post Office where sneaky Johnnie Mae tripped him to the floor. He wasn't in Pete's parking lot where Bessie Black and her Hatchet Ladies attacked him with switchblade knives, neither was he at the Dover Avenue subway station where they tried to push him onto the tracks in front of the speeding 7 AM B train. He was away out south on Grove Avenue in front of the apartment building where he lived.

Nevertheless, he suddenly picked up his pace and rushed for the door. But it was too late. He made it through the outer door into the vestibule, but could not get his key into the lock of the inner door in time to open it.

A monster of a man, wearing a black shiny coat, black glossy boots, a black knitted ski mask, and black satin leather gloves, rushed in behind him. With an enormously heavy hand, and brandishing a big black 45 Automatic, he grabbed Jimmie by the shoulder and pointed with the gun to the door.

Why go back out into the zero weather, Jimmie wondered. He reached into his hip pocket and pulled out his wallet. He fished out all the bills and motioned then to the big man. "Here, take it," he said. "That's all I have."

But the monster of a man slapped the bills from his hand to the floor. "I don't want your money," he snapped, and pointed with the gun to the door again. "Out."

Jimmie picked his money up from off the floor and, disjointedly, headed for the door.

"Move it," the big man said. "Let's go."

Who is this man? he wondered. If he isn't a mugger and doesn't want my money, what does he want? Where is he taking me? And for what reason? Especially this time of the morning?

As Jimmie walked past the massive man and back out toward the outer door, a mental picture of the five black managers seated at the very long and wide table the night Brim summoned him in to see Sonny Blake several months before flashed before his eyes. One of those black managers was a very big man, he recalled. Colossal, he was. Could this be the same guy? Looking back at the big ski faced man and slowly pulling the outer door open, Jimmie asked in a terribly unsteady voice: "Let's go where?"

"Just go," the big man demanded, forcefully pushing him out into the street. "This way," he ordered, pointing with his 45 to the gangway between the first and second sections of the huge Grove courtway building.

In a fearful, reluctant stride, Jimmie started toward the gangway, continuing with his speculation. The big man in the conference room was sitting at a table; Jimmie could not see the full figure of the man. He could only see from the waist up. And this big man is wearing a ski mask; he can't see his face, only his eyes peeking through. He must be the same person, though, he figured. He's not a mugger, because he won't take my money. He's not a rapist, because I'm a man. So, he must be the guy from the conference room. Sonny Blake and G.F. Brim must have sent him out here to throw a scare into me.

The conference room episode was probably just a ploy. They called it only for this guy to get a good gander at me so he'd know what I look like. That way he wouldn't go chasing all across town in the early morning 20 degree zero weather pulling his gun out on the wrong person. As he entered the gangway, he turned around to get another look at the big man.

"Keep going," the big man shouted. "What the hell you looking back here for?"

"Bring 'em on in, Protector One," someone from the back of the gangway said to the big man. "Right on back here."

Although Jimmie didn't believe it, declaring forthrightly that it wasn't true, he recognized the voice.

"You heard 'er, so get your black ass on in there," the big man said, giving Jimmie a fast running push.

The big man's actions caught Jimmie off guard. He stumbled helplessly through the gangway's cluttered debris, as he tried desperately to maintain his balance. He stretched out his arms for buoyancy, but to no avail. He left his feet and fell flat on his stomach. And with the help of empty beer cans and wine bottles acting as casters, like a baseball player making a hand slide into second base, he sailed speedily down the icy gangway, head first. When he finally came to a halt, the familiar voice spoke out again.

"Well, if it ain't Mr. Jones hisself." the voice said. "Look, ladies, it's our good friend, the traitor. Come on out and give him a warm welcome."

Jimmie looked up into their faces. Fully armed with their switchblade knives, it was Bessie Black and her Hatchet Ladies. And with Jimmie immobile and prone on the ground, they immediately did what they had been unable to do on the morning several years before when they ambushed him out in Pete's parking lot. They formed a ring around him, with Bessie Black in the middle standing over him.

He was sure now that the big man was sent by Operations Director Sonny Blake and General Foreman Brim.

Bessie Black had referred to him as Protector One, and Jimmie remembered having heard something about a five member group being organized called the Protectors. One of those five managers who sat at that long, wide conference table saying nothing, was a big man like this guy here. And Jimmie wondered. Were they the Protectors? Yeah, he said, they are the same men, I'd bet on it. But what do they protect? And is this how they do it?

"Get up, you black bastard," Bessie shouted at Jimmie.

He stood up and noticed that a new dimension had been added to her group of Hatchet Ladies, a fifth member, Johnnie Mae, his section mate.

"Oh, so you've become a member of this bunch of cut throats now, too, huh?" Jimmie asked, then added: "Birds of a feather."

"She ain't jes become no member uh nothing," Bessie Black disputed Jimmie. "She been one uh us all the time. She ain't let nobody know 'cause I told her not to. That way, she could watch your black ass without you knowing it. And she did jes that. She got the book on you, baby."

Johnnie Mae, who on most occasions was quite vocal, said nothing. Like the other Hatchet Ladies, she just stood in the circle formation squeezing the handle of her long, glaring switchblade.

"Come on, Johnnie, let's get the show on the road," Bessie Black said, grabbing Jimmie's left arm and twisting it back behind him.

Johnnie Mae came into the middle of the circle with Bessie Black and did the same with his right arm, only more forcefully. She was a strong woman, especially in her grip. As Slick put it, her section mate, and Jimmie's, too. "That old man woman broad don't know her own strength. With them 210 pounds she's carrying 'round here, she's stronger than uh ox."

She and Bessie Black pushed Jimmie through the circle of Hatchet Ladies, backed him up against the old Grove building's crumbling brick wall, and beckoned for the Hatchet Ladies to follow. And they closed in with what would now become a combination circle of humans and a crumbling brick wall.

"Protector One?" Bessie Black called out. "Come on in here."

And Protector One responded by asking: "You ready?"

"Yeah, we ready."

Protector One walked into the circle, took a pair of brass knuckles out of his pocket and slipped them onto his hands.

Jimmie tried to wriggle free of the Bessie-Johnnie hammerlock, but to no avail. Then, he opened up his mouth very wide; he'd yell loud enough to wake up the whole city.

But before he could throw his vocal cords into gear, with all the finesse and quickness of a flashy, highly trained professional prize-fighter, Protector One ripped off what seemed an invisible right shot, and, then, a left one to his head, banging it fast back up against the crumbling brick wall. Jimmie knew what it meant: don't try it, buddy. Shut up.

Protector One took a long look at Jimmie, turned his back, looked away and moved about. "So, you're the can't tell a lie anti-black efficiency expert, huh?" he snapped.

Jimmie was busy trying to blink away the thousands of specks of light he saw dancing before his eyes, and to cast off the awful throbbing pain in his aching head. Just the same, though, he attempted to shape his lips in order to ask Protector One what he meant by can't tell a lie anti-black efficiency expert, as if he didn't know.

But the big man wheeled back around and dangerously vaunted his striking right hand through the air. "You are taking jobs away from black people," he told Jimmie. "All the other supervisors cooperate, what's your problem? Why won't you balance your production sheets as they do?"

Jimmie didn't make any more attempts at speaking. The big man had made it very clear that he shouldn't. If he tried to speak, though, the very first thing he'd say would be something in the way of correcting Protector One. What the big man really meant, he said to himself, wasn't to balance the production sheets but to pad them.

He stopped momentarily and checked out his predicament: Bessie Black and Johnnie Mae each holding tightly their hammerlock with one hand and squeezing their switchblades with the other. The rest of the Hatchet Ladies, with the help of the crumbling brick wall, forming a tight circle around him, and Protector One just standing there itching to use his shiny brass knuckles. This was no time to be smart lipped, he counseled himself. It was a time to think about whether or not he was going to get out of that gangway alive. Irritating these heinous cutthroats, he thought, certainly was not the way to do it.

"My job is to help you change your mind," Protector One told Jimmie. "And if you don't change your mind, well, tonight will be only the beginning."

"It's cold as hell out here, Protector One," Bessie Black chimed out at the big man. "Do what you got to do, and let's get the hell out of here."

What Protector One had to do, he did quickly and professionally. He slammed two hard rights and lefts to Jimmie's abdomen.

Jimmie made a kind of muffled grunting sound as the upper part of his body bent forward. And as his drooping head followed after his bending body, the big man, with lightening speed, came in again upper cutting with lefts and rights that sent his head and body back up-right again.

Protector One was sure he had done his job He turned and walked away without looking back. Bessie Black and Johnnie Mae let go of their hammerlock hold and they, too, walked away without looking back. Jimmie's limp, crouching body, like an untethered slab of fresh meat market beef, fell flat to the alley's icy concrete floor.

Later, he climbed to his feet. And like a man sloppy drunk, he staggered around to the building's front entrance. He fumbled his key into the lock of the vestibule door and, with great dependence on hand-railing support, he slowly pulled himself up to his third floor apartment. Boy, was he feeling tough.

An aching tooth, as well as a sore toe, can be omnivorous producers of debilitating pains; they can really do a guy in, he remembered. On several separate occasions he had experienced the wrath of them both. Although they had sometimes seemed all embracing, the separate pains precipitated by those tooth aches and sore toes were localized pains. Each affected only one small part of the body.

Those tooth aches and sore toes had never consolidated their forces and together attacked him at the same time. If they had done so, he was not so sure that he would have been able to distinguish one pain from the other. Like now, his whole body ached terribly from two different pains. It ached from the exposure to the frost biting zero weather. And it ached from the brutal beating given to him by Protecteor-One.

But he couldn't tell the difference. All he knew now was that he was feeling one big nasty dose of consummate pain. Not one inch of his body, inside nor outside, was free of pain. And it was a killing kind of pain, especially the part of it that was spinning around in his head.

Once inside his apartment, he got his water bottle, filled it with ice cubes, headed for the medicine cabinet in the bathroom and closed the door behind him. He tugged his clothes off, douched his wounds with healing preparations, ran the bathtub heaping full of soapy water that began steaming up the room, and gingerly crawled into it. If only he could bring himself to pad those darn production sheets, he would not have this problem. His face and abdomen would not be badly bruised, he would not be aching all over, his head would not be spinning. His body would not be chilled through and through, and he'd be in there, now, in his big, warm queensize bed dropping off to sleep.

Suddenly, though, the pain started to subside. The healing preparations began to sooth the bruises on his face and abdomen. The ice pack, combining with the steam swirling about the room, proceeded to clear his spinning head. And the heaping tub of hot lathery water started thawing out his bent, frozen body. He let out a sigh of relief, fully stretched out a now flexible body and leaned back in the tub to a more relaxed position. It was a moment for a kind of celebration, for a good lung filling drag from a name brand cigarette, or a slow tangy sip from a tall glass of rare champagne.

But, just as he settled down to partake fully of the delightful healing event, he heard an anxious voice coming from the hallway outside the bathroom. Then, as the bathroom door swiftly opened, he felt a cool breeze rushing in. And he fanned frenetically with both hands at the room's soothing, steaming clouds trying to see who the brash intruder was.

Naturally, It was Mary Belle. "What the hell you doing taking a bath this time uh morning 'fore you go to bed!" she screamed out at Jimmie. "You don't never take no bath 'til night, 'fore you go to work. What choo trying to wipe off you? Been out ho-fucking, huh? "Wait a minute," she ordered. "Don't wash another lick. Not 'til I checks you out." She walked over to the bathtub, reached her hand down into the water, and suddenly drew it back as she caught a glimpse of his badly bruised face. "What happened to you!" she yelled.

"Nothing happened to me," he said. "Nothing."

"Yeah, I can see nothing happened." She bantered him for a second, then went into a lengthy tirade. "I knowed something lak thrs was going to happen to you. I keep telling you to jes go down there and do your job and quit trying to run everything everywhere you go. Serves you right, too," she sniggled out, throwing her wet hand over her mouth to dampen it. Then she headed back toward the bedroom, still trying to muffle the sniggle, which was now fizzing out more profusely. And she repeated the words: "Yeah, serves you right, with them damn crazy ideas that don't do nothing but take jobs away from black folks. And they ain't through with your black ass yet, neither," she yelled, then warned him. "You better wise up."

As Jimmie listened to the rusty bed springs screeching beneath Mary Belle as she crawled back into bed, it seemed to him that in Metro City, there was no place of solace or understanding, not even in his own home. In every nook and corner, it was one big metropolis of singlemindedness. Not any one individual he knew had a mind of his or her own, he thought Like docile heads of cattle out on a barren plane, they all had been hearded up into a nebulous cloud of emotional misunderstanding.

Mary Belle was his wife; she didn't work at the Post Office; and she didn't walk around the house with a glaring switchblade knife in her hand. But with her cold impermeable heart, her abrasive personality, and her foul language, everyday, she let him know exactly where she stood. Deep inside her she was more of a Hatchet Lady than even Bessie Black herself, he thought.

Later that day, Jimmie got up out of bed, gingerly washed his battered face, carefully slithered his clothes on over a punching bag body and headed out to see Billie Ross, head of the postal supervisor's union. There were two such organizations, one integrated, the other all black. Billie Ross was union boss of the all black one. And Jimmie thought, perhaps, Ross could help him with his problem. He should do something for the money I pay him in dues every month, he declared.

But Billie Ross was of little help. He stood solidly behind the black agenda. "I understand your problem," he told Jimmie. "But creating jobs for black people takes prescedence over all else. My advice to you is to pad the production sheet. When you do, your problems will be over.

But that night back at work, it was the same story. Jimmie still refused to pad his production sheet.

Without informing Jimmie, General Foreman Brim advised mail supplier, Scooter Rob, to double the amount of mail he'd deliver to Jimmie's section. "For every truck of forty trays you give him, write eighty on his sheet," he told Scooter Rob.

But, during the course of the night, Jimmie saw what Scooter Rob was doing, and at the end of the tour, before signing the sheet, he made the necessary corrections.

On the way home from work early the next morning, sober of mind now, Jimmie skirmished a bit with harsh reality. His obsession with truth and honesty would one day cause him serious trouble. And speaking of trouble, he wondered if Protector One, and Bessie Black and her Hatchet Ladies would be waiting for him this morning? He hoped not, not this morning or ever again, but especially not this morning. Yesterday morning it was zero. This morning it's 10 below. Maybe he could get a parking spot in front of the door. If so, he'd hop out of the car and rush into the building before Protector One could catch him.

Finding the parking spot to his liking, Jimmie quickly cut off the car's motor, yanked the key from the ignition, got out, slammed the door lock-shut and headed directly for the building's entrance. He fingered hurriedly through his bunch of keys and pointedly singled out one from the rest. Once inside the vestibule, he'd ram that key into the inner door's lock and up the stairs he'd go. So long to brass knuckled Protector One and his switchblade Hatchet Lady companions.

But, to Jimmie's surprise, Protector One and the Hatchet Ladies were expecting some such elusive behavior from him. They had planned their clandestine response and were patiently awaiting his arrival.

He quickly swished the outer door open and rushed right into the arms of Protector One who greeted him with: "Good morning Mr. Can't Tell a Lie Anti Black Efficiency Expert. What kept you so long? The Hatchet Ladies, out in the gangway, and I have been waiting quite awhile for you to come home. We want to have another little chat with you."

"About what?" Jimmie asked.

"Let's just go back outside around to where the Hatchet Ladies are and discuss it there," he said taking him by the arm. "They would like to take part in the festivities, too."

Jimmie tried to pull away from Protector One, but he clutched his arm more tightly and pushed him back outside throught the open door. "I don't have anything to say to you, or to the Hatchet Ladies, either," he blurted out.

"Oh yes you have," the man shot back, "and it better be good, too. Something like, 'Yes, I'm going to cooperate. I'm going to help create jobs for blacks. That is, I'm going to call more workers into my section than I need. I'm going to pad my production sheets. I'm going to up the count on mail-received sheets. And, then, I'm going to willingly sign those sheets.' That's what I advise you to say," Protector One threatened. "You hear me, nigger? And if you don't, you're gonna be sorry. Our meeting with you yesterday morning was just to warn you. This morning, we mean business!" he shouted.

Jimmie ripped his arm free of Protector One's grasp and ran swiftly back toward the building's entrance. It was a foolish thing for him to attempt, but he made it. He yanked the outer door open and streaked across the vestibule floor to the inner door. He still held the bunch of keys in his hand. Now, though, they were all jumbled up. And in a frenetic effort to single out the inner door key again from the rest, one of his nervous, flapping fingers got caught in the ring and flipped the entire bunch of keys to the floor. He stooped hurriedly to retrieve them. But it was too late.

His impromptu escape had come to an abrupt end. As he reached the bottom of his speedy descent, he saw, straddling the sprawling bunch of keys, Protector One's two black shiny boots. He stared up in fright. And for the first time that morning he saw Protector One take his 45-Automatic out of its holster. He pointed the long, over size barrel at Jimmie. And, with a devilish grin on his face, he pulled back the hammer and stormed at him, "Do that again and you're a dead man! Now, get the hell back out there and around to the gangway to where the Hatchet Ladies are patiently awaiting to greet you."

Jimmie became sullen and did not immediately respond. He just stood there. Protector One was holding the 45-Automatic in his right hand. He shifted it over to his left hand and took one of the brass knuckles out of his pocket. He expertly wriggled it onto his right hand and quickly gave Jimmie a short jab to the left side of his face. "Let's go, dammit, outside," he barked.

Jimmie walked out of the vestibule, but very slowly. Bleeding from reopened cuts and bruises, he thought about the morning before, the beating Protector One gave him while the circling Hatchet Ladies, with their drawn switchblade knives, backed him up, how they left him lying there on the gangway's icy, tin can, broken bottled floor. And a subtle, slow but mean streak sprang up in him.

"Come on, step up, move it," Protector One yelled, skillfully planting a hard swift kick to Jimmie's behind. "Let's get going. We haven't got all day."

Without cowling from the quick, short jab to his jaw, or wincing from the swift, hard kick to his behind, Jimmie was becoming a stoic being, void of feeling. Looking back at the towering giant of a man with gradual departing fear, his face was a furrowed mass.

"Get going, sucker!" Protector One shouted at Jimmie, giving him a rushing push. "What the hell are you looking back here at me for? Move it, dammit "

Jimmie became more slothful, deliberately dragging himself along and continuing to stare back at the big man.

Protector One placed the 45-Automatic back into it's holster, carefully slipped the other brass knuckle onto his left hand and declared, "I see what you need, a little coaxing."

The audacious posture of the man prompted Jimmie to engage in some self analysis, and to size up of the situation he now found himself in. What am I? he sternly asked himself. This guy is a hulk of man, and, along with his gun and brass knuckles, a brute and a big bullie. But what the hell am I! with great disgust he asked himself again. Then, surely, surprising to Protector One, and even to himself, he indignantly turned fully around. He made a fist, coiled his body backward almost to the ground and came up swinging at the big man with a classic, wide sweeping, school yard haymaker. He missed. The intended blow went past Protector One's head as fast as a bullet fired from his 45-Automatic would have.

But Protector One did not miss. He saw the telegraphing haymaker coming from a mile away. He stepped to one side to let it go by and quickly chopped Jimmie with a barrage of lefts and rights hard to the head and face, which dropped him to the cold, concrete walkway. Jimmie hopped right back up, though, and started carefully analyzing himself again. He was a man, all man, not a coward. Squaring off at this brash, reckless monster, he knew he was out of his league, that he may not win. But he damned sure had to try. He wasn't going to tuck in his tail and take a beating from any, one, single individual, man or beast, which this guy partly was, without fighting back.

The Hatchet Ladies, waiting around in the gangway, weren't there to back him up with their switchblade knives. It was just the two of them. One on one. So why shouldn't he resist the beastly beating this superciliously, presumptuous ass was now planning to give him? He may take me out again as he did yesterday morning, he reluctantly admitted. But this morning he's damned sure gonna have to earn it. No freebies today.

Jimmie reached deep, down into his big bag of tricks again and, without doing any fine tuning, or making any adjustments at all, he came up with another one of those outrageously wide sweeping school yard haymakers. Again, it spiraled through the air like a shot out of Protector One's 45-Automatic. Again Protector One saw it coming from a mile away and stepped to one side. Also again, it went right past its intended mark. And again, Protector One chopped Jimmie with a barrage of vicious lefts and rights hard to the head and face. And again, Jimmie dropped to the cold concrete walkway. But this time he did not hop right back up. He laid there like a man who was dead.

"Get up, nigger!" Protector One yelled at Jimmie. "Don't konk out on me yet, the party is just beginning. So, get on up. You hear me? The Hatchet Ladies by now. I know, are getting pretty impatient, and damn cold, too. So, let's not keep them waiting any longer. Okay?"

Jimmie did not respond. He did not say a word, nor move a muscle. He just laid there.

Protector One walked over, looked down on him with disgust, then, swiftly kicked him in the ribs. "Get up, nigger!" he yelled again. "Get on up, now!"

From the cuts and bruises caused by the pounding brass knuckles, Jimmie's head and face were bleeding profusely. And from the vicious kickings Protector One had given him, his ribs were now paining, too. He did not respond with sound or movement, though. He just laid there. But he was fully conscious, sensitive to all that was happening around and to him. What he was doing lying there was listening to a head that was rapidly spinning, but more from thought than from pain

He had tried solving his problem with the two wide sweeping haymakers. They didn't work. Maybe he should try to make it into the building. Naw, he tried that, too. It didn't work, either. And if it didn't work before, now that I'm all banged up, it certainly won't work now. But if I have the right key separated from the rest when I get into the vestibule, I probably could make it. Naw, he argued, too weak now.

Protector One reached down and took Jimmie by the arm. "Come on," he said. "Let me give you a hand. Stand up. Walk around for awhile. And by the time we get to the gangway where the Hatchet Ladies are waiting, you'll be okay. Come on, now, get up, let's go."

Jimmie got up all right, but not in the weak, flagging mode Protector One expected him to. Suddenly, he called for a massive wave of great strength to quickly surge through his body. He told his bleeding, bruised up head and face and his caved in ribs in no uncertain terms to get the hell away from him. And he convinced himself that if Joe Louis, in the peak of his pugilistic career, at that very moment, squared off at him, he would beat the living hell out of him. And to Protector One, he did just that. He beat the living hell out of him. Protector One's disintegration was short, precise, and for Jimmie, very very sweet, and oh so timely.

His wide sweeping haymakers were replaced with short, seem-ingly, invisible jabs that Protector One this time, apparently, did not see coming from a mile away. At least, he did not avoid them by stepping to one side. They did not go past, but landed on the intended mark. And for a brief few moments, as if he thought he'd better finish the job today because there'd probably be no tomorrow, Jimmie was a very busy man. Protector One was very busy, too, in a futile attempt to ward off Jimmie's·damaging blows. When he'd throw his defensive hands up to protect his head, Jimmie would go to the body

"Hey, Protector One?" Bessie Black yelled from the gangway, "bring that traitor on around here and let's get this damned thing over with so we can get the hell home, out of this damned cold ass weather."

Protector One didn't answer, he just laid there, out cold.

"Protector One!" Bessie Black yelled again. "What you stalling 'round for? Come on, let's get the show on the road. Bring his black ass on 'round here so we can get this shit over with. It's cold out here, man. Do you know it's 10 degrees below zero, and getting colder all the time?"

Surprisingly, Jimmie suddenly became a brazen clone. He towered over Protector One as Protector One had towered over him. Physically and emotionally, he hastily changed places with his fallen adversary. He reached down, brashly yanked the gun out of Protector One's holster and roughly ordered him to, "Get up, nigger." And when Protector One failed to respond, he did to Protector One what Protector One had done to him. He took his right foot and banged him hard in the ribs. Still getting no response, he took his left foot and banged him in the ribs again.

Protector One was lying face down. Jimmie flipped him over, took his brass knuckles from his pocket, slipped them on his hands and crouched to his knees for better leverage. And for the hell of it, he pulled another one of those previous wide sweeping school yard haymakers out of his trick bag and landed it quick, fast and hard to Protector One's head and face.

Bessie Black yelled again for Protector One to, "Bring that damned traitor on 'round here. What the hell you doing out there?"

Protector One still did not answer, and Bessie Black, with Unlearned Hatchet Lady Mamie Smith tagging along behind, came from the gangway out to the front to find out why.

She saw Protector One sprawled on the cold, concrete walkway, now a miserable clone of Jimmie, with his head and face all bruised and cut up and oozing of blood. Expressing bewilderment and utter disappointment, she exclaimed: "What the hell!"

"Well I'll be damned," Mamie Smith let out. "And they call him Protector One. What the hell is he protecting laying down there on that cold ass ground spitting up blood and shit?"

"And that's where you onerous Hatchet Ladies are going to be, too," Jimmie warned, pointing the 45-Automatic straight at them, "right down where he is, if you don't get the hell out of here right now. And take him with you. I mean it."

Mamie Smith brandished her switchblade knife through the air several times and started walking slowly toward Jimmie. She had an anxious look on her face as if she probably thought that, luckily, there would come a favorable unguarded flicker in which she could successfully rush Jimmie. No doubt, her plan was to move in fast, to one side out of the direct line of fire, and rip into Jimmie before he'd have time to make an accurate readjustment.

"Come on, Mamie," Bessie Black urged her. "Let's get the hell out of here." She stared down at Protector One in disgust and reached a hand to him as he tried desperately to get to his feet. "And help me get this ass out of here, too," she ordered Mamie Smith. "Come on, now."

But Mamie Smith, grinning now and appearing looney about the eyes, and still brandishing her switchblade, kept inching along toward Jimmie.

"Come on, Mamie!" Bessie Black screamed, catching her by the arm trying to pull her back. "Don't be no fool. Cain't you see he gotta gun?"

"Yeah, I see that thing he got in his hand," Mamie Smith answered. "So, he gonna try to put us to sleep lak he did that morning out in Pete's parking lot, huh? Well, I got news for 'em. Before he can pull the trigger on that little pop gun of his, I'm gonna be in there on top of him ripping 'em open lak he was a red-ripe watermelon."

Jimmie pulled back the cock-hammer on the long barrel 45 Automatic until it caught and held steady. Then, releasing it and coiling his finger closely around its trigger, he said to Bessie Black, "You'd better take this maniac out of here, now, while you can. Otherwise, it's gonna be the undertaker taking her out of here..."

"Ah naw, buddy, Mamie Smith cut in. "It ain't gonna be me they's gonna take out of here, it's gonna be you. And piece by piece," she stipulated.

Bessie Black let go of Mamie Smith's arm and banged her fast to the head with a hard right hand. "Listen you fool, cain't you see that that ain't no play gun. That's Protector One's 45-Automatic he got. And if he puts you to sleep with that, honey, it's gonna be forever."

Mamie Smith's eyes popped open tea-cup wide. And she started backing away, and breathing hard. "That's what!" she yelped. "What you say, Bessie!"

"That's this fool's 45-Automatic he got, that's what I said," she responded, grabbing Protector One by the arm and moving away. "We getting out of here, and if you got any damn sense you will, too. Come on, and holler back there and tell them others to come on, too."

It was now June, 1973, six years since Bill Brown became the first black Postmaster of the Metro City Post Office, and six years, almost to the month, since Jimmie submitted his Blockbuster to the Awards Committe. He neither retracted any part of the Blockbuster, nor did he ever pad any production sheets. And Bessie Black and her Hatchet ladies, and General Foreman Brim and his Protector One did not ever let up one bit of their pressure on him. So, on this 1973 June moonlit night, Jimmie came to the job as he had done every single work night since 1967: watchfully alert. Early tomorrow morning, entering his apartment building, he's do the same.

Jimmie was still supervising at Section 150, but he was now back on the 10:12 set. He stepped off the elevator on to the fourth floor expecting to be greeted by early arriving Bessie Black and her Hatchet Ladies, and throngs of other colleagues yelling out as they usually did: "There he is, the traitor, there he is." But they were not there, not Bessie Black, her Hatchet Ladies nor anyone else, except Ronnie and Oscar. They were there. With great concern on their faces, they were anxiously awaiting Jimmie's comimg. Ronnie took him by one arm and Oscar took him by the other. And they walked south toward their lockers. "Have you heard the news?" Ronnie asked.

"What news?"

"That Postmaster Bill Brown is going to be replaced by a white Postmaster?"

"No, I haven't," Jimmie answered with great surprise. "Where did you hear that?"

"It's all over the building," Ronnie informed him. "Everybody's talking about it. You mean you really haven't heard?"

"No, I haven't," Jimmie responced, then cocked his head to one side in a recalling gesture. "But now I know why the people coming up in the elevator were so quiet."

"Yeah, they knows 'bout it. That's why they wasn't saying nothing," Oscar said, joining in. "They done heard the news that boss Riley is 'bout to make his move. Now that the civil rights movement is dead, niggers ain't sitting in, demonstrating and marching no more, and ain't gonna tear up his town, he don't need no black front man no more. So, Bill Brown's gotta go. That's all. He's gotta go."

"Well now, I don't know about all of that," Jimmie objected, but not forcefully, and not with a great amount of confidence, either, not even to himself. "Ed Riley is only the mayor of Metro City. He's not God".

"Naw," Oscar agreed. "He ain't God. You got that right. But what he say in this town, is God's word. And if you don't believe it, jes you don't do what he say."

Jimmie tried to pull from his chin a beard he did't have, and pondered for a second. "Ed Riley is a big city boss," he said. "But he's not a gangster. He's not going to send a couple of hoods in here with guns drawn to tell Bill Brown to take a hike. If indeed Ed Riley is involved. Which no one is really sure about. But if these rumors are true, whether it's Ed Riley or the white power structure, generally, what concerns me is: what would be their strategy? It would have to be something believable, probably a strong procedural argument of some kind."

"You wouldn't believe what their strategy is," Ronnie told Jimmie.

"With the torment I've been through these last six years with Bessie Black and her switchblade wielding Hatchet Ladies, and with G.F. Brim and his brass knuckled Protector One I'll believe anything you have to say," Jimmie grumbled out. "So out with it. Tell me. What is their strategy?"

"What do you think," Ronnie asked Jimmie. "Come on, take a guess."

"I have no idea. Ed Riley is just going to name someone else, I guess. Is that what you're going to tell me?"

"No, they are not going to be that bold," Ronnie disagreed.

"Why not?" Oscar interjected. "He was that bold with Bill Brown. He reached in a hat and pulled him out. So, he'll just put him back in that hat and pull out somebody else now, a white dude."

"Well, we don't know that Ed Riley really had anything to do with Bill Brown's appointment," Jimmie objected. "It's just a rumor, nothing more."

"Maybe it was just a rumor," Ronnie thoughtfully disagreed. "But I don't know. He's got the power to do it. And I believe he would do it..."

"You better believe it, buddy," Oscar cut in. "He got the power all right. That dude can make or break anybody in this town. All he got to do is snap his finger, and it's goodbye Bill Brown."

"You mentioned something about a white man, why do you think that," Jimmie asked.

"I done told you, man," Oscar emphasized. "Civil rights is dead.

You don't hear nothing 'bout nobody sitting in no more. And you don't see nobody 'round here marching or demonstrating no more. Civil rights is dead, baby, gone with the wind. Them black dudes that said it back in 1967 was right. Bill Brown ain't nothing but a front man. They been using 'em. Ed Riley knowed 'bout the low morale down here. And he knowed, too, that all you had to do was to get these niggers riled up down here and it would spread across town in nothing flat. So, he put a nigger in charge of us to keep us from burning this sucker down. And it worked, too, huh? Didn't it...?"

"I just can't believe it," Jimmie cut in. "We've got a 98 percent black workforce here. I can't visualize us going back to a white man boss. I'm afraid it would cause a lot of difficulty in this town. You say the civil rights movement is dead. If a white Postmaster is appointed here, I am sure that would be more than enough to bring it back to life. The sit-ins, demonstrations and marches you say no longer are viable would probably return, too. And God help us all. Who knows? Returning with all of that could very well come: 'Burn baby burn.'"

"You're probably right, Jimmie," Ronnie agreed. "I think it would cause a lot of tension, too..."

"Tension my ass," Oscar cut in. "We's in control now. And we ain't gonna give it up. You jes let 'em try some shit lak that and all hell's gonna break loose 'round here."

"Just the same, it sounds serious," Ronnie warned. "I wouldn't be surprised if they tried it..."

"Well, now, let's not jump to conclusions," Jimmie cautioned. He thought about the insubordinate management team, how they refuse to cooperate with Postmaster Bill Brown. "Just because there's talk of a replacement doesn't necessarily mean that the new guy is going to be white. They probably just want to improve the relationship between the Postmaster and his management team. Don't worry. The next guy will be black, too."

"What about Cliff Morley," Oscar asked, putting a damper on the discussion. "That sound black to you?"

"Cliff Morley?" Jimmie responded in astonishment. "You mean the white guy that used to be the superintendent up on the ninth floor? The one that's now in charge of the southside Sectional Center Facility? What about him?"

"That's right, Jimmie," Ronnie interjected. "That's the name that's floating around. Looks like he may be our next Postmaster. And there's no doubt that he wants it," he stipulated.

"What do you mean there's no doubt he wants it?" Jimmie asked.

"You wanted to know what the white strategy was," Ronnie reminded him, "what kind of scheme they were going to come up with to make the Postmaster grab look legitimate..."

"You mean to make it look lak it ain't no racial thing," Oscar cut in, "and that's what they's working on right now. They gonna make it look real good. The fuckers."

"Rumor has it," Ronnie continued, "that Cliff Morley claims to have a lot of records to prove the point about poor management here..."

"Hey, man, dig the time," Oscar said. "Almost time to hit in." And they all left the locker room for the time card rack.

When Jimmie reached his post at Section 150, Slick met him at the entrance. A 7:12 clerk who had been on the job three hours now, Slick had some inside news that 10:12 Jimmie, Ronnie and Oscar were not yet privy to. "Well, how is the celebrity tonight?" he asked.

"Celebrity?" Jimmie asked back, looking over his shoulder as if searching for some VIP to suddenly appear behind him. "And what's that all about?" he asked.

"You know what it's all about. The big meeting tomorrow."

"Meeting? what meeting?"

"The big meeting between Postmaster Bill Brown and his management team."

"So? How does that make me a celebrity?"

"They gonna talk about ways for blacks to stay in power down here, how to keep whitey from comimg back in here and taking over again. And you knows the only way they gonna pull that off is by doing most uh them things you say they ought to do in your Blockbuster."

"I'm flattered by your remarks, Slick. But I doubt that they'll consider using any of my stuff. If they did they wouldn't admit it, not openly anyway. They haven't so far, So why would they do it now?"

"'Cause whitey is closing in on they black asses, that's one reason. The other reason is, if there's a problem you didn't talk about in your Blockbuster, you better believe it ain't down here. It's jes that simple,

Jimmie. You touched all the bases, baby. Ain't nothing out there the brothers can come up with, about improving conditions 'round here, that gonna help 'em to hold on to they power that you didn't cover in your Blockbuster. The question ain't is they gonna use your shit. What chu gotta worry 'bout is if the black asses gonna give you credit. That's the question."

Slick stopped for a moment. It seemed that he was pondering whether or not he should say what he was about to say. Then he continued. "Now, I heard last week, when this shit first started going 'round 'bout a white Postmaster coming back in here, that Bill Brown was having some copies of your Blockbuster run off..."

"You did!" Jimmie asked, cutting him off. "Why didn't you tell me?"

"I didn't think nothing 'bout it at the time," Slick tried to justify. "They's always running off copies of suggestions and stuff down there in his office. But when I heard 'bout this big meeting, it dawned on me that that must uh been the reason they was running off them copies of your stuff."

"Well, if they use something from my Blockbuster, it won't be the first time they've used my stuff. They're always stealing my ideas."

"That's what I'm talking 'bout," Slick warned. "That's jes what they's gonna do down there tomorrow, steal your stuff. You know something?" he said thoughtfully. "You seen on TV when the President of the United States is making a speech to the Congress, ain't you. Well, You see all them dudes reading something right along with 'em, huh? Them's copies of his speech they's got. That's what that is they's reading. And that's what gonna happen down there tomorrow. All them black ass dudes on Bill Brown's management team who been fucking over you all these six years, is gonna be setting there reading your shit right along with Bill Brown and yelling like fools: 'Yeah, let's do it. Look right here on page 21, what a great idea. Why didn't I think of that. Come on, let's do it. If ideas like that won't keep us blacks in power, I don't know what will.'"

"You may be right," Jimmie agreed. "They might do just that. From what I've seen from them in the last six years, I'd put nothing beneath them."

"I know I'm right I ain't old as you is, but I been 'round these brothers long enough to know what makes 'em tick. They got a taste of power now. They laks the way it feels. And they ain't gonna give it up too easy. Even if they gotta step on another brother's neck to keep it, well, lak it or not, that's what they's gonna do."

"I saw General Foreman Brim a minute ago," Jimmie told Slick. "For the first time in six years, he greeted me with a face that was not all frowned up. In fact, he actually smiled at me."

"Why not? He's a part of management, ain't he? You's his buddy, now. Your Blockbuster is gonna keep him in power. Lots uh them brothers and sisters who been giving you a hard time is gonna be grinning at you everytime they sees you now. 'Course you can bet it ain't gonna last too long. Soon's they think they back in power, them frowns is gonna be back on they faces lak they never was before..."

"Speaking of brothers and sisters who have given me a hard time for the last six years, I wonder where Bessie Black and her Hatchet Ladies are. I haven't seen them, at all, tonight. Strange. They usually meet me at the elevator every night when I come in, or somewhere close by, yelling 'Hey traitor' at me."

"Oh, they's 'round here somewhere. I seen 'em earlier."

"Why haven't I seen them?"

"Maybe they's hiding from you, 'cause the way they been treating you. They done heard 'bout that meeting tomorrow. That's where I seen 'em, coming out of Sonny Blake's office. They knows all about what's gonna happen down there tomorrow. Maybe they know now you was right all along 'bout what you said 'bout this place needing greater efficiency and improved productivity."

Jimmie wasn't sure that Slick's prediction would actually come true. But it did. Bill Brown and his recalcitrant management team did in fact meet the following day. And, like Jimmie and Goldie coming out of the Lakeland Hotel after having sex together for the first time in seven years, they came out of the meeting arm in arm.

Immediately, Postmaster Bill Brown issued a statement to "All employes" that considerable changes in operations would soon be made. He didn't mention anything about the black-white power struggle. He simply said that the changes were being made in order to improve productivity and to give to the people of Metro City better, faster and more efficient service.

He ended the statement by saying: "In a very few days I will inform you in more detail of just what the improvement plan will be about and in what ways we must proceed to make it work."

And, as he promised, in less than five days, Bill Brown was ready and waiting to make known the program he had so quickly come up with. Workers were alerted to stop in their tracks whatever they were doing and listen to what he had to say.

"As you know," the Postmaster began, "normally, each of the twelve floors here have their own public address system, separate and unattached from the others. But for this occasion, I have ordered a one line hookup established throughout the building so that all main installation employes will have a chance to hear first hand what I have to say. Also," he added, "my message to you is being taped. A copy will be sent out to each of the 55 carrier stations, to the numerous contract stations and to all local postal entities. They will be instructed to play the tapes at a selected time when the full complement of their employes are available to listen to them.

"In a written message to you several days ago," Bill Brown continued, "I spoke to you about the need to increase productivity, about how changes in our operations would be necessary to meet that need. I promised you that I would devise a program in that regard. And I have come up with such a program, which at this time I will spell out in detail to you. I titled the program The Five Point Improvement Plan," he said. "And it will go into effect as of one week from this date, July 1, 1973.

"Point one," he advised his listeners, "is that letter sorting machines, as long as machineable mail is available, will operate up to full capacity, around the clock. Point two, ZS-1 and all such sections where mail is needlessly resorted, will be shut down permanently. Point three, all germane primary and secondary sections, especially those where third class mail is processed, will be consolidated. Point four, floor suppliers found guilty of padding mail-received sheets will be dealt with severely. And point five, supervisors who pad production sheets will find themselves in line for immediate demotion.

"Now, about the around-the-clock use of LSM machines when machineable mail is available..." the Postmaster continued.

"See? What did I tell you?" Slick said to Jimmie. He had come up to section 150 where Jimmie was supervising. He seemed to have come just to say, I told you so.

Ronnie and Oscar were there, too. "Slick's right, man," Oscar agreed. "Everything he said come right out of your Blockbuster. He ain't said nothing you ain't said..."

"Yeah," Slick cut back in. "His Five Point Improvement Plan, is your Five Point Improvement Plan, not his."

"I second that motion," Ronnie chimed in. You ought to be on that public address system right along with him. And he should be telling the people who came up with those ideas."

"Well, he ain't gonna get away with it," Slick interjected, "'cause I'm gonna tell everybody I know that them's Jimmie Jones's ideas he's using, not his. "

"Everybody do know," Oscar cut in. "They all done heard about his Blockbuster."

"I ain't talking 'bout jes down here. I'm talking 'bout people I know in the neighborhood, out in the streets, that's what I'm talking 'bout. I want everybody in Metro City to know what's going on down here in this lousy joint, what they done done to this man. I want everybody to know that these black ass bastards in charge of this place down here ain't no damn different from the white sonofa-bitches that went and moved out of here. I'm gonna print me a sign," Slick promised, "strap it over my shoulder and jes march up and down the streets, all through the neighborhood. Let everybody know how dirty these damned no good niggers is."

"That's jes what I'm gonna do, too," Oscar said. "What you gonna say on your sign?"

"That's a good idea, fellows," Jimmie agreed, "but, for now, let's just listen to what else he has to say."

"You may hear it rumored that the changes will create a reduction in force," the Postmaster said "It's true and it's not true. Current career employes whose records are in good standing and don't dictate otherwise, have nothing to worry about. What I'm really saying is, we have an over-staffing problem here. It must be brought under control, but we are going to try and do it in the least harmful way. To be exact, in two ways. First, we will initiate a hiring freeze, then an attrition program. So, if you are a career employe, unless you have some intolerable blemish on your record, don't worry about being laid off."

Bill Brown wasted no time in putting the operations changes into effect. The Five Point Improvement Plan did the trick. It gave Bill Brown the ammunition he needed to win the battle. Greater efficien-cy and improved productivity became a reality. And The Would Be Take Over White Opposition, having no substantive charge now to wage against the black administration, reluctantly, but irrefutably, backed off. And Bill Brown and his newly rediscovered management team remained firmly in power.

The End